3/20

DEATH, DIAMONDS, AND FREEZER BURN

Grime Pays Mystery Book 2

TRICIA L. SANDERS

SOUL MATE PUBLISHING

New York

DEATH, DIAMONDS, AND FREEZER BURN

TRICIA L. SANDERS

Cover Design by Rae Monet, Inc.

Published in the United States of America by
Soul Mate Publishing
P.O. Box 24
Macedon, New York, 14502

ISBN: 978-1-68291-806-7

ebook ISBN: 978-1-68291-777-0

www.SoulMatePublishing.com

Acknowledgments

As always, family comes first. Without them, I wouldn't have the inspiration or inclination to write. Thanks Ray and Amy!

To my readers, thank you for following along on Cece's journey. If not for you, I'd be cooking or cleaning house. So, thanks for the opportunity to do something more creative. Please, please keep reading.

Next, my friend, Alice Muschany, your helpful feedback and critique makes me a better writer. I truly appreciate your thoughtfulness and red pen. You wield it well.

Camille, Margo, Grace, Sarah, and Brandi—the Lit Ladies. There are never enough words to say thanks to you wonderful ladies.

Many thanks and hugs to my advanced reader group for Murder is a Dirty Business—Dianne Prinster, Cathy Setinsik, Dixie Dart, Maggie Herrel, Valya Mobley, Kathryn Symank. I appreciate you taking the time to read and review my debut novel.

To all my fabulous girlfriends, there's a little bit of Angie (and Nancy) in all of you. I'll let you figure out which one. I cherish our friendships. Time spent with friends is always a treat.

A special thanks to Deborah Gilbert, my editor and publisher at Soul Mate Publishing, Inc.

Chapter 1

"At my age, I never dreamed I'd be getting a divorce, starting a business, or finding myself attracted to a man who wasn't my husband."
Cece Cavanaugh

I hauled my aching body through the front door of Weezie's Bar and Grill, in serious need of alcohol. The hostess led me to a table in the back, where my neighbor and best friend Angie Valenti, Wickford's first female cop, sat nursing a beer. Three shot glasses lined the edge of the table, harkening back to our party days, many, many years ago. By the way, she was not on duty, and the shot glasses were not empty. Yet!

Her eyes filled with concern, Angie said, "Cece, you look beat."

"I am. Between Phillip's constant badgering and working my butt off, I'm wrung out." I bent for a hug. I'd been at work before dawn cleaning condos at Hunter Springs, my backup job—the *only* job currently paying the bills while I worked toward turning my new cleaning business into a profitable venture.

"Hang in there," Angie said. "Once your divorce is final, things will get easier."

"Can't get worse, Ang. I'm scared." I slung my purse over the chair and dropped onto the seat. "I've never been on my own."

"Not true. Before you married Phillip, you took care of your mother. At sixteen, you were more of an adult than her. How many teenagers do you know who can do that? If it weren't for you, your mom might not even be alive. You were the glue, Cece. You have to stop selling yourself short. You worked two jobs while going to school. After you got married, you managed to get yourself through nursing school with a toddler." Angie pushed a menu across the table to me. "And no one says you have to be alone."

"If you're trying to sell me on Detective Alder again, you can stop. I'm not divorced." I blew out a breath, ruffling the menu in front of me. Immediately after Phillip left me, Angie started a two-month-long campaign to set me up with a detective from her department.

"You're not divorced yet because it took you so long to wise up to Phillip's antics. But you're working in the right direction."

Before I let myself spiral into an endless cycle of self-pity, which I'd become quite good at lately, I changed the subject. "Where's Carla?" I waved my hand to get the lone server's attention. "She's always late, I swear."

"She's on her way," Angie replied. "Cut her some slack. She sounded frazzled to the bone when I talked to her. This deal with her mom is wearing on her. Looks like we all could use some downtime."

Our friend Carla had arrived in Wickford on a morning flight after a call from the hospital. Delores Redmond, Carla's elderly mother, had fallen and broken her hip. The three of us, Carla, Angie, and I, had grown up together, but Carla relocated to Hillsborough, North Carolina, after her first husband died in a car accident. She'd enrolled in classes at the university, where she'd met and eventually married Max Edison, three years after I'd wed Phillip Cavanaugh. Her marriage still thrived. Mine didn't, which explained the condo job and my increasing frustration. Phillip let our mortgage payment fall six months in arrears. He'd also cleaned out our bank account before leaving me for a floozie named Willow, half his age and half my weight. To set the record straight, Willow appeared to be anorexic. She had big feet too. And thanks to Phillip, she now had boobs to match.

Sure enough, Carla breezed in carrying an air of havoc. Her usual disposition.

"What a 'freaking nightmare.'" She made little quote marks in the air. "Crap piled everywhere. Hundreds of fast-food ketchup packets, three boxes of empty toilet paper tubes, and a drawer full of bread ties. How long does it take to eat enough bread to fill a whole drawer?" She slowed down long enough to bestow hugs.

"What's going on?" Angie asked, waving again for the waitress.

"All the touristy kitsch my brother sends her is piled everywhere. Hula girls, state magnets, tapestry rugs, and dozens of cheap statues and plastic trinkets."

Angie held up a hand to slow her down. "What are you jabbering about?"

"Mom's house is a disaster. There's a condemned sign on the front door for the whole neighborhood to see." Carla fanned herself with a menu. "I've got thirty days to make it livable."

"That doesn't sound like Delores," I said. "I feel bad for not stopping by to see her."

"She's turned into a hermit. A messy one," Carla said.

Our waitress arrived and stood at the table tapping her foot. Weezie's had great food, but the wait staff bordered on obnoxious. A huge, silver ring hung from the girl's lower lip and a safety pin stuck through her eyebrow.

"I already know what I want. Ever since my plane landed, I've been craving Weezie's toasted ravioli. And I'll take a double cheeseburger. Oh, and a margarita."

"Dang, you must have good metabolism. I thought Angie ate a lot," I teased, trying to lighten the mood.

Carla stuck out her tongue.

Angie and I ordered, and I handed the menu to the adorable safety-pin girl. "Tell the bartender to make me something with those little umbrella thingies and toothpicks full of fruit. Umm, a Missouri Tornado sounds good. And tell him not to skimp on the rum." My body ached from working muscles I rarely used. I'd taken a muscle relaxer, earlier in the day, which limited my alcohol intake. If I could only have one drink, I might as well make it count.

She shoved the menus under her arm and stalked off, muttering something about old, dried-up grandmas.

"None of us are old enough to be grandmas, squirt," Angie called after her.

"You wish," I said. We were all old enough, except I was the only one for whom it was a possibility. Carla and Max had chosen to not have children. For Angie and Dave, the first years of their marriage had been an endless barrage of disappointing fertility treatments. They weren't childless by choice. But at our age, they'd given up hope.

Carla cackled, which in turn cracked me up. Angie joined in, and we laughed until we teared up.

I pulled myself together first. "How's your mom?"

"She's coping. I spent the morning with her. Afterward, I went to her house, and talk about the shock of my life!" Carla sighed. "My mother's a hoarder. Like the ones you see on TV. When I saw the mess, I couldn't breathe. I started shaking and felt a heaviness in my chest. It's quite possible I had the early warning signs of a stroke."

"I've got a prescription to make you happy, or at least numb your pain." Angie grabbed a shot glass from the trio at the end of the table and pushed the other two toward Carla and me. "Kamikazes to the rescue. Last one down's a loser," she said, making an L out of her thumb and pointer finger and holding it against her forehead. She tossed the shot back and slammed the glass on the table. "It's between you two weenies."

It had been years since I'd done a shot, but I tipped my glass and drained it. "We all know who the loser is," I said with a smug tone, thinking to myself, *okay, two. Two drinks and no more.*

Carla toyed with hers. After finally downing it, she promptly burst into tears. "This is too much. I don't know how I can deal with it. It's bad enough she's in the hospital, but now this. I'll never get it all cleaned up."

"Do you think Lloyd leaving triggered any of this?" I asked, referring to Delores' husband, Lloyd Redmond, who had run off with their younger next-door neighbor several years ago.

Carla sniffled and swiped her eyes. "Who knows? She changed so much after she met him. I'm sure my dad rolled over in his grave the day she married Lloyd." Carla waved her hands like she was trying to erase history. "Getting back to the house, it's a nightmare. I don't even know if I can make a dent in thirty days."

Angie shook her head. "Carla, it's not as easy as tidying up to give her a clean slate. Your mom needs help. I worked a case a couple of years ago. An old woman died when a gargantuan pile of garbage bags stuffed with who-knows-what fell on top of her and suffocated her while she slept. We had to shovel our way in to get to her." She closed her eyes and shivered. "I can still smell the filth."

"Let's talk about something else. I need to get my mind off it," Carla said.

We shifted our conversation to old times until our drinks arrived. Mine glistened an enticing electric blue.

"Bio-hazard blue. Think I'll pass and stick to something more civilized." Angie wrinkled her nose. "Speaking of bio-hazard, did Cece tell you about her crime scene cleaning gig? One job almost got her killed."

Carla's eyes widened, and she leaned in. "You? Of all people. Do tell."

Angie chattered on while I squirmed. Physical labor wasn't my forte, but I'd traded in my tennis racquet and social calendar for a new lifestyle. A lifestyle barely keeping me afloat. I still wasn't comfortable with my newly acquired career, especially with Angie blabbing to Carla and making me feel like a chump. Maybe the wound was too fresh. Losing my husband and my financial freedom all at once had left me feeling vulnerable. Sharing my vulnerability, even with friends, stung. I gave Angie the stink eye, hoping she'd get the hint, but she continued. Carla lapped it up like fresh milk, or should I say, margarita. She had already drained her first and ordered a second when safety-pin girl brought our food.

"Maybe Cece can help at your mom's," Angie offered.

I sank into my seat. It wasn't like I didn't need the work, I did. But I needed paying work, and in good conscience, I wouldn't be able to charge Carla.

Carla nodded. "I know it's a lot to ask, but the three of us could knock it out in no time."

Angie held up a hand. "Count me out. The department's short on manpower. They've got me working twelve-hour days."

"Carla, any other time, I'd be all in," I said. "But my finances are in the toilet, and I have this huge project at Hunter Springs I need to focus on."

"I understand," Carla said.

I breathed a sigh of relief and took a sip of my drink, relaxing as the smooth liquid made its way down my throat. Seconds later, tears welled in the corners of Carla's eyes. She brushed them aside and took a big bite of her burger.

A moment of guilt almost made me rethink my decision. What kind of friend refused to help? I wanted to, but my family came first.

"Is anything salvageable?" Angie poked around her salad, fishing out chunks of chicken.

"I can sort the good from the trash, but it will take a while to get it manageable. There's a lot headed straight to the dump. She has boxes of old books and magazines from the Friends of the Library sales. The library had retired them all, and Mom couldn't bear to throw them out. She never intended to read them. I'm not going through all those boxes. And I don't have time for a garage sale; besides, no one wants them. There's a whole set of encyclopedias like we used in grade school. My new motto is dump and forget. I can't get bogged down. I'll salvage the sentimental things like photos and her jewelry and anything of value, of course."

I nodded in approval. "No sense wasting time, if you know it's not worth it."

Carla paused between bites. "I think I need a lawyer."

I sat straighter. "What for?" If she and Max were having trouble, I'd feel even guiltier. I knew all about imploding marriages.

"Technically, I have Mom's power of attorney, but the house is still in Lloyd's name. When they married, Mom sold her house, the one Noah and I grew up in, and moved in with Lloyd."

Lloyd Redmond swept into our tiny town of Wickford, Missouri twelve years ago with a pocketful of cash. Before he'd unpacked a single suitcase, he set his sights on Delores, the widowed town librarian. Six months later, Lloyd and Delores married in a quiet ceremony attended by Carla and her older brother, Noah.

Delores idolized Lloyd, and he seemed to share the sentiment. Until five years later, when he left a note on the kitchen table telling Delores that it had been fun, but he was headed to California with their much-younger neighbor, Rhonda Bray.

Angie dropped her fork. "You mean Delores and Lloyd are still married? How many years has he been gone?"

"They are. He left six or seven years ago."

"Who knew? Seems like yesterday," I said, remembering how crushed Delores had been.

"I know, it's crazy how quickly time goes," Carla said. "It would make my life a whole lot easier if we found out the old coot had died." Carla leaned back in her chair and yawned.

I shivered. "Yikes, knock on wood. Don't even think about it." With Angie's connections at the department, she might have access to locate him. "Any suggestions on where to begin a search, Angie?"

"My first thought would be the Internet, unless he's changed his identity. Or you could hire a private investigator. I can give you a name." Angie pulled a pen from her bag, scribbled on a napkin, and pushed it in front of Carla. "She's not cheap, but she's good. If Lloyd can be found, she'll find him. I can run a check at the office as a last resort. Does Rhonda's ex still live next door to Delores? He might know something."

"I'm not sure. Mom hasn't mentioned him, but I understand why." Carla nodded for the waitress to bring another round of drinks.

Angie cut her off. "I've had my limit; besides, I have to work in the morning."

"I'll have another," I said. My resolve officially scampered out of the building. This was the first outing I'd had since Phillip left, and it felt good to sit with my friends and push my problems aside.

By the time our drinks arrived, our talk had transitioned to divorce—mine.

I jerked the fruit from my drink and dove in.

Angie frowned. "Maybe you ought to go easy on the booze."

Carla turned to Angie and said, "Since when are you the party pooper?" Then she added, "Cece, can you still tie a cherry stem with your tongue?"

"Cherry-stem tying isn't exactly smiled upon at the country club," I said.

Angie leaned forward, elbows on the table. "You're no longer a member." To Carla she said, "Her mother-in-law had her membership canceled. Probably rusty anyway."

Thoughts of Hazel Cavanaugh ruling my life surfaced. Money was power, and Hazel had both. I doubted Weezie's had enough alcohol to erase Hazel from my memory.

"Do I detect a triple-dog dare?" I asked. *What the heck?* I couldn't remember the last time I'd had a good laugh or a triple-dog dare. What better way than by making a fool of myself with friends? Plucking the cherry from my drink, I twisted off the stem and poked it in my mouth.

It took a few tries, but I finally stuck out my tongue with a neatly tied stem.

"Impressive," said a familiar male voice from behind my chair.

I gulped, and the stem lodged in my throat. The dang thing wouldn't come up, wouldn't go down. My gag reflex kicked in. *Cough. Gag. Cough. Gag.* Tears rolled, and more tears rolled.

Angie and Carla hooted with laughter. Seconds away from peeing my pants, I grabbed my throat to show them I wasn't joking.

"Alder, give her the Heimlich!" Angie yelled.

Next thing I knew, I felt myself yanked from the chair. Strong arms grabbed me under my boobs and jerked my stomach into my backbone. The stem shot from my mouth.

I didn't have to see him to know who rescued me. It was the second time in two months he'd saved me from my own stupidity.

"Are you okay?" Detective Case Alder whispered in my ear.

My face grew warm. I nodded and shot a sour look at Angie. *What's he doing here?* I mouthed.

The corners of Angie's mouth hiked in a knowing grin. Of course, she'd invited him. Another attempt to fix me up with the eligible bachelor—even though my divorce wasn't final. I'd been fighting feelings for Detective Alder since I'd met him back in April on a job. The one where I'd almost been killed.

"I'll deal with you later," I whispered to Angie.

Carla batted her eyelashes. "Aren't you going to introduce me?"

I rolled my eyes, removed the fruit from my drink, and took a long swig.

"Carla, this is Detective Case Alder." Angie made the introduction, and Alder slid into the chair next to me.

Carla shoved her hand across the table. "I'm Carla Edison, from North Carolina," she said in a phony southern drawl. She may have lived there for more than twenty years, but she still talked like a Midwesterner, except, apparently, in the company of an attractive man. An attractive man with incredibly blue eyes, black hair shot through with enough silver to make him look cultured, and a mustache that made me quiver.

Alder grasped her hand and shook. "Nice to meet ya, ma'am." He must have caught on to her bogus accent. Alder had a fine southern drawl, the kind which makes you crave sweet tea, but he'd gone overboard on the twang.

Angie stood. "I hate to break up the party, but I've got an early day tomorrow. Good to see you again, Alder. Since you went on evenings, I haven't seen much of you."

Ah, that explained why she hadn't been on my back to go out with him. Out of sight, out of mind.

Carla's cell rang, and she excused herself to take the call. We were still saying our goodbyes to Angie when Carla came back to the table, visibly shaken, tears in her eyes.

"Max had a heart attack," she said with an unsteady voice. "He's in the ICU. I need to get home."

Alder stood. I started to, but my knees buckled, and I fell back onto the chair.

"Too much to drink?" Alder asked me.

I held two fingers in the air. "I only had a couple," I said.

Angie hugged Carla. "Is there anything we can do?"

"Can you follow me to Mom's? I have to drop off her van." Carla curled her lower lip and frowned. "But I also need a ride to the airport. I booked the last seat on a flight that leaves in two and a half hours."

Angie nudged her with a hip and said, "Come on. I'll take you."

"Okay," Carla whispered. "But, what am I going to do about Mom's house? I only have thirty days." Tears welled in the corners of her eyes again. "Never mind, I can't even think straight. I need to get to Max."

I knew I shouldn't have, but my mouth opened, and the words rushed out. "I don't have anything going on at Hunter Springs until the day after tomorrow. The least I can do is get it started until you figure something out."

"Are you sure?" Carla asked.

"Yes," I said, mentally kicking my butt.

"The key is under the ceramic frog on the front porch." Carla's hand shook as she pulled a piece of paper from her purse and handed it to me. "I started a to-do list."

"I've got this. Don't worry," I said with bravado. "And I can take you to the airport, if Angie has to work in the morning." I grabbed my purse and started to follow, but Alder nudged my chair with his knee.

"You're not driving anywhere." He motioned for Angie and Carla to go ahead. "You ladies go on. I'll make sure Cece gets home."

"Are you kidding? I'm fine." I pushed against him until he relented and moved out of my way.

"I'll take Carla to the airport. Don't worry." Angie winked and practically shoved Carla out the door.

Alder took my elbow. “We’ll get your car in the morning.”

My knees wobbled, and I stumbled.

“See?” Alder steered me toward the door.

My head went woozy, and my insides went woozier. A Missouri Tornado was fixing to touch down in my stomach.

Outside, Alder led me to his car and buckled me in. My head spun like a funnel cloud. I leaned against the door and closed my eyes. A deep, black hole opened in front of me, and I spiraled down. Alder waited, arms open, at the bottom of the tunnel. I slid farther and farther and farther.

Chapter 2

"I don't feel the least bit ashamed of whitewashing Mrs. Cavanaugh's personal life to her mother-in-law. Spying on your daughter-in-law is pretty low in my book."

Beatrice Giovannetti

I awoke in bed with the covers pulled to my neck. The morning sun glared from the open drapes. My eyes slammed shut, and I wiggled deeper beneath my quilt. The sound of the shower in my bathroom jerked me fully awake. I lay there for a minute, listening. The water stopped, and seconds later, the toilet flushed. I remembered walking out the door of Weezies. I remembered Alder helping me into my house last night. I didn't remember Alder leaving. Had he left?

You dork. Not even divorced and already sleeping with another man. I wasn't any better than Phillip. And what kind of man takes advantage of a drunken woman? Alder was a cop and supposed to uphold the law, and order, and everything. I slowly lifted the covers, expecting to see nothing but my nakedness. Thank goodness, I still had on the outfit I'd worn last night.

Throwing off the quilt, I stumbled out of bed and stomped across the floor to the bathroom. The doorknob turned, and I stopped, glued to the floor. If I was ever thankful for anything, I was glad my youngest daughter, Michelle, was vacationing on Cape Cod with her best friend Delia Foster's family. I didn't need my seventeen-year-old witnessing her mother's debauchery.

Could I face Alder? I smacked my forehead, which made my throbbing brain hurt worse. *Think, Cece.* Obviously, I hadn't slept with him, unless he dressed me after he had his way with me. Why didn't he leave? Why hadn't he tried anything? Was he a saint or something? He had an intoxicated woman in bed, and he didn't try anything. What was wrong with him? What was wrong with me? If I went downstairs, he'd join me on neutral ground, not in my bedroom. Well, sort of neutral, considering I lived here. Then I'd kick his sorry butt out.

The door opened.

"It's about time you woke up." Beatrice, my housekeeper, stood in my bathroom with her cleaning bucket and the toilet brush. "It's nearly nine. I've been tiptoeing around for an hour."

"It's you." I almost passed out with relief.

Beatrice screwed up her face and shook the brush at me. "Did you expect a handsome gentleman caller?" She looked me up and down. "Is there something I need to report to your mother-in-law?"

Long story short, after my husband left, my mother-in-law Hazel hired Beatrice to clean my house, so she could spy on me and report back with all my inadequacies. But to my good fortune, Beatrice disliked my mother-in-law almost as much as I did. Even though Hazel paid Beatrice's salary, Beatrice and I had formed a bond to sidetrack Hazel. It couldn't get any better. Beatrice fabricated little stories to throw Hazel off, and I didn't have to worry about my mother-in-law coming around and snooping.

I tugged my shirt and ran a hand through my hair. "Don't be silly. I drank too much. Girls' night out."

"Now I know why your car isn't in the garage." She paused. "I didn't think you were home until I came in and saw you buried under your blankets like a mole."

"Will you drive me to Weezie's after I take a shower?"

"Can't. My old heap's in the shop. My sister dropped me off." She shoved the brush in the bucket and wagged her finger. "I got your bathroom all sparkly. Make sure you wipe down the tile when you're done. I hate water spots."

I had finished my shower and towel-dried my hair when the phone rang. I glanced at the screen and recognized Carla's number.

Balancing the phone between my shoulder and my chin, I answered, "Hello."

Remembering Beatrice's admonishment, I went back to the bathroom to wipe down the shower.

"My flight landed in Raleigh a few hours ago. I'll let you know what's going on as soon as I talk to the doctors."

I sank onto the side of the tub. "Take care of yourself, and Max."

Carla sobbed into the phone.

"Don't worry," I whispered.

"Thanks, Cece." She blew her nose. "I'll find a way to repay you."

"Go. Max needs you. I'll be fine."

"You have the list I gave you, plus I left a few more instructions on the kitchen counter."

"Of course." I threw the towel in the hamper. Beatrice could deal with the water spots.

The thought of standing knee-deep in a hoarder's house made me lightheaded. I contemplated my predicament and how to get my car. Wickford didn't have Uber, and Mr. Guffey, the taxi driver, had an expired driver's license. Calling Guffey for a ride always ended with him getting a ticket from the Wickford Police. The doorbell rang. I pulled on a pair of khaki shorts and a T-shirt and ran a brush through my hair.

"You got a visitor," Beatrice yelled up the stairs.

When I came around to the top of the landing, Beatrice sat on the bottom step, shoe off, rubbing a bunion on her big toe. Alder stood in the foyer dressed in jeans, a polo shirt, and a cocky smile plastered on his face. "You ready?" He also had on a leather jacket which seemed like overkill on a seventy-degree day in June.

"Ready for what?"

"I told you I'd take you to Weezie's to get your car." He smiled, and I felt a flicker of electricity surge in my mid-section. "Umm, you may not remember. You better change into long pants. I brought my motorcycle."

Great. Motorcycle cop to the rescue.

Beatrice stopped rubbing her foot and craned her head in my direction. "You going to make the man stand here all day? Go get some pants on, while I concoct a story to report to you-know-who. If you're not back before I leave, remember that I'm off the next two days for my granddaughter's wedding."

I wondered if having Beatrice was worth the effort. Though, she could sure fabricate some whoppers for Hazel to keep my privacy intact. I would rue the day Hazel caught onto our scheme. She'd fire Beatrice in a flash, and I'd have to find it in my finances to be able to keep her employed. Loyalty does not come cheap.

Did I mention I haven't been on a motorcycle in . . . ? Never. It's never been one of my burning desires. If I didn't need my car so badly, I wouldn't be contemplating it now. The thought of sitting close to Alder made me shiver. I backtracked to my bedroom to change.

~ ~ ~

I pulled into Delores' drive behind her red minivan, the one Carla used when she was in town, and headed next door to the Bray house. I hoped Peter Bray still lived there. Carla had warned me to tread lightly around him, because he wasn't a generally pleasant person. Who was I to judge? We shared a common ground with the cheating spouse thing. At least I could offer him the benefit of the doubt.

Peter Bray opened the door, and before I could open my mouth, he said, "Whatever you're selling, you can take it on down the street. I'm not interested."

My resolve quivered, but I gulped and extended my hand. "Not selling anything. I'm Cece Cavanaugh, a friend of Delores Redmond. I'm helping Carla clean out the house."

When Bray didn't move to shake my hand, I pulled it back. "Got a minute? I'd like to talk to you about Delores. More specifically, her husband Lloyd."

A muscle in Bray's jaw jumped, and he clenched his hand into a fist. "What about Lloyd?"

"Delores is recuperating from a broken hip. She may not be able to live on her own when she's released."

His face relaxed, and he pulled the door open wider and invited me in. "What's that got to do with me?" he asked. "I always liked Delores, everyone in Wickford does, but I'm sure you know about Lloyd and my wife. If this has anything to do with helping Lloyd, don't go there. We were best friends until my wife got the roving eye."

I followed Bray to the kitchen, where he pulled out a chair and motioned for me to sit.

"The thing is," he said. "Lloyd and I became fast friends when he first moved in next door. He and I had a lot in common, and we formed a real friendship. Delores and Rhonda, not so much, but the four of us got together once a week and played cards. We'd barbecue in the summer and have potluck in the winter." He tensed, then let his shoulders sag.

"When it became obvious there was more to our get-togethers than friendly neighbors, I begged Rhonda to stay away from him." Bray seated himself across from me and seemed to take time to form his words. "But she had a thing for older men. Rhonda is . . . I don't know, naive, maybe. She's fifteen years younger than me. Probably twenty years younger than Lloyd. I always thought she wanted a father figure instead of a husband. She kept after Lloyd. He acted lovestruck and helpless around her. Once Rhonda sank her claws in—she got what she wanted, and she wanted Lloyd."

I nodded. "Lloyd talked Delores into selling her family home, and he used her money to buy this house, which cost considerably less. The thing is, he didn't put her name on the deed. Unless we find him, Delores is stuck with a house she can't sell or live in. Her daughter wants to sell it and move Delores to North Carolina to live with her."

The phone rang, and Bray stood. "Sorry, got to take this."

While he left the room, I noticed a couple of photos stuck in the glass door of a china hutch. I pushed out of my chair and went to inspect them. One of the photos pictured Bray and a woman I suspected to be Rhonda. She seemed familiar. The other photo was the woman by herself in a Weezie Bar and Grill T-shirt, and now I knew why I recognized the face. Rhonda had worked at Weezie's years ago.

Bray cleared his throat, and I jumped.

"Oh, sorry. I saw the photos and couldn't help myself," I said.

He waved his hand, dismissing my apology. "Rhonda," he said, addressing the photo. "The one where she's by herself was taken a month or two before she left. She made a fool out of me. The whole neighborhood knew about Rhonda and Lloyd's affair."

"I'm sorry," I said, feeling the pain ooze from him.

"Meh. Life goes on, doesn't it?"

"She worked at Weezie's?" I asked.

"Yes, the two of them would meet there. A friend of mine saw them and clued me in. When I confronted her, she didn't deny it. And you know the rest of the story," Bray said. "Not long after, they left town."

"I know this is a bit personal, but did you divorce her?" I asked. "The reason I ask is because Lloyd and Delores are still married."

"No, she never asked, and I didn't have the energy. Not like I want to get married again and put myself in another bad situation." Bray's chin quivered. "And if you're going to ask if I know where they are, the answer is no. Don't know, don't want to know. I'm sorry about Delores. She's a nice person, but if you find them, don't tell me where they're living. I've made my peace and would rather not have to deal with all those feelings again. Nothing good will come from dredging up the past. Leave it alone."

I told him I couldn't do that and left him standing in his kitchen. Clearly, Delores wasn't the only one affected by what Lloyd and Rhonda had done.

~ ~ ~

The condemned sign nailed to the front door might have scared me off a few months ago, before I'd cleaned a crap-covered restroom at The Bargain Hut. I shrugged it off and shoved the key in the lock. How bad could it be? Mold? Mice? Maggots?

Talk about creepy. I took a step backward and bumped into Eleanor Wafford, the across-the-street neighbor.

"Why lands-a-mercy, we never had a house condemned in Wickford before. No wonder Delores didn't want her neighbors to come visiting," Mrs. Wafford said. "After her gigolo of a husband left, she buckled up her house and became anty-social. And who wouldn't? Only saw her when she came out for the mail. Until she didn't. Then I called the cops. I said to myself, 'Eleanor, sumptin' ain't right.'" Mrs. Wafford pulled a wad of tissue from the sleeve of her pilly cardigan and blew her nose. "Summer cold. I get one every year. Anyways, sure enough, there she was, a-laying in her own pee water, all crippled and moaning for help. Broken hip, happens all the time when you don't take your calcium. Me, I take two a day and walk several miles ever—"

I stepped inside and let the storm door shut after me, putting some distance and glass between me and the yammering Mrs. Wafford.

The little bungalow contained mountains and piles of clutter. No, clutter didn't do justice to the chaos in front of me. Stacks of junk filled the small rooms. I shimmied past a chair and stumbled into a mound of Wickford's daily newspaper, dusty, yellowed, and torn. The *Daily News* straddled a thin line between scandal sheet and society pages. On top of the pile lay a dead mouse. The thought of someone living like this made me sick to my stomach. Oh, wait, it also could've been the fruity drink and the kamikaze I drank last night.

"Yoo-hoo." Mrs. Wafford stood with her nose pressed against the storm door, creating little foggy images every time she exhaled, hands shading her eyes to get a gander. I should have known Eleanor Wafford wouldn't leave before she'd gathered a gossip-worthy eyeful. Wickford thrived on rumor, gossip, and innuendo, and Mrs. Wafford faced the challenge head on.

"You need anything?" She wiped fog from the glass and continued to stare. "I've got freshly made lemonade and tea cookies."

I took another step into the room and heard the storm door squeak open, followed by footsteps. "Stay there, Mrs. Wafford." I turned too quick, twisted my ankle, and grabbed at a bookshelf to catch myself. The whole thing toppled forward, barely missing Mrs. Wafford, who stood mouth agape.

"Lordy mercy, I never seen nothing like this in all my born days. It looks like somebody done threw a hissy fit and tore this place to pieces." The old biddy took a tentative step forward, craning her head to get a better look.

"Don't come any closer," I yelled. "It's not safe." I felt my way around the bookcase and ushered Mrs. Wafford out the storm door, turning the lock as I did.

Mrs. Wafford shoved the tissue back in her sleeve and stood her ground.

"I'll stop by and try some of those cookies before I leave," I promised. *Please leave. Now.*

"If you need my help, I'm right across the street." Her wrinkled face drooped into a frown. She readjusted the white, stretchy headband which held her wiry gray hair in place, tucking in a few scraggly strands.

"Okay," I called after her, stifling a curse word.

She pulled the ratty sweater around her and shuffled in her slow octogenarian gait across the street, up the three steps on her porch, and into the house. Her door had no sooner closed when the drapes in her living room parted slightly.

I shook my head and turned back into the living room. The house had a used bookstore smell—musty and old. I pulled open the front drapes and light spilled into the tiny space, illuminating bundles of foam egg cartons, stacks of mail, and more knickknacks than I'd seen in my life.

Chapter 3

"I've been infatuated with Cece since the day she walked into my construction trailer looking for work. I can only hope the feelings will someday be mutual."
Grant Hunter

Me and my stupid big mouth. I stood in Delores' kitchen, practically hyperventilating. Canned goods, dishes, utensils of every size and shape, and laundry baskets exploding with clothing filled every counter, table, and square inch of the floor, except for the space I'd cleared in front of the ancient beige refrigerator.

Carla had left a pile of empty cardboard boxes stacked on the porch, and I'd brought two with me when I cleared a path down the hall from the living room. I'd already filled one carton with forty packages of expired AAA batteries, seventeen rolls of Kodak film, and twelve tubes of some off-brand toothpaste—all items I'd found in the fridge. Who used film these days, and why would Delores keep toothpaste in the refrigerator?

By two, I'd picked through and sorted the piles of clothing in the baskets and delivered a load to the women's shelter. The volunteers would have to launder everything, but by the looks of the rest of the house, Delores had plenty to wear.

At this rate, I'd still be carting stuff next week. Grant Hunter owned a truck, and I knew he'd let me borrow it, but I hesitated to ask. Shortly after I'd started cleaning condos for him, he'd invited me to coffee. I thought he wanted to discuss a job, but he had expressed more than a business interest. His attention flattered me, but once I explained about my pending divorce, he'd settled for being friends. I knew he wanted more than friendship, but I was grateful Grant never pushed the issue.

At two-thirty I broke down and called. While I waited for Grant, curiosity led me to the little garage out back. It listed to the left, and the roof sagged like it had shouldered a huge weight. A length of gutter had given loose at one end and swayed precariously in the breeze. The garage also had a CONDEMNED sign plastered across the door.

I walked with guarded steps along the cracked pavers leading to the back. I tried the side door, but it didn't budge. Darkness crowded the windows, making it impossible to see inside. Clearly, I couldn't handle the garage by myself. I went back to the house and before long heard vehicles out front. Help had arrived in the form of two trucks, a flatbed trailer, two young men, and Grant Hunter himself.

I held the door open and invited them in. "Welcome to hoarder's paradise," I said.

Grant, a sweet, affectionate giant of a man with coffee-colored eyes, glanced around the living room and whistled. "Holy smokes, woman. What have you gotten yourself into?"

I sighed and shook my head. "Apparently a big mess."

Grant put an arm around my shoulder. "Fellows, this is Mrs. Cavanaugh."

His crew wore jeans, T-shirts, and work boots. The tallest of the two smiled. "I'm Brad James, and this is Larry Welsh." Brad might have been the tallest, but I gave them both an A+ in the looks department, though they were total opposites. Brad had sandy-colored hair and big green eyes with the longest lashes I'd ever seen on a man. The smaller fellow, Larry, sported dark brown hair and sparkling brown eyes.

"Thanks for coming. As you can see, I'm in over my head," I said.

"Cece, tell them what you want done." He turned to his men and said, "Anything she asks, you do it. If Ms. Cavanaugh isn't happy, then I'm not happy. You guys understand?" Grant hugged me to him.

"Sure thing, Mr. Hunter," Brad said.

We left the guys in the living room and walked to Grant's truck.

"You're a lifesaver. I'll make it up to you," I promised.

He rubbed his chin and winked. "Yeah, I think I know what you can do to pay me back."

I felt heat rise to my cheeks and couldn't blame it on a hot flash. Exactly the reason I didn't want to ask for his help. "Grant."

"Dinner." He smiled, and his eyes twinkled. "Unless you had something else in mind."

I cuffed him on the shoulder. "Get your mind out of the gutter."

"Okay, then. I've got to get back to work." He climbed in his truck and waved. "You've got help as long as you need it."

I put the guys to work. Brad went to the kitchen with an armload of boxes and instructions to clear off the countertops. Larry loaded his truck with water-stained boxes from the spare bedroom. I'd opened a couple of them and found warped books. A call to the library confirmed they had been rescued several years ago after a water pipe had burst and flooded the building. Delores apparently couldn't stand the thought of throwing them out, and she'd salvaged them and increased her hoard. No doubt, they were the culprits responsible for the musty smell in the house.

I found an undamaged box of cookbooks in the kitchen and had Larry haul them to my car. Carla could ship them to North Carolina if she wanted. I didn't want to chance throwing out family recipes. Delores cooked and baked like a professional chef. She always had unique recipes for the library bake sales.

When they had the truck loaded, I sent the guys to the dump and continued to pack away the more delicate items. Two curio cabinets in the living room contained soapstone rhinos, bronze Buddha statues, trinket boxes, and an assortment of exquisite Asian fans. Most likely more souvenirs from Noah. In the bottom of the last cabinet, I found a dozen jade elephants.

I'd loaded the last box in my car when Brad and Larry returned with a Café du Soleil sack. Brad removed three coffees. "Mr. Hunter said we'd make extra brownie points if we brought you one of these." He handed me a café special, a creamy coffee and chocolate concoction laced with cinnamon and nutmeg. I'd never been a coffee drinker until Grant introduced me to this heavenly potion, but now I was hooked.

"You guys sure know how to make a gal feel special. Either one of you married?" I asked, thinking maybe I'd found some son-in-law material. Jessie had turned twenty-five on her last birthday and had yet to find *the one.*

They both blushed.

"I'm not ma'am, but I sort of thought you and the boss were a thing," Brad said.

"You're kind, but I'm old enough to be—" I laughed. "I'm definitely old enough be your older sister. But I'd be willing to fix you up with my daughter—providing you work real hard today. She's a perky blonde with a career in nursing."

Jessie would kill me. She'd warned me more than once about matchmaking. I didn't listen. Most of my friends were grandmothers, or at least had a son-in-law and the potential for grandchildren. Me? I sat around waiting for Jessie's eggs to dry up.

"She sounds nice," Brad said.

I scrolled to her photo on my cell phone and shoved it in his hand. "She got the looks in the family."

Larry whistled. "Man, you better take her out. You haven't had a date in months."

I circled in for the prize. "How about coming by the house Thursday? I'm grilling steaks, and she'll be there."

"Uh, okay. I guess so." Brad handed me the phone and grinned. "She is cute."

"Let's get back to work," I said. "Larry, you finish in the kitchen, and Brad, I need help getting into the garage. The door's jammed."

~ ~ ~

Brad pushed and tugged the side door with no results. Beads of sweat spotted his T-shirt. He released the knob and headed around to the front of the garage. "Let me give the overhead door a try," he said.

He grabbed the handle of the rickety garage door and gave it a yank. The door screeched and rose an inch or two before sliding back to the ground.

"This one's as bad as the side door and as stubborn as Larry," he said. His left cheek dipped in the center, showing me a hint of dimple. Dimples, the perfect trait for my future towheaded grandchildren. Grandchildren he and Jessie would give me. Provided I could introduce them, convince them they were soul mates, and get them married off while I was still young enough to enjoy grandchildren. If only—

"Mrs. Cavanaugh, did you hear me?"

I shook the imaginary grandchildren out of my head and blinked. "What?"

"Stand back. I'm going to put some muscle into it. No telling what's jammed. Don't want you getting hurt."

I took a few steps back and admired the set of his shoulders. Another picture flickered to life. Brad's strong arms holding my grandchild in the air. Laughter and giggles filled my ears. Yes, I would definitely have to work on getting Brad and Jessie together.

He bent low and yanked the handle. This time the door bumped and groaned, rose a foot, and stopped. Brad wrapped his other hand around the handle and jerked. The door squealed, and shrieked, and squalled. An ear-splitting percussion followed by a sound like a giant spoon, a whole bushel of giant spoons, grinding and grating in an industrial-sized garbage disposal. The door broke free and flew up the track. A mound of black trash bags convulsed, and shuddered, and swayed.

Brad pulled me to the side in time to keep us from being buried when the entire pile rumbled and spewed from the garage.

"Holy crap," I shouted.

Several of the brittle bags burst, disgorging the contents. Hundreds of cans of chili con carne, pork and beans, and double cans of chow mein rolled and careened down the driveway, crashing at the curb in a smorgasbord of red and blue and orange labels.

A noxious odor pulled my attention toward the tiny garage. "What in the name of everything holy smells so nasty?" I tugged the neck of my shirt to cover my nose, taking in small, shallow breaths.

"Dead," Brad said. "Something dead for sure. A mouse? An army of mice. Maybe a raccoon or 'possom? In this mess, could be anything."

I scanned the garage, checking beyond the initial log jam of trash bags. Every square inch of space contained boxes, or plastic totes, or more trash bags.

"Here's a freezer." Brad made a path, then lifted boxes from the top of the freezer and set them on the floor. When he lifted the last one, the bottom gave way, and a bloated rat thudded to the ground.

I screamed and stumbled backward.

"Now we know what smells," Brad said. "He's dead. Can't hurt us now."

Brad put a plastic tote on top of the offensive rat and hauled it outside. While he disposed of the rodent, I opened the windows, then ran back to the house and found a can of air freshener I'd brought. The industrial kind, guaranteed to eliminate even the most offensive of odors. Brad had gotten the side door open. Once I sprayed, the breeze began to stir, and the smell faded. Brad lifted the lid of the rust-pitted, off-white vintage freezer. The hum and whir of the motor filled the garage.

I sidestepped a box and peered inside. Stacks of TV dinners and frozen desserts lay encrusted in years of frost. I pictured Lloyd and Delores watching old *Bonanza* reruns and chowing down on turkey, mashed potatoes, and cranberries, followed by a slice of semi-frozen coconut cake. The odd thing—Delores was an amazing cook. I'd bet she hadn't eaten a frozen dinner since Lloyd left. I pulled the plug from the wall and the motor squealed to a halt.

"We should let this thing defrost." I stretched and massaged a kink from my back.

Brad picked up a crowbar he'd found and began chipping away at the layers of ice and food. "Might as well get on with it. As hot as it is in here, it'll defrost while we work." Pausing, he pushed his ball cap back and swiped at his forehead with the back of his arm.

Thirty minutes later, we had dislodged and removed half the freezer contents and gotten to the point where the packages gave way to a layer of newspaper.

"Strange." Brad poked at the crusty mess, peeling back a corner with the crowbar.

I stood on my tiptoes and bent in to see better. We scraped away the frozen newspapers and unearthed a plastic tarp.

"Who knows what goes on in the mind of a hoarder," I said. "Delores plain wigged out after her husband left." I might have gone a little cray-cray when Phillip ran off with his assistant, but hoarding wasn't on the horizon now that I'd seen this mess. I might need to get Beatrice to do some serious decluttering. Maybe hold a yard sale. Anything to keep from getting into this kind of funk. One thing was sure, I wouldn't be wigging out on frozen dinners. I pulled at layers of plastic while Brad urged the pry bar into the corners and under the tarp.

He tugged, grunted, and removed a huge section, revealing a frost-covered shoe. He wiped the iciness away and tugged on the tarp, exposing another shoe. He watched me with wide eyes. "Why would she put shoes in the freezer?"

"What?" I asked. My fingers ached from the cold. I shivered as I slid them beneath the edge of the tarp and wrenched it away. What Brad said finally clicked in my brain. A sinking feeling snagged my heart, dropped to my stomach, and rippled to my knees, which had begun to shake and tremble. I allowed my gaze to travel from the shoe to pant legs frozen into stiff pleats. Little ripples of nausea churned in my gut and turned into rolling waves.

I shrieked, slammed the lid, and lost my lunch.

Chapter 4

"Cece is both infuriating and adorable at the same time. She has me at arm's-length for the time being, but I'm not going anywhere."
Detective Case Alder

Larry came running when I screamed. Brad lifted the lid of the freezer and confirmed we'd found a real body and not some Halloween dummy. While Larry called 911, Brad pulled a chair from the kitchen and sat me down on the front porch. When I started shivering, he retrieved a jacket from his truck and wrapped it around my shoulders.

Two patrol cars showed up almost immediately. The officers cleared the area and gave orders for us to stay where we were. When Detective Alder arrived on the scene, I hadn't moved from my spot. He stopped to talk to an officer at the end of the driveway and then made straight for me.

"Are you okay?" he asked, worry in his blue eyes.

I answered with a shiver and buried my face in my hands. In my forty-eight years of life, I'd seen plenty of dead bodies in the hospital when I worked as a nurse or at funeral visitations. Never once had I seen one frozen stiff.

Alder knelt beside me. "What happened? Why are you here?"

I looked at him, seeing for the first time a small, jagged scar at the edge of his upper lip, partially hidden by his mustache. I longed to reach out and trace its path with my finger. A jolt of electricity passed between us. He cleared his throat and stood. I wanted to crawl into his arms and disappear. Instead, I tried to make my mouth move and failed. I'd never been at such a loss for words before.

"We're cleaning the house for Mrs. Cavanaugh's friend," Brad answered.

Alder cut a glance toward the two young men. "Who are you?"

"We work—"

Alder cut him off. "I didn't ask what you were doing. I asked who you were."

Brad gulped. "I'm Brad James, sir."

"I'm Larry Welsh."

Alder jotted something in the notebook he'd pulled from his shirt pocket. He took addresses and phone numbers for both.

"This is-is," I stuttered. "Carla's mom's house."

"Your friend at the bar?" he asked.

"Her mother, Delores Redmond lives here."

Alder smiled an encouraging smile while he wrote those details in his notebook. "Who found the victim?"

"Me." I winced. "Brad too. He helped me in the garage. Who is it?" I finally formed a coherent sentence. "Who's in the freezer?"

"Don't know," Alder said, in a low soothing tone. "At least, not yet. The coroner will take care of identification."

Larry patted my shoulder. "I called the boss, ma'am. He's on his way. Is there anything else we can do for you?"

I pulled the jacket from my shoulders, but Brad shook his head. "Keep it as long as you need it. You can give it to Mr. Hunter."

"You driving the truck out there?" Alder asked, pointing to the Hunter Construction vehicle parked at the curb.

"Yes, sir," Brad replied.

"Will you both go have a seat in it while I talk to Mrs. Cavanaugh? I'll be down to talk to the two of you in a minute."

Brad and Larry nodded and hurried to their truck.

Crap. I slumped against the chair and pulled the jacket tighter. Despite the seventy-degree temperature, my teeth chattered. If I'd been a betting person, I would've bet the dead body was only the beginning of my problems.

I received my answer when Grant's truck skidded to a halt on the street. Alder cut him off halfway up the yard. I couldn't hear what they were saying, but I saw the scowl on Grant's face. He sidestepped Alder and marched to the porch with the detective right behind him.

Trouble seemed to follow me like my mother's cheap perfume. I needed Alder and Grant on the same turf like I needed advice from my mother-in-law. An invisible thread intersecting our paths drew me to one man, Alder. The other, Grant Hunter, had reached out to me for companionship. Could my day get any worse?

"Sir, you need to leave," Alder said. "This is an active investigation."

Grant bristled. "Not until I make sure Mrs. Cavanaugh is okay."

Alder turned to me. "Who is this?"

"My boss," I said, then corrected myself when I saw Grant's shoulders slump. "A friend."

Grant puffed his chest and stood taller. "The guys said you found a body. Are you okay?"

I shook my head, then nodded. "I don't know."

The two men came face-to-face for the first time today, and a sick feeling slithered into my stomach and took up residence.

If I'd been Dorothy with ruby-red slippers, I would've clicked my heels right then. Toto be damned, I prayed for a tornado to swoop down and scatter us to the four winds. Or at least pick up the house and drop it on me. It could happen. Late spring in Missouri meant tornado season.

My brain kicked into gear. I pushed off the jacket and stood on wobbly legs. “No one needs to worry about me. I’m perfectly capable of taking care of myself. I’m a little shocked maybe, but I’m fine. Alder, do you need me to stay, or may I leave?”

Alder closed his notebook and slid it into his pocket. “I still have questions, but they can wait.”

“My purse and keys are inside,” I said, hating how my voice quivered.

Alder shook his head. “I’ll have one of the uniforms retrieve it.”

Grant slipped an arm around my shoulder and pulled me in protectively. “I’ll take you home.”

I pulled away. “I’m finc. Really.”

Alder stared at me and then Grant. “You two figure it out. I’ve got work to do. I’ll stop by later if you’re okay answering more questions.”

“I’ll be home,” I said.

He took off down the driveway to where Larry and Brad were seated in their truck.

When the officer came outside with my purse, I thanked Grant for sending Brad and Larry, told him goodbye, and drove off. After I turned out of the neighborhood, I pulled into a convenience store parking lot, where I laid my head against the steering wheel and started shaking all over again.

I thought of Delores. How long had she lived in her house with a dead body in the freezer? Who was it, anyway? Carla had her hands full with Max, but she needed to know what had happened—though she couldn’t do anything from North Carolina. Still, if it were me, I’d want to know. Alder would question her soon enough. Better to hear the news from me.

When I’d gotten myself under control, I pulled onto the road and drove home. Beatrice had already gone for the day. She’d left a note on the breakfast bar. *The Barracuda’s evil spawn came by.* (Translation: My mother-in-law's son, Phillip, and my soon-to-be-ex had graced me with his presence at my home. It was a long, boring story.) *Wants you to call him.* I crumpled the note and threw it in the trash. Phillip could wait. Forever.

~ ~ ~

Once I'd showered and changed, I carried in the boxes of souvenirs and books I'd removed from Delores' house and placed them on my breakfast bar. The first box contained a dozen jade elephants. The second held twenty soapstone rhinos in various sizes. A third had Asian fans, Buddha statues, and a dozen intricately carved trinket boxes. The last carton contained cookbooks.

I waited for a pot of water to boil and called Carla to fill her in. The call went straight to voice mail. I left a vague message and carried the tea to my office. My office, formerly Phillip's, sat across from my living room. I had claimed it when he left. It still had his masculine decor, but as soon as I could see fit financially, I intended to make this room scream Cece Cavanaugh. His loss, my gain.

When I had first needed a job, I'd been lukewarm to the idea of cleaning, much less cleaning crime scenes. Bruce Fletcher at Bonafide CSC (I'd been so naive that I hadn't realized CSC stood for Crime Scene Cleaners) had hired me, and after a couple of generous paychecks, I slowly began to catch up on my bills. I'd decided a little blood wouldn't deter me from a well-paying job. The downside meant dealing with his irritable, gum-popping secretary, Nancy. She'd treated me as if I had cooties. I hadn't liked her much either.

Then I'd mistaken the elderly Mr. Fletcher for a mugger and sprayed him with pepper spray. Not having much of a sense of humor, he'd fired me, but the work had inspired me to think about starting my own business. If I could make a good wage working for him, I'd be able to do even better working for myself. Plus, whatever money I made would belong to me. The upside meant I didn't have to deal with Nancy anymore.

Jessie had created my business plan and encouraged me from the outset. Michelle had not only been against the idea, she'd all but stopped speaking to me, after a scholarship kid at her school teased her about my line of employment. Lately everything out of her mouth was a snarky remark. I'd almost been glad when school ended for the summer and she'd gone on vacation with her friend Delia's family. I had a whole month free from her moodiness. We needed a break, and it hadn't come soon enough. I still missed her like crazy, though. Even with Beatrice here three days a week, the house felt empty with Michelle gone.

I was browsing my email when the doorbell rang. I expected Alder to come in and launch a zillion questions about Delores and Lloyd. I plodded to the door, not ready to face him, especially after Grant had arrived on the scene. The closer I got to the door, the madder I got. Neither one of them had any claim on me.

I jerked the door open, and Nancy pushed into my foyer, suitcases clutched tightly in her hands. Nancy, the gum-popping secretary from my former employer's office. I'd rather take a punch in the gut than be staring at her. Had thinking about Nancy summoned her to my home? Was that even possible? I sure hoped not. *Note to self: Never, ever think about Nancy, Hazel, or Phillip.* If I had the power to make people appear, I could think of dozens of people to send for, like the Publishers Clearing House people with a big, fat check made out to me. Or on a more nefarious note—a hit squad for my nasty mother-in-law.

"I need a place to stay," Nancy announced, jaw working overtime on a wad of gum. The evening sun glinted off her gold lamé halter.

My mouth dropped open while I took in the sight of her hip-hugging, skin-tight white jeans complete with gold studs and heart cutouts alternating down each leg.

She pushed by me and dropped her bags. "Aren't you going to invite me in? It's been like forever since we've seen each other."

If she comes in for a hug, I'll deck her flat out. Whatever this nightmare is, wake me right now. She had baggage, as in two suitcases. I continued to stare, not sure what to say. The word *friendship* didn't suit the spirit of our relationship. No, *antagonistic* and *scary* summed it up better. Plus, I hadn't seen her in a month, and we'd never even held a personal conversation.

She popped a bubble and sashayed into my living room. "This is some humongo house you got."

When I regained my voice, I asked, "Why are you here? How did you find me?"

"I told you, I need a place to stay." She picked up a vase from the table and turned it over, inspecting the bottom. "I saw your résumé at Bonafide, remember? You never know when an address will come in handy. Ta-da!"

"Excuse me." I took the vase from her and placed it on the table. "It's a gift from my women's group."

She puckered her lower lip. "You always were such a snob. I figured you were the country club sort."

Before I could usher her to the door, she took off toward my kitchen, her nasally voice trailing behind. "Man, so this is how the rich and famous live. Do you have a Jacuzzi? I'd love to soak naked in a big old tub full of swirling water, with little candles and a big glass of fancy champagne."

The thought of naked Nancy lounging in my Jacuzzi caused a wave of queasiness in my already unsettled stomach. *Not in my lifetime.* I followed her down the hall. When she stopped at the breakfast bar, I positioned myself in front of her. "Nancy, what's going on?"

"Fletcher kicked me out, and it's all your fault. I figure you owe me." She eased onto a barstool and flung her purse onto the counter. "After you maced the old coot, he decided to close the office. Wanted to retire while he could enjoy it. Next thing I know, he's sold the duplex and told me I had thirty days to move."

I almost stopped breathing. Did she honestly think I'd let her move in here? I didn't even like the woman.

"So, I ask you," she continued, "without a job, where am I going to find a place to live? When I got to checking and found out you live right smack in the middle of La-Di-Da Land, I thought to myself, I said, 'Nancy, the Cavanaugh woman surely has an extra bedroom she could put you up in.'"

"Well, did you think you might be wrong?" I grabbed her purse and pushed it into her lap. "You can't stay here."

Nancy started crying. Not just little tears collecting in the corner of her eyes, but big glistening rivers, leaving ruts in her makeup. "I don't have any place else to go," she said through sobs and hiccups.

Nancy's demonstration in my kitchen explained why men went crazy when women cried to get their way. It was downright manipulative, but it worked. The more Nancy bawled, the more my resolve disintegrated. "One night," I said. "You can stay one night, but you have to find someplace else. Do you understand?"

Nancy nodded and hugged me.

I pulled back, wanting to maintain my distance. "I mean it, Nancy. This isn't a bed and breakfast."

She pulled a tissue from her purse and dabbed her eyes. "Thank you. I won't be any trouble, you'll see."

"You're not going to be here long enough to be trouble," I said. "Understand? Do you have a plan? Have you applied for any jobs? Did you come here first?" My questions went unheeded, because she was busy rooting through the boxes I'd brought from Delores' house.

She grabbed an elephant and turned it in her hand. "This is sooo pretty."

"Good grief. Would you put it down?" I said. "It doesn't belong to me. What is it with you having to touch everything you see like a two-year-old?"

She continued to twirl it around and 'ooh' and 'aah.' Then she picked up another and pretended to have them kissing by pushing their trunks together, making smoochy sounds with her own lips.

"Stop!" I yelled.

Nancy jumped, and both elephants flew out of her hands. One landed unscathed on a legal pad on the counter. The other crashed to the floor and fractured. *Crap! Carla's going to kill me.* It probably cost a mint, and Nancy ruined it.

"Do. Not. Touch. Anything," I said through clenched teeth. I began to gather the pieces and noticed a shimmer in the debris. I sorted through the small bits and pulled out perfectly shaped stones that looked suspiciously like diamonds. Big diamonds.

Nancy bent down to inspect. "Are those what I think they are?"

If they weren't diamonds, they were a good imitation. I scooped a handful of the sparkly gems. "I don't know what you think they are, but they're none of your business."

I gathered the remaining stones and spread them across the breakfast bar, smoothing them into a single layer.

Something shattered behind me, and I turned. Nancy had thrown the other elephant to the floor, and it exploded with the same result. Tiny, glittering gems sparkled at us.

"I told you to leave them alone!" I stooped to gather this latest trove of jewels.

Bang! Another elephant hit the floor.

"Are you nuts, or deaf, or both?" I yelled, but Nancy paid me no heed and slung another pachyderm with the same result.

"Quit it!" I threw myself across the box. "What have you done? These don't belong to me." *Crap, crap, double crap. How am I going to explain this to Carla? To Delores?* My mind swirled. A dead body in Delores' freezer and diamonds in her elephants. What did all of it mean?

Carla's words came back to me. *Pack all the valuables, and I'll take them back to North Carolina for Mom.* Did Carla know about the diamonds? Had she made me an accomplice in some nefarious plot to scam Delores?

"Why are you getting all bent out of shape? These dumb old things are loaded." Nancy picked up one of the stones and held it on top of her ring finger. "Don't it fit me perfect?"

"Don't get any ideas." I snatched the gem away and pulled one of the trinket boxes from the carton, sliding the diamonds inside. "Until I figure out what this is all about, do not say a word to anyone."

"I knew it. These are diamonds, aren't they? Where did they come from?" Nancy asked.

"I don't know," I hissed. "Keep your mouth shut. Do you understand?"

Nancy placed her forefinger on her chin and tapped lightly. "What's it worth to you for me to keep quiet?"

"What?" I frowned.

"Well, I need a place to stay. For more than one night. And it sounds like you need me to zip my lip." She winked. "We could maybe work a deal."

"Oh, for crap's sake. Are you serious?" I asked, dreading her answer. "No how. No way. One night is the only deal on the table."

The doorbell rang.

"Well, I guess it's possible my lips might loosen up." Nancy's mouth quirked at the corners. "I never could keep a secret."

The doorbell chimed again, and my heart lurched at the thought of giving in to Nancy. I knew Alder would be making an appearance to ask more questions about the body in the freezer. And now Nancy was blackmailing me into letting her stay longer. What choice did I have?

"Okay, deal. Only until we figure this out." What a bad, a terrible idea, possibly the worst one I'd ever had. As a caveat, I added, "Then you're out of here. Do you understand?"

Nancy nodded.

"And do not touch this box until I get back. No, don't touch it period. And stay here. If you make one sound you're out of here. Understand?"

Nancy held a finger to her lip. "Gotcha."

Egad! *Cece Cavanaugh, you have rocks in your stupid head.*

Chapter 5

"People think I'm not smart, but I got a lot going on they don't know about. Take deciding to move in with Cece, for instance."

Nancy, former secretary

I scooted Nancy's bags into the hall closet before opening the front door. Detective Alder stood there with his notebook and pen ready for action. The firm set to his jaw alluded to business and only business. He followed me to the living room, where I motioned for him to sit on the sofa. I chose the wing-back chair, so I wouldn't be sitting next to him, which would have been distracting, to say the least. He gave off a vibe which worked its way to all my nerve-endings at inappropriate times.

"Let's get this over with. Okay?" he asked without looking at me. "What time did you arrive at the Redmond house?"

"Oh, come on. Quit acting all cop-like," I said, trying to lighten the mood. "And you know when I arrived. You took me to my car this morning, so I could go to Delores' house. Remember?"

His shoulders relaxed, and he shut his notebook. "Cece, I know we left things unresolved."

Unresolved pretty much covered it. He was referring to my request for space while I sorted out my feelings and worked my way through my pending divorce. We'd shared a spark during the last murder investigation, the one at Harmony Inn, but I'd been newly separated and not ready to plunge into a relationship. We'd both acknowledged feelings for one another, but he'd agreed to give me the time I needed to process my pending divorce.

He continued, "But if you're seeing someone else, all you have to do is tell me."

"Ugh! No. Grant Hunter is a friend. He's also my boss. I'm cleaning condos at one of his developments. There's nothing going on. I can assure you." I kicked my shoes off and pulled my feet beneath me. "He'd like there to be, but I nixed the idea. When I told you I needed time, I meant it. It's only been two months, and I'm drowning in legal paperwork. Fletcher fired me, so I'm trying to make a go of it on my own. Phillip is making me crazy with his demands, and his evil mother has me banished from every social activity in Wickford."

I laughed, trying to inject some humor into what felt like a lecture. "I don't have time for a social life anyway. My dance card is filled with cleaning, cleaning, and more cleaning. And now a dead body, apparently."

I tried to gauge Alder's reactions, but his face gave nothing away. Not even a hint. If he was angry or fed up with my whole situation, he didn't show it. "I asked you to be patient with me. I'm trying to do the best thing for both of us. I cannot run headlong into a relationship until I've finalized my divorce and am able to fend for myself. It wouldn't be fair to me or you."

Alder raised his hands in the air. "Okay, I give. Sorry. The guy seemed overly protective, and it got my hackles up. You need your space. I get it."

"Thanks," I said, a feeling of relief settling over me. "There is nothing going on with Grant other than a friendly work relationship."

Something crashed in the back of the house, and I froze. Nancy! I had forgotten she was still in the kitchen. "I'll be right back. I need to check something," I said.

Alder rose from the couch.

"Nope." I held my hand out like a traffic cop. "No, you stay put. I'll be right back."

I scurried to the kitchen, where I found another elephant smashed on the floor. "Didn't I tell you to keep quiet and leave those alone?" I pulled a key from the junk drawer and handed it to Nancy. "Go out the back door. There's a set of stairs which lead to an apartment over the garage. Make yourself at home. You can get your bags later."

"As soon as you get rid of your boyfriend, you mean." Nancy made kissy noises.

"Go!"

Nancy took the key and shuffled out the back door.

"Everything okay?" Alder said from behind me.

I startled but maintained my composure. "Fine, everything's fine."

"What's this?" Alder asked, walking closer.

"N-Nothing," I stuttered.

Alder eyed the floor, then me. He bent and retrieved a handful of sparkling stones. "Where did these come from?"

A few lies took shape in my head, but eventually the truth won out. "They came from Delores Redmond's house. Carla wanted me to bring anything of value to my house to determine whether to ship it to her in North Carolina or not. I had no idea they were anything but statues and knickknacks, until I accidentally dropped one and it broke."

He cocked his head. "Ah."

"You met Carla at Weezie's." Why had I brought Weezie's up? I remembered thinking I'd slept with him. My insides turned to jelly. Good thing he couldn't read my mind.

"At the infamous cherry-stem tying event?"

"Funny," I said.

"You removed evidence from a crime scene," Alder said, his tone sounding serious.

"Not technically," I said. "I took the boxes out before I found the body. Along with the dozens I delivered to the food pantry and the women's shelter clothing drive. I cleaned and hauled stuff away the whole day. These appeared to have sentimental value, so I set them aside for Carla. I had no idea they were filled with diamonds. They looked higher quality than the other souvenirs I'd found." I opened the other boxes and showed Alder the rest of the stash.

"I'm going to tag everything as evidence. If it turns out it's not, your friend can claim it at the station." Alder went to his car and came back with evidence bags.

When he had everything bagged and tagged, he secured the evidence and returned to the living room where I waited.

"You had me worried this afternoon. I've never seen you speechless," he said.

"Ha! Probably a first," I said. "I've seen my share of dead bodies from my days at the hospital, but never quite like this. So . . . the body. Did you identify it?"

Alder leaned forward and clasped his hands together, making a steeple out of his index fingers.

I thought of the old rhyme I'd heard as a kid about the church and the steeple.

"The identification we found on the body belonged to Lloyd Redmond."

I gasped. "What? Lloyd's been gone for years. He ran off with a neighbor. He broke Delores' heart." My mind churned with possibilities. Maybe Delores killed Lloyd and shoved him in the freezer. But why? What about Rhonda? I hadn't even opened the other two freezers in Delores' garage.

Alder checked his notes. "Where is Mrs. Redmond again?"

"In the hospital," I said. "She broke a hip."

I heard the backdoor slide shut and footsteps clomp across the ceramic tile. Why hadn't I locked the door behind

Nancy? "I'll be right back." I jumped up and raced to the kitchen.

The refrigerator door stood open, and I could see Nancy's backside bobbing up and down. The rest of her was busy rummaging the food selections.

"What are you doing?" I asked.

When she didn't answer, I pushed the fridge door into her, knocking her off balance.

"What the he . . . . Oh, it's you." She straightened. "You got anything to eat in here besides yogurt and leftovers?"

She had an iPod strapped to her arm. I pulled the earbuds from her ears. "I told you, this is not a bed and breakfast. You are a temporary boarder and not an invited one! My house, my kitchen, my food—off limits."

"Well, you don't have to be such a poop about it." She teetered across the floor on knee-high, glittered spiky-heeled boots.

I ushered her out the door and locked it behind her.

"Was that your daughter?" Alder asked.

I spun around and saw him standing in the doorway with his arms folded across his chest.

The man must have had cat genes, creeping around all stealthy. Between him and Nancy, my nerves were shot. "Her," I blurted out. "Not hardly. She's a big . . . She's like a rock in my shoe. Annoying. Trouble with a capital T."

"Trouble always seems to find you in one form or another, doesn't it?" He tapped his notebook with a pen. "What kind of trouble? Anything I can help with?"

"Nothing, she's a tenant I have staying in the garage apartment. One who has overstayed her welcome. Did you have more questions?"

"She have anything to do with the evidence you found?" he asked.

"No, she showed up on my doorstep this afternoon. As

much as I'd like to pin something on her, the boxes were already here."

Alder lifted one corner of his mouth in a grin. "You are something, Cece Cavanaugh. I haven't decided what yet, but you definitely are something."

I fixed two glasses of tea and ushered him back to the living room. People needed to stay put and stop wandering around my house.

Alder cleared his throat. "Tell me more about Carla."

I told him about Delores' broken hip and Carla's worries that her mom might not be able to live on her own. If Delores wasn't able, Carla planned to sell Delores' house and move her to North Carolina. While he wrote, I told him about Rhonda and Peter Bray, and Lloyd leaving Delores for Rhonda. Before I'd stopped, I'd given him a blow-by-blow of my involvement.

"You are quite a treasure trove of information, aren't you, missy?" He rubbed his chin. "You aren't going to leave this alone, are you?"

I bristled at his words. "What are you insinuating?"

"You know exactly what I mean. You stuck your nose so far into my last investigation that you almost got yourself killed. For your sake, and for my peace of mind, let me handle this one, would you?"

His lecture fell on deaf ears. "Someone needs to tell Delores," I said, changing the subject. "Lloyd broke her heart when he left. I can't imagine how she'll take the news of his death, especially when he's been right there in her garage all along."

"Now that I know where Mrs. Redmond is, I'll talk to her myself." He glanced at his watch. "It's too late now, and I have court tomorrow morning." His shoulders drooped. "I don't suppose you'd go with me to talk to her?"

"You want me to get involved? I seem to recall you ask me to let you handle this. Am I mistaken?"

"You're yanking my chain, darlin', and I'm not taking the bait. Do you want to go along or not?"

"Delores is in a fragile state. It might help to have someone she's familiar with deliver the news. And since Carla isn't here, I guess I'm it," I said.

"Great! You available around four tomorrow?" he asked.

I nodded. "I'll be ready."

When we were standing at the door, Alder said, "One more thing. *Do not* say anything about finding the body in the freezer. I already cautioned the fellows who were helping you, but I'm playing it close to the vest with that information."

~ ~ ~

After Alder drove off, I called Carla again. While leaving a message, I noticed the box of cookbooks I'd brought from Delores' house. Before all the commotion with Nancy and the elephants, I'd started to place the boxes beneath the desk in the little alcove off the kitchen. I'd gotten interrupted and never put the rest of them away before Nancy started her smashing frenzy. Now I debated whether to call Alder and tell him. I decided I couldn't tolerate another lecture. Besides, I had other things to do.

I hadn't gone to check on Nancy. I wondered if I'd done the right thing by letting her stay. On one hand, I felt sorry for her. I'd been desperate when I took the job with Bruce Fletcher at Bonafide. I knew the fear of having no money. At least I had a place to live. Nancy didn't. But she'd been snappy and rude to me. Could I see past her attitude? What did I know about her? She'd been good to Fletcher, and he'd returned the favor by leaving her stranded without a job or a place to live. For all I knew, she could be a scam artist. Or she could be a scared person hiding behind a rude, inconsiderate attitude. I voted for the second.

I dialed Angie's cell and left a message. She could find out if Nancy had a record. That was the nice thing about having a cop for a neighbor and best friend, one who I had enough dirt on to make asking for a favor worthwhile. The dirt wasn't one-sided. Angie and I had known each other since first grade. We knew each other's dirty secrets. Not terrible things, but antics I didn't want my girls knowing and Angie would prefer her employer not learn. Like the incident at our senior skip-day, which may have included skinny-dipping in the mayor's pool while he skied in Vermont, underage drinking, and a crumpled fender on Angie's dad's classic Camaro. Those wild days were well behind us. Angie had a respectable job, and I chaired several committees at the country club. Strike that. I no longer retained a membership at the country club, thanks to Witch Hazel.

Angie strolled in my back door, phone to her ear. She liked to do that. Said it gave new meaning to the word *mobile*.

"You're quick," I said.

"Your message sounds urgent," she said. "What's the big problem you alluded to? Phillip giving you fits again? I keep telling you to change the locks. You're such a wimp. Sometimes, I think you want him to come crawling back."

The first couple of weeks after Phillip had left, he'd kept his distance, but lately he'd been showing up unannounced at the most inconvenient times. He hadn't threatened me, and I knew he wouldn't, but he still wanted to come home, and each time he became more insistent. I would've already changed the locks, but I didn't want to get him riled before our lawyers had worked out a settlement, hopefully a hefty one. After all, Phillip was the one who ran off with a woman half his age. When all the details had been worked out, I'd have a locksmith here before I cashed my first settlement check.

"No. No. No. He's not why I called," I said. "There are two reasons. The first is I found Lloyd Redmond. At least I think it's Lloyd."

"Where's he been all these years?" Angie asked.

"Right here in Wickford," I said.

"Seriously?"

"On ice. In Delores' garage."

"What are you talking about?" Angie gave me her cop stare. The one you don't want to see when you've had one too many beers and decided to drive home, because it's only a couple of blocks.

I relayed the story about the freezer and how I'd found a body underneath a stack of frozen coconut cakes. "Kind of pokes holes in the theory that he ran away with Rhonda Bray. Wonder what happened to her? Her husband still lives next door to Delores," I said. "If it is Lloyd?"

"It'll sure have people checking their freezers for missing spouses." She eyed my refrigerator suspiciously. "Naw, you would've put Phillip in the trash compactor."

"Yeah. No chance he's missing. He keeps showing his pathetic face around here. But if he disappears—"

"Don't even joke about it. Talk about a mess even I couldn't get you out of!"

"Do you think Delores could have killed Lloyd?" I asked.

Angie sat down on a barstool. "Stranger things have happened. You know her better than me."

Growing up, Delores was like my second mother. More like a first mother, since mine passed her time at the local bar. Delores came into my life when I entered fourth grade. She held the position of head librarian at the town library. I was a latchkey kid long before the term existed. To keep from going home, I'd head to the library to quench my passion for reading.

Most days, I'd huddle in a corner to read and forget all about the time. Delores would find me asleep when she made her rounds to close the building for the evening. She'd bundle me up and drive me to her house, because she couldn't stand the thought of me being home alone. No, Delores didn't have a speck of unkindness in her.

"Well, there's no use speculating. You said they don't know for sure it's Lloyd," Angie said. "Don't go getting any crazy notions. Last time you got involved, it was a disaster." She shook her head. "Leave this one to the department. Is Alder working the case?" The glint in her eyes obvious.

I felt my neck heat up. "Yes."

"He brought you home from Weezie's. I saw you leave with him this morning." She winked several times in rapid succession. "Good thing Michelle is gone."

"He didn't spend the night. Nothing happened." I didn't tell her I woke up thinking I'd slept with him. It would work right into her game plan, which was to get me dating someone as quickly as possible.

"You need to snag him before someone else does. He's too good a catch to leave dangling," she said. "He doesn't normally date, and he's interested in you. Significant!"

"You forget, I'm married. Besides, I need a favor. Remember the rude secretary from Bonafide CSC that I told you about?"

"The gum-smacker?"

"Yep. She's here."

Angie hiked an eyebrow and glanced around the kitchen. "Riiight."

"Not here, here. Upstairs here. In the apartment." I told her about Nancy showing up and blaming me for Fletcher taking off to Florida.

"Are you crazy? What do you know about her?" Angie shook her head. "Tell her to leave. You're not her mother."

"I can't make her leave. It's my fault she lost her job," I said, leaving out the blackmailing me over the diamonds part. "She's only staying a little while."

"We'll see. I know you. She'll be here six years from now. Look how long it took you to get rid of Phillip." Angie went to the front door and got the license plate from Nancy's Jeep. "I'm calling the station to run a check on her."

I grinned. "I hoped you would."

Angie gave me the finger. "What's her name?"

I hesitated. "Uh, Nancy."

"Nancy what?" Angie smacked her forehead. "You don't even know her last name, do you?"

"No, but if you run her plate, it'll tell you, won't it?" I crossed my fingers. Phillip had always chided me for being too naive. I preferred to think of it as giving people the benefit of the doubt. In Phillip's case, I'd been too stupid to admit to myself he'd been cheating.

"Yes." Angie relayed the information to dispatch and then drummed her fingers on the counter while she waited for the information. "You better hope she comes back clean," she said. "Or else, I'll have to go upstairs and arrest her. I don't know why I let you talk me into this stuff."

She let me talk her into it because we were best friends. The same reason I didn't blast her when she tried to fix me up with Alder, even when I wasn't divorced. We had each other's best interests at heart, even though we drove each other crazy.

She disconnected and placed the phone in her pocket. "You lucked out. She has a lead foot and enough speeding tickets to paper the apartment upstairs. But there's nothing outstanding on her."

"I owe you one," I said. "What's her last name?"

"You're going to love this. It's Lustbader," she said. "But I tell you, you better make sure she hits the road tomorrow. Not having a record doesn't mean she's not a con artist looking for an easy target."

"Don't worry. She's out of here as soon as the sun comes up." Alder had the diamonds, which meant Nancy had nothing to hold over my head. Oh yeah!

A soft tap on the back door made both of us turn around. Nancy had her face pressed to the glass.

Angie groaned. "Must be Ms. Lustbader herself. You might want to let her know if she gets too loud with the gum, I'll shoot her."

I waved Nancy in.

"What's up?" She sidled to the breakfast bar, pulled out a stool, and sat. Immediately a huge bubble parted her lips. She sucked it in and chewed vigorously.

Angie shot me a look but didn't say a word. Instead, she went to the fridge and rummaged around while I dealt with Nancy.

"Is there something you needed?" I probably should have qualified what I meant before I asked. This wasn't a mini-mart. Unless she needed advice, she could trot right back to the apartment.

Angie pulled out a beer and waved it in my direction. "Want one?"

Nancy nodded until I thought her head would fall off. "I'd love one. It's hotter than Death Valley up there."

Angie looked at me with a *what am I supposed to do?* expression.

I'd probably be sorry for this, but I knew it was sweltering in the apartment. It had been vacant since April, when I'd let my live-in housekeeper, Esther, go. Beatrice only worked three days a week and didn't use it. I'd never opened the vents once the summer temperatures started rising. Without the benefit of air, stifling heat lingered in the space.

"Sure. Why not?" I said.

Angie twisted off the caps and slid two bottles across the counter. She followed with a bag of pretzels from the pantry. Have I mentioned she always makes herself at home? And she loves to eat.

"Little bitty pretzels. They're my favorite." Nancy

pulled the wad of gum out of her mouth and stuck it to the label on her bottle.

I rolled my eyes toward the ceiling, and Angie burst out laughing.

"What's so funny?" Nancy asked.

"Disgusting," I said, pushing the napkin holder toward her. "Why don't you wrap it in a napkin? The trash can is in the pantry."

"Jeez, don't get your panties—"

I squinted and said, "Get rid of it."

She peeled the gum from the label and wrapped it in a napkin. "Happy?"

"Yes," I said. "Nancy, this is my neighbor, Angie."

Nancy stuck out her hand, the same one she'd used to pull the gum off her bottle. "Nice to meet you. I guess we'll be neighbors too."

Angie glowered but didn't offer to shake. "Did I mention I'm a cop?"

Nancy drew her hand back. "I used to date a cop. You work in Wickford?"

"Yes," Angie said.

"You know Joe Rafferty?" Nancy grabbed a handful of pretzels and spread them out on the counter in front of her.

"You dated Joe?" Angie leaned back and took a swig of beer. "Really? He's a great guy. What happened?"

The two of them chattered about Joe while I sat and watched the exchange. Two beers later, Angie glanced at her watch. "I'd better go. Dave will be home soon. Nice to meet you, Nancy. Don't be a stranger. I live right next door."

Nancy came around the bar and hugged Angie. I figured Angie would stroke out, but she hugged Nancy back. In all the time I'd known her, I'd never seen Angie make friends so quickly.

When we got to the patio, they hugged again and went their separate ways. Neither one said goodbye to me. I slid the door shut with a grunt and threw the bottles in the recycling bin.

Crap!

The phone rang while I was wiping down the breakfast bar. I checked the display in case it was Phillip or my mother-in-law. When I saw Carla's number, I answered.

"What in all that is holy is going on?" Carla could barely contain her agitation. "Mrs. Wafford called and said the police had Mom's house surrounded after a shootout. Then the ambulance took someone away."

"Calm down," I said. "First things first: How's Max?"

"He had a freaking panic attack. They're still running tests, but so far, everything has come back negative. His publisher's been leaning on him. I guess the deadlines got to be too much."

"At least you have good news," I said.

She snorted. "Yeah, Max is not good with pressure. What happened at Mom's?"

"There wasn't a shootout. Mrs. Wafford exaggerated."

"Thank goodness." She exhaled. "What *is* wrong with the dingbat?"

I took a deep breath. "Well, something did occur. It seems Lloyd might not have run away with Rhonda Bray after all."

"What? How is Lloyd involved?"

"Lloyd's been on ice." I swear I couldn't help it. After the day I'd had, I needed some comic relief, even if it came at Lloyd's expense. "I found him, or someone with his identification, in one of the freezers in your mom's garage, underneath a stack of frozen desserts." *Crap,* Alder had told me not to mention the freezer. I figured it hadn't hurt to tell Angie, she was a cop, but telling Carla was another matter.

Carla didn't say anything. Then she laughed. "I think we have a bad connection. It sounded like you said you found frozen desserts in my mother's freezer. That can't be right." Carla paused. "Wait. What *did* you say?"

"Look, I wasn't supposed to talk about it, so please don't say anything. The detective will fry my butt. You did not hear this from me, okay?"

"Okay, now you have me intrigued."

"I found a dead body in the old chest freezer in Delores' garage. The cops think he's been there a while." I took the phone to the great room, dropped into the recliner, and flipped up the footrest. This conversation would take a while.

Carla sucked in an audible breath. "Dear Lord, you found Lloyd? In my mother's garage? In the freezer? You're joking, right?"

"Nope, not a joke," I replied.

"I can't even process what you're saying," Carla said. "Must have scared the bejeebbers out of you."

"I'll never open a freezer again without seeing him," I said. "The police won't let anyone in the house, so cleanup is on hold."

"I cannot deal with this. I wanted to find the jerk, but not like this. It must be him. Right? Who else could it be? Regardless, I need to get the house on the market. While I was home, I reviewed Mom's financial records, and other than her checking account, Mom's broke. All her investments were cashed out. The doctor says she can't live on her own. It's either a nursing home or my house." Carla paused, and I heard her breath hitch. "I can't, in good conscience, put her in a nursing home in Wickford. Not with me being in North Carolina. And like usual, Noah won't be around. If it is Lloyd, it solves my problem. At least one problem. As Lloyd's wife, the house goes to her."

"Beats me. I don't know anything about wills or lack of wills. Let's take this one step at a time." I took a giant swig of my beer. "How can she be broke? She gets a monthly pension from the library, plus her social security, doesn't she?" I asked. "And what about the huge payout when your dad died?" Carla's dad had died years ago in a freak accident at the concrete plant. The resulting lawsuit meant Delores would never have to worry about money.

"Exactly what I'm talking about. I've checked all her accounts. I talked to her financial planner, and he said she withdrew everything before Lloyd left. Err . . . . Well, you know what I mean."

"Do you suppose Lloyd did something hinky before . . ." I stumbled on my words. "Before he umm . . . died?" I asked. "Could he have withdrawn it?"

"Oh, Cece, you're not thinking he scammed her out of her money. I've been meaning to talk finances with her, but she always changes the subject. She gave me power of attorney a few years ago only because I made a stink," Carla said. "That's when I found out the house wasn't in her name, but she refused to do anything about it. She assured me Lloyd would do right by her. And seriously, with the kind of money she had, it didn't bother me. The value of the house is nothing to speak of. Except, now, I don't know how I'm going to take care of her if I can't find out what happened to her investments. At least selling the house would provide some additional resources to her pension and Social Security benefit."

Carla asked how much I'd been able to do, and I told her about Brad and Larry helping me. I was about to mention the diamonds when she blurted out, "How much of Mom's personal stuff did you get boxed up?"

"I brought a couple boxes home with me, but most of it's still at her house. A lot of the junk got hauled to the dump, along with some clothing to the women's shelter, but we're making progress." I didn't mention the evidence Alder had taken into custody. I needed to tell her face-to-face.

"Ship what you have. I'll pay you," she said.

My heart sank. "About those—"

"On second thought, hang onto them. I'm coming out as soon as I can get the okay from Max's doctor. By the way, if you hear from Noah, don't tell him anything. And *do not*, for any reason, give him the key to the house."

"I left the key under the frog. Why would I hear from Noah?" I asked. "Isn't he off gallivanting around the globe?"

"You never know with him. He shows up at the oddest times. I left a message when I learned Mom had fallen. Haven't heard back. I'm assuming he's unreachable. But who knows? I need to get Mom's affairs in order before he goes sticking his nose in," Carla said. "He always wants to do the opposite. Ever since Mom gave me power of attorney, he's held a grudge. And he's never around to help. He wants to make decisions and then disappear, leaving me to pick up the pieces. If he finds out her settlement is gone, he'll go ballistic. I will not let him get involved in this."

"Understandable," I said. "I'll get back there as soon as I can. No telling how long the cops will have the place off limits."

"Maybe Angie can help you get in sooner. Or what about your good-looking detective? I only have thirty days."

"I don't know. I'll see. But I'm not pushing the issue." I took another slug of my beer. "I better get going."

"Hey, wait. Don't hang up. If it is Lloyd in the freezer, and he didn't run off with Rhonda Bray, what happened to her?" Carla asked.

"Good question." I was wondering the same thing. "I talked to Rhonda's husband before I knew about Lloyd. Maybe I'll pay him another visit. It's been on the news all morning about a body being discovered at Delores'. Maybe Rhonda's been in touch. Who knows?"

"The old Wickford rumor mill will be going full force. Poor Mom." Carla sighed. "I'll be back as soon as I can. If Max's tests turn out okay, he'll be able to come home, and I'll be on the next flight out. Thanks for everything you're doing."

I disconnected, wondering why she wanted me to ship Delores' personal things now when it hadn't been a priority earlier. Even if she'd seen the elephants, she had no way of knowing about their hidden treasure. Or did she? I hated feeling suspicious of Carla. And what about Noah? He and Carla had always had a strained relationship.

I could only imagine the tension an elderly parent might cause. Having no brothers or sisters, I didn't have to worry about sibling rivalry. Except maybe my two kids and their constant squabbles, which I hoped would not cause problems when they were both grown. When the time came for my mom to need help, it would fall solely on me. Unless she'd found a new man to share her life. I didn't know which thought I dreaded most, worrying about Mom getting older, or worrying about her having a new man in her life.

Chapter 6

"When I was a teenager, Noah Feldman acted like I didn't exist. Yet I had a photo of him stuck in my notebook, and I kissed it every night before going to bed. Is that sick or what?"
Cece Cavanaugh

During the night, I woke several times to howling winds and heavy rain. The sky seemed as unsettled as my nerves. When I wasn't at the window watching lightning chase across the sky, I slept fitfully, dreaming of elephants spewing diamonds from their trunks while a bearded man chased me. It seemed so real; I woke up shaking. I knew I had to tell Carla about the diamonds. Alder would question her when she returned, and it would be better coming from me first. But she had enough on her hands without worrying about what her mom had gotten herself involved with. And I wasn't sure whether Carla already knew.

While I was contemplating breakfast, the doorbell rang. I half-expected Phillip to show up, but instead I opened the door to a man sporting a beard. The hairs on the back of my neck rose. My dream came barreling back. The beard, the diamonds. Had I inadvertently summoned the man from my dream? *Listen to yourself. Have you gone nuts?* No, it had to be coincidence. Didn't it? First, Nancy appeared out of nowhere after I thought about her, now this. I needed to stop opening doors.

He had a backpack slung across one shoulder and wore wrinkled khakis with an equally wrinkled button-down shirt. I thought about slamming the door and throwing the deadbolt, but when my eyes traveled to his, I recognized them instantly.

"Hey Cece," he said. "Are you going to stand there, or are you going to invite an old friend in?"

The voice I recognized too, even fifteen years after the last time I laid eyes on him.

"Noah," I said. "Of all the people. What are you doing here?"

"Carla left a message about Mom," he replied. "I was in Chicago for a conference and decided to swing by to see if I could help."

"Oh." Carla's warning about Noah sent an alarm straight up my spine. Had he really come to help? Or did he have an ulterior motive? I thought about the diamonds and a feeling of dread and a tingle of excitement snuggled together next to my heart. My first teen crush stood on my porch.

"Well, aren't you going to invite me in?" he repeated.

I pulled the door open and stood aside, gaping at him. The years had been kind. His brown hair, a little thinner on top, had gone silver in a good way. He wore a close-cropped beard in the same shade of silver. His tanned skin set off chestnut eyes which were as bright and playful as ever. I smoothed my hair back and sucked in my stomach. The best I could do at the moment, since he was standing right in front of me.

He dropped his backpack in the foyer and wrapped his arms around me. "You're as gorgeous as ever, Cece," he whispered into my ear.

I filed his words away in the *things Noah Feldman would never in a million years say to me* category. My crush had gone unrequited. Noah had never given me a second glance. "You still know how to turn on the charm." Apparently, he'd never made it stick, as he wore no wedding ring.

"I *still* can't believe you chose Phillip Cavanaugh instead of me. What he did to deserve you, I'll never know," he teased.

My hand instinctively went to my bare ring finger. I jerked it away quickly but not fast enough. "Ah, is there a sad tale to tell?" he asked, glancing at my hand.

Typical sarcastic remark for Noah. He hadn't changed. "Nothing I can't deal with," I said.

"Still under his mother's thumb? I can't imagine the Cece I knew taking Hazel Cavanaugh's guff."

I changed the subject and invited him in. "Does Carla know you're here?"

"Here?" he asked, sweeping his arm around my foyer. "Or here, as in Wickford?"

"Either," I said.

He shrugged. "I don't keep track of her, and I try my best to fly below the radar, so she can't keep track of me."

I frowned and shook my head. "In other words, sibling rivalry at its best. I guess I hold no hope my two will outgrow it."

"And how are your girls? Pretty as their mama, I'm betting."

"They're good." I gave him a brief rundown on what my daughters were doing with their lives.

He followed me down the hall to the kitchen, admiring the artwork Phillip had collected during our marriage. "You get the house in the divorce?" he asked with a touch of smugness in his voice.

"We're not divorced," I said. "Yet. Besides, it's none of your business." I needed to put my guard up. Noah could sweet talk a nun into improper acts. We had a history, and not a pretty one. Until I found out his motive for showing up, if he had one, I planned to maintain my distance.

"I came by because I've called Carla several times and left messages, but she hasn't returned my calls. I went by

Mom's house and saw a condemned sign on the front door and crime scene tape. I figured you or Angie would know—what the hell is going on?" Noah settled at the table and ran a hand through his hair, ruffling it in the process.

"What has Carla told you?"

"Mom fell, broke her hip, and landed in the hospital. Nothing else. Not a thing, Cece. Not a blasted thing. I stopped by the hospital first thing."

"How was your mom?" I asked.

"Her usual sunny self. We talked a while, and she dozed off. She gave no indication what I'd find at her house. It looks like a scene out of a horror movie." Noah folded his arms across his chest. "What happened?"

I put two glasses of tea on the table and filled Noah in on Delores' hoarding and the reason for the condemned sign. "Carla asked me to help clean up the clutter. You wouldn't believe the chaos. I've been hauling away old books and clothing. I've brought back some of her collectibles, so they don't get mixed in." *Why had I told him that?* My mouth had a way of shooting itself off before my brain figured out what it needed to hold back. "You know, like family photos and your mom's cookbooks."

"I trust you to make those decision, but you shouldn't have to. Carla should be here. Mom is picky about her personal belongings. You know she dearly loves her collections," Noah said. "She's like a kid any time I send her something new."

"Everything of sentimental value or otherwise is set aside. Carla can determine what to keep," I said. "I have a box of your mom's cookbooks here, if you'd like to see them."

"No," Noah said. "It's fine. Not like I cook anyway. Though, I do miss her pie. No one bakes like Mom. But I do want to see everything you've salvaged to see if it should be saved or not."

"We'll see." I hedged. "Carla will be back soon. Then the two of you can hash it out." I changed the topic and told him about finding a body at his mom's. The possibly-Lloyd body. This time I didn't mention the freezer.

"Body?" The shock registering on Noah's face seemed genuine. "At Mom's? Has she gone 'round the bend? She seemed fine this morning. Lonely maybe, but not like she'd gone crackers. And when did Lloyd come back? What about the neighbor? The one he ran off with? Where is Carla? What's she doing about this?"

"Those are all questions I have no answers for except for Carla and Lloyd's whereabouts," I said. "If it's Lloyd, it appears he never left. Carla flew back to North Carolina because she received a call saying Max had suffered a heart attack, which turned out to be a panic attack." I paused to take a breath and a sip of tea. "She's on her way back to deal with your mom, the house, and, I presume, Lloyd's remains."

Noah pushed his glass away and stood. "Thanks for the tea. I'm headed back to the hospital and Mom's house after I have lunch," Noah said. "You wouldn't want to join me, would you?"

"For lunch, or to visit your mom?" I asked.

"Either. Both." He let out a throaty sigh. In my mind he ran his hands through his hair, a simple gesture, but one that had always made me weak in the knees. Only the man I saw in my mind was much younger, the boy I had once had an intense crush on. I wondered if he likewise imagined a much younger me as we spoke. Or if he only saw the pesky kid who always made goo-goo eyes at him. I could still picture myself tossing my hair over my shoulder and trying to act older than my age. Anything to get his attention. *Stop it, Cece. You have enough on your plate, and Alder to boot. Noah is leaving in a few days.*

If he'd asked me to lunch a million years ago, there would be no doubt in my mind. But I hesitated, worried Alder or my mother-in-law might spot us. I didn't need tongues wagging about my personal life. I had nothing to hide, but with Noah, caution was my motto.

"Don't read anything into it. I have to eat, you have to eat. If you join me for lunch, we can eat together. We can talk about old times and catch up." He followed me to the foyer and slipped his backpack on his shoulder. "Fill me in on what's been happening in Wickford. I kind of miss small-town gossip."

"Umm." I waffled. "I don't know."

Noah leaned down and kissed me on the cheek. "Why so hesitant? Maybe I'll give Phillip his comeuppance."

The fifteen-year-old Cece would have melted at a peck on the cheek, but the adult—not so much.

"Too much on my to-do list today. How about a rain check?" I asked, hoping it would fail to materialize.

He shrugged. "Okay. Well, I need to get back to the hospital and then find a place to stay, since it appears I can't crash at Mom's place. Any recommendations?"

"The old Wickford Gardens apartment building on Main Street is now a hotel called The Riverside Sanctuary. I don't know about the rooms, but they have a fantastic restaurant."

"I'll check it out," he said. "Once I'm settled, the least I can do is buy you dinner, considering all the help you've been to Carla."

"Okay," I replied. "Call me. We'll work out a time. In the meantime, your mother doesn't know about Lloyd, and the police want to talk to her this afternoon."

"The police?" Noah asked. "They don't think Mom had anything to do with Lloyd's death, do they?"

"I'm sure it's routine." I paused. "She had her dead husband in her garage."

"I suppose, but I'll be there for her," he said. "With an attorney."

Alder and Carla would kill me for telling Noah, but I hadn't even thought about the possibility of Delores needing a lawyer. And it made sense. Considering the circumstance, I wouldn't want my mother questioned.

Now I wished I hadn't told Alder I would go with him to visit Delores.

Noah left as Beatrice was arriving. She gave him the once over, parked her car, and scurried up the sidewalk with a massive grin on her face.

"What are you doing here on a Saturday?" I asked. "Thought you had a wedding."

"I do. Ran off and left my readers here yesterday, and without them I can't read the program or anything else."

"I think I remember seeing them on the desk in the alcove," I said.

"Another gentleman caller, I see? You're making quite a reputation for yourself. Care to elaborate, so I can come up with a good story for your mother-in-law?" Beatrice asked, her eyes twinkling at the thought of espionage.

"Old boyfriend from my school days," I said, knowing Beatrice would spin a good tale for Hazel. "He's in town because his mother is in the hospital. But he did ask me to dinner. There's nothing to it."

"He got a name?" Beatrice asked.

"Noah Feldman," I said.

"Don't you worry about a thing. This will get back to The Barracuda before you can bat your eyelashes."

I loved the nickname the gals at Maids a-Plenty had given my mother-in-law. Hazel cycled through housekeepers like I go through a good bottle of wine—fast! Beatrice had escaped working for her until Hazel decided she needed a snitch in my house while my divorce was pending. All the other housekeepers had already met the wrath of Hazel and begged off, leaving Beatrice for the dirty work. Only

Beatrice and I hit it off and decided to turn the tables on Hazel by feeding her fake information. Childish, I know, but I loved antagonizing my mother-in-law.

~ ~ ~

Police tape surrounded the little garage behind Delores' house. I circled the block twice to make sure Alder wasn't around. He'd said he worked evenings, but I wasn't willing to take a chance on running into him. I told Carla I would talk to Peter Bray to see if he'd heard from Rhonda. I parked in Delores' driveway and cut between the hedges separating the two lawns.

"Stop. Stop right there. Get off the grass." Peter Bray knelt in front of an impressive flower garden planting marigolds. He jumped to his feet, grabbed the hose, and turned the nozzle on. "Get off my lawn before I squirt you."

"Mr. Bray, it's me, Cece Cavanaugh. From the other day. Can I talk to you?" I asked.

"Are you deaf? Do you have no respect for turf, woman?" he asked, pointing the spray in my direction. "There's a sign. 'DO NOT WALK ON THE GRASS.' Are you blind too? Do I have to install a billboard to keep you people off my lawn?"

I ran back to Delores' driveway before he drenched me. Peeking through the hedge, I said, "Mr. Bray, I need to talk to you."

"You and everyone else. Come around on the street." He turned off the hose and met me in the driveway.

"Your lawn is beautiful," I said, hoping to get on his good side. This time of year, dandelions were the bane of landscapers all over Missouri. Not even one dared show itself in his yard. Only perfectly manicured grass lived here.

"Yeah, well, it takes effort, and when people like you and those cops and the news people tromp across it, it doubles my work. I'll never undo the damage those photographers did trying to get a good angle." He pulled off his hat and scratched his balding head. "You can fertilize, water, trim, and baby all you want. All it takes is one careless trespasser to make it all for nothing."

Jeez, I wondered if I would have to get down on my knees and beg forgiveness. Maybe offer up a sacrificial rake. "Please, could I have a minute of your time?" I asked.

He scowled.

"It won't take long, I promise."

"What? Oh, fine." He stared over my shoulder. "Take a picture, you old hag. Get back in your house and shove those binoculars."

"Excuse me?" I spun around.

"It's the old biddy from across the street. She thinks she has to know everything going on around here. Doesn't have a life, so she sticks her nose in everyone else's. A person can't smoke a cigarette on his own front porch without her sending out a neighborhood news flash."

Mrs. Wafford scurried back into her house. Of course, the drapes separated instantly. I wondered if she had microphones scattered around the neighborhood, or maybe she read lips.

"Now, what do you want?" Bray asked while winding the hose into a coil.

I followed him to the house as he wound, being careful to stay on the sidewalk. "Obviously, you know about the body they found at Delores'."

"You mean, Lloyd? Couldn't miss it if I wanted to. They carted him right across the driveway into the ambulance. Then I had to defend my lawn from all the looky-loos. Well, it's too bad. He must have pushed Delores—fine lady she is—right over the edge. I never saw the day coming when she'd seek revenge. She's always been mild-mannered and forgiving. But who knows what makes a person snap?"

Tell me what you really think, I thought.

Bray turned around and shook his trowel at me. “A person can only put up with a cheating, lying imposter for so long.”

“Oh, Mr. Bray, you can’t possibly think Delores killed Lloyd,” I said.

“What’s your explanation?” he asked. “Her garage, her freezer, her husband. Doesn’t take an Einstein to figure out what happened. I hate to say it about someone as nice as Delores, but everyone has a breaking point.”

“What’s your take on Rhonda?” I asked.

“What does she have to do with this?”

“If Lloyd never left, then why did your wife leave?”

Bray pulled a towel from his back pocket and swiped it across his forehead. “Darn good question. You think Rhonda’s involved? I don’t see the connection, but she could be.”

“How can you not see a connection?” I asked. “Lloyd and Rhonda disappear at the same time, and even you assumed they ran off together. Aren’t you curious where she is? What if she never left either?”

“Frankly, I don’t care where she is. And she did leave. You don’t see her hanging around here, do you?”

“Has she contacted you since Lloyd turned up?” I asked. “Like you said, it’s been all over the news.”

“Why on earth would she contact me? For all I know, she killed Lloyd and then took off. Now that would make sense, wouldn’t it? Maybe he decided not to leave after all. Or maybe Rhonda made it all up about them running off. If I had known back then what I know now, I would never have married her.”

“How long were you married?” I asked.

“Married her about a year before Lloyd and Delores hooked up. Rhonda was a cute little number but man-crazy. Worst mistake I ever made. And maybe the worst mistake old Lloyd ever made.”

Chapter 7

"Haven't seen my buddy with a woman in a long time. For him to bring Cece in for a burger, must mean she's pretty special."
Dicky Dickerson

Alder drove me by the morgue to see if I could do a visual identification. The day I'd discovered the body, I never looked past the shoes and pant legs. The attendant led me to a room and shoved a close-up photo of the dead man in my face. I made the identification based on several things I knew about Lloyd. He had a creepy-looking goatee, was bald on top with an atrocious comb-over, and had the bushiest, blackest eyebrows I'd ever seen. Like two fuzzy caterpillars meeting in the middle over the bridge of his nose. Definitely Lloyd Redmond.

On the way to Delores' room, I broke the news to Alder about Noah and the attorney.

"Well, it adds a new wrinkle, but nothing I can't handle," Alder said. "I need to question the son anyway. What do you know about him?"

Egad! *Nothing, Alder. Not a thing!* "He's lived out of the country for years," I said, gulping before continuing, "He grew up here. I had a thing for him in high school, but it was years ago." *Why did I feel it necessary to share personal information?*

A muscle jumped in Alder's jaw, but when he turned his smile seemed as genuine as ever. "I wish I had known you back then. Were you two serious?"

"Ha! I wished. He acted like I didn't exist," I said. "To him I was one more pest in his sister's social circle. Teenage drama on my part." My heart wasn't ready for a replay of unrequited love, and my head wasn't all the way in the game with Alder. I didn't know how long it would take to get where I needed to be. I only hoped Alder could see his way to waiting me out.

Alder smiled. "Let's go get this over with."

When we walked into the room, Delores' face brightened. When she realized she didn't know Alder, she narrowed her eyes. "Who's he?"

Noah hadn't arrived, nor had the attorney he promised.

I scooted a chair next to her bed. "Delores, this is Detective Alder. He's a friend of mine."

Delores leaned forward and looked Alder squarely in the eyes. "You're a detective?"

Alder nodded, but to his credit, he remained quiet.

"Did you enjoy your visit with Noah?" I pulled Delores' hand into mine and rubbed my fingers over her wrinkled skin.

She sat straighter. "Noah is here? My boy is in Wickford?" Then she frowned. "Why? Am I dying? Are they keeping something from me?"

"No," I said. "You're going to be fine." I glanced at Alder, and he shrugged. "Noah hasn't been to see you?"

"No. I think I'd remember my own son coming to visit," Delores said.

"We have something to tell you," I said. "It's about Lloyd."

Delores' eyes grew wide. "Has he come back?"

"I'm afraid not." I stroked across the age spots with my thumb. During my nursing career, I'd witnessed plenty of death notifications to spouses, but this was the first time I'd be delivering the message.

Delores jerked her hand back and pulled the sheet to her chin. "What is it? It's that woman Rhonda isn't it? Is she back? She never liked me, you know? She pretended to be my friend to get close to my husband. Did Lloyd leave her too?"

"It appears he never left Wickford, Mrs. Redmond," Alder cut in.

"Lloyd's still here?" Delores cried out, her face brightening.

I shushed Alder. "You said I could do this." I took a deep breath and swallowed the knot in my throat, before leaning in and saying, "Delores, Lloyd didn't leave you for Rhonda. I'm sorry to give you this bad news, but Lloyd is dead."

Delores shook her head. "Impossible." Tears appeared at the corner of her eyes and rolled down her cheeks. "I get a letter from him every year. He's in Texas or maybe California with her. But he still checks in on me."

"When was the last time you heard from your husband?" Alder asked.

Delores swiped at her cheeks and eyed Alder. I pulled a tissue from the box by her bed and pressed it into her hand. "It's okay Delores. He's here to help. You can trust him. He'll find out what happened to Lloyd."

"I love him, you know? Even though he left me, I still love him." She blew her nose and stared at the window. "Are you sure it's Lloyd?"

"Yes ma'am," Alder said with sadness in his voice. "We did a visual identification this morning."

"Delores, when did you hear from Lloyd?" I asked.

Alder shot me a grateful smile.

She paused in thought. "Last month. On my birthday."

"Delores, your birthday is in November. This is June." She and Jessie shared the same birthday. Jessie and I had always made a big deal of baking cupcakes and taking one to her birthday buddy Delores. The library staff had always gotten a kick out of Delores and Jessie eating their matching cupcakes.

"No, it was Mother's Day. I still have the card. Get my pocketbook out of the closet."

I did as she requested. She dug into her purse and extracted a stack of yellowed envelopes.

Alder glanced at me. I shrugged. Delores pulled off the pink ribbon which held the bundle together. She thumbed through the stack several times.

Confusion creased her face. "I know it's here somewhere. I got it last week."

"Would you like me to check?" I asked.

She clutched the envelopes to her chest. "No. Leave me alone. Please leave me alone."

Alder placed a hand on my shoulder. "All we're doing is upsetting her. We should leave."

"Give me a minute, please?" I asked.

He nodded and left me alone with Delores.

I sat next to her bed. "I'm going to leave, but Noah will be by to see you. He's in town, and Carla will be back soon."

Delores ignored me and stared at the ceiling.

I waited a few minutes, but when she didn't respond, I said goodbye and joined Alder in the hall.

"She's confused. I can't stand seeing her like this. Do you think she really heard from Lloyd recently?" I asked Alder.

"You saw him. If I had to guess, I'd say she hasn't heard from Lloyd in a long time. Did you see any return addresses on those envelopes?" Alder asked.

"No," I said. "But I wasn't looking."

Alder glanced at his watch. "Let's regroup and figure out how to approach this. Have you eaten?"

I shook my head.

"Want to grab a burger? I'm still on duty, but a guy's got to eat."

I considered the chemistry I'd been trying to ignore. "I don't think it's a good idea."

"It's a burger. I'm not proposing marriage." He waggled his eyebrows.

Nancy had been right about the contents of my refrigerator. Since I didn't have to worry about feeding Michelle, I'd been living on yogurt. I was afraid to open the takeout containers. Beatrice kept my house immaculate, but she refused to clean the fridge, citing she feared the green, fuzzy stuff.

"Let's do it." *What is wrong with me*? Had my brain shut off communication with my mouth?

"Now you're talking." He chuckled.

We stopped at the nurses' station on the way out and told one of the floor nurses about Delores' agitation.

As we were walking to the parking lot, Brett Havil, a local attorney, rounded the corner with Noah beside him. Havil stepped forward and blocked our way. "Hello, Cece. Detective Alder. Mr. Feldman has hired me to represent his mother, Delores Redmond."

"Down, boy," Alder said. "I've already talked to your client. You're a bit late."

"I'm putting you on notice, Alder. No further conversations unless I'm present. Am I clear?"

Alder stepped around him. "Perfectly. Now if you don't mind, there's a burger with my name on it waiting for me."

Noah pulled me aside. "What happened? Why did you let him question my mother? You knew I was hiring an attorney."

"I'm sorry. It just happened," I said. "She didn't say anything. She's too upset about Lloyd."

"Why didn't you let me tell her?" Noah raked a hand around the back of his neck.

"Honestly, I don't know. But, Noah, she doesn't remember you being here. Were you here?" I asked.

"Of course. I told you I came by this morning."

"There's something going on with her memory. She thought it was December, and she thought Lloyd had sent her greeting cards. Has she been diagnosed with Alzheimer's?"

"How would I know? Carla doesn't tell me anything. I don't know what all she's been hiding, but I aim to find out," he said in a curt tone. "Until then, I want the cop to stay away from my mother, unless her attorney is present."

I nodded. "For her sake, it's probably a good idea. I'm sorry about today, but I assumed you'd be here, and when you weren't . . . I apologize."

"Don't worry about it, this has us all rattled," Noah said. "I'd better go see her and see what's what. Don't forget about dinner."

"Call me," I said.

Alder joined us. "Mr. Feldman, will you come by the station tomorrow? I have a few questions about the deceased."

~ ~ ~

Alder drove to the neighboring town of Ferris, not far from the county line, and pulled into the parking lot of a nondescript cinder block building. A flashing neon sign with several burnt-out letters winked "icky's" in purple script. Not the kind of place I wanted to get a burger, or any meal for that matter.

"I hope the sign isn't an advertisement for the quality of this place," I said.

Alder laughed. "Dicky isn't much for décor or ambience, but he has the best burgers in the state."

I pushed down a judgmental thought and reached for the door handle.

"Hang on. I'll get it." Alder walked around the car and opened my door.

Phillip's idea of being a gentleman meant not letting the

door slam in my face when he rushed into a building before me. It's not like he had never opened a door for me; he had, but only if he wanted to impress someone. Someone other than me. Otherwise, his philosophy was that I had two hands and two feet, and they both worked fine, so I could do it myself.

The lack of lighting inside 'icky' Dicky's worried me. Any place with lights this dim must be hiding something. They certainly didn't do it for the atmosphere. A well-worn bar skirted one side of the building. Formica-topped tables rounded out the dining area and hosted a variety of chairs in every shape and color imaginable. I could see through a beaded curtain to a back area with people crowded around pool tables.

A burly, bald guy in a muscle shirt waved from behind the bar. "Hey, Alder. What's new, man?"

Alder waved back. He took my hand and guided me past the tables to a booth at the end of the bar. I slid in, and he scooched in beside me, forcing me to make room. When his leg brushed against mine, I tensed. The familiar surge rushed to my core. I moved closer to the wall.

"Why are you so jumpy?" He leaned back and stretched his arms along the back of my seat. "Relax."

"Relax? I'm not sure I understand the word. I found a dead body. I have a nut case living above my garage. And my almost-ex-husband is trying to drive me into the poorhouse." I pulled a menu marked "BIG DICK'S SPECIALS" from behind the napkin holder and pretended to scan the selections, faking relaxation.

"What's a 'Big Dick's'?" *Did I say that out loud?* My face burned all the way to the tips of my ears from embarrassment.

Alder chuckled. "Relax, will you? I'm not the enemy." He paused. "You don't need this." He reached for the menu, which I held in a death grip, and snagged my pinky finger. I raised my head and looked into his eyes. I felt like I had fallen under a spell, one I couldn't end. *Relax? I don't think so.*

"Who's your lady friend?" The bald guy set two cups of coffee in front of us.

Alder and I both jumped, the trance broken. The worn menu I'd been holding split right down the middle. Alder made busy unrolling the paper napkin from around his utensils.

"Dick, this is Cece." Alder shook hands with the big guy. "Dick and I served in Desert Storm. He saved my sorry self on more than one occasion."

I nodded. "Nice to meet you. Umm, sorry about the menu." I shoved the two pieces behind the napkin holder.

He bowed slightly. "No worries. I need to replace them anyway. Don't listen to a word Alder says. He embellishes his stories. You want to know the real one?"

Alder held up a hand and shook his head.

"Sorry." Dick wiped his beefy hands on the spotless white apron tied around his marshmallow middle. "What can I get you two?"

"Make us a couple of 'Big Dicks' and run 'em through the garden. Throw in some of those twisty fries with lots of seasoning and bring Cece a hot tea." Alder pushed my coffee away. "She's not a coffee drinker."

I cocked my head at him. "How'd you know?"

"I drank the swill you made me when I worked the Anderson case. Anyone who makes coffee as bad as you do cannot take coffee seriously."

I felt a blush coming on or a hot flash. Either way, thank goodness the lights were dim.

"Don't stay away so long. I'm still running a weekly poker game, if you want in."

"Maybe so," Alder said.

Dick cuffed Alder on the shoulder and left with our order.

Alder shifted toward me. "Thanks for going to the hospital. You were good with Mrs. Redmond."

"I've known Delores a long time. It hurts to see how she's gone downhill. The confusion could be dementia or Alzheimer's. I wonder if she'll remember what we told her about Lloyd? She hadn't recalled Noah visiting."

"How much do you know about her son? Besides the teenage stuff." He winked.

"I've known him all my life. He grew up in Wickford too," I said. "He and Carla had a normal enough family life. The sibling rivalry between the two has always been ferocious. They've been horribly jealous of one another as long as I can remember. Their father died in an accident at the concrete plant many years ago. Noah took his dad's death hard. And both Carla and Noah resented Delores marrying Lloyd."

Alder lifted his cup and took a long swig. "Mmm. Now this is how coffee should taste."

The blush I'd developed turned into a vicious hot flash. Heat lapped at the nape of my neck. It took everything I had not to fan myself.

Alder flashed his devastatingly handsome grin, then sobered. "Would you say he got along with Lloyd?"

"Noah wasn't around much due to his job. He does international relief work," I said. "They were cordial enough, I guess. Not best friends, but Noah came to accept him while Carla never did."

Alder continued his questions, "Did Lloyd ever get abusive with Delores?"

I thought for a moment. The smell of burgers cooking on the grill caused me to lose my concentration. I couldn't remember the last time I'd had a burger, and my stomach rumbled, anticipating the juicy goodness.

Alder nudged my knee.

The innocent contact sent my mind in another direction. A direction where Alder and I weren't hashing out a murder investigation. A direction where my divorce was in the past.

The nudge became more insistent. "Hey, where are you?"

I left those thoughts and forced my mind back to the current topic. "Sorry, the aromas in here are heavenly," I said, tamping down my feelings and focusing on Alder's question. I'd been around Lloyd a lot in the beginning of their marriage, but they both seemed to grow more reclusive after they moved into the bungalow. "Was Lloyd abusive? I don't think so. Of course, Delores would never have said anything. But there were never any visible signs."

A slew of customers came and filled several tables at once, and Dick had gotten busy behind the bar. A waitress about my age delivered our order. She pulled a ketchup bottle from her apron and set it on the table with a *plunk*.

"Thanks, Mary Grace," Alder said.

"You're welcome, hun'. Don't stay away so long. Dick gets lonesome for your company," she replied, before heading to another table.

Alder squeezed a puddle of ketchup onto his plate. "Did Carla ever change her feelings for Lloyd?"

I cut my burger in half and contemplated his question. Carla and I hadn't seen each other for years. Since Delores always made the trip to North Carolina, and Carla had no other family in the area, she hadn't had a reason to visit. We stayed in touch mostly by phone and email.

"She never understood their relationship. Delores had always been a strong, independent woman, but when Lloyd came along, she gave in to his every whim. Including giving up the home she loved to move into the place on Castleman Lane, which Lloyd never bothered to put her name on. Carla told me today how Delores' investments are gone. She received a huge insurance settlement when Carla's dad died, and it's disappeared. Carla's been working with Delores' financial advisor trying to track down why she withdrew the funds," I said.

"When Lloyd left, Carla didn't have anything good to say about him." I pulled a fry through the ketchup and popped it in my mouth, savoring the salty goodness. "From what I've heard, Noah started visiting more often, and it didn't sit well with Carla. Like I told you, the siblings have never gotten along."

Wow, I had turned chatty suddenly, but Alder made it easy to talk. He didn't interrupt and wasn't distracting. Nix that. He was distracting in a good sort of way. He finished his burger and wiped a dab of ketchup with his last fry.

I pushed my plate toward him. "You want mine? I can't eat another bite."

He grinned and scraped my fries onto his plate.

I told him everything I could think of about Noah, Carla, and the Redmonds. I hadn't said anything to Carla or Noah about the diamonds or the elephants. There could be a perfectly reasonable explanation for elephants with gems in their bellies. There had to be. Maybe Delores had hidden them for safekeeping. Maybe Lloyd had invested in diamonds for his retirement.

A twinge of guilt hit, but I shrugged it off. When we'd first come in, I'd promised myself that if I touched the table and it was sticky, I'd ask Alder to drive me home. I had. It wasn't. Maybe looks were deceiving. Since I'd married Phillip, I'd been doing a lot of judging from first appearances. Sometimes a deeper view was necessary.

Alder pushed his plate away. "What'd you think?"

"Excellent. I never knew this place existed," I said.

"One of life's hidden treasures." He reached over and touched my lip. "You got a little ketchup here."

If I'd been standing, I would've fainted dead away. Instead, I groaned and savored the moment. Good thing we were in public. I was having a difficult time maintaining my focus.

His mouth twitched, and the corners of his mustache lifted in a smile. "Better get you home." He laid a twenty on the table and walked me to the car. All the way, he had his hand on the small of my back, and I didn't want him to take it away.

We drove home in silence. I debated asking him inside for coffee, but he knew I couldn't make a decent cup. He'd know why I asked him in. Chances were, he'd be right. I could still feel the tingle from where he'd touched my lip.

With my court date around the corner, I refused to give Phillip any ammunition. The divorce would be final soon, and I needed to cool my jets! As it sat now, he'd been the one who cheated and walked out on our marriage. It was a tough decision, but I decided not to invite Alder in. Besides, he was still on duty.

When we pulled into my driveway, he shut off the engine. "I'm off duty in ten minutes. How about I show you how to make a decent cup of coffee?"

He must have been reading my mind.

Funny how quickly resolve melted. Had I shaved my legs recently? Then I started worrying about protection. I might be hot flashing, but I could still get pregnant. Perish the thought! If I slept with him in the bed I had shared with Phillip, how weird would it be? Did Alder carry around condoms in his wallet? Angie said he didn't date. If he did carry condoms, were they old condoms? Was this what it was like to be single? Maybe Alder only wanted to teach me how to make coffee. I saw the faint glow of a cigarette on my front porch, sat upright, and squinted my eyes. "Nancy?"

"What?" Alder asked.

I opened the car door and stomped up the sidewalk. "Get rid of the cigarette and get off my porch."

Alder followed, staring bug-eyed at Nancy, who had draped herself across my ladder-backed rocker dressed in a filmy hot-pink negligee.

Chapter 8

"It's probably for the best that Nancy was on the front porch when I brought Cece home. I don't want her to have any regrets. Though, I'll be taking a few cold showers until she decides she's ready for a relationship."
Case Alder

My dreams, or should I say fears of a romantic interlude, sputtered to a halt. Nancy dropped the cigarette, rubbed it out with the toe of her fuzzy, hot pink house slipper, and kicked it into the decorative bark in my flower bed.

I glared at her. She gulped, rose from the chair, and retrieved the butt.

"Thank you," I said. "Now get off my porch, especially since you're dressed like a centerfold-of-the-month."

Alder stifled a laugh. I shot him a scowl.

Nancy extended her hand to Alder. "Hi, I'm—"

"Leaving," I interrupted. "You are leaving."

"Okay, okay." Not bothering to wrap her filmy negligee around her, Nancy flounced into the house, chiffon and silk waving in the breeze.

"No telling how long she's been out here, or how many of my tightly wound neighbors have seen her," I said. The neighborhood swarmed with impressionable teenage boys, not to mention their sex-deprived fathers. The moms would ring my phone off the hook.

"Well, she certainly put on a show," Alder said. "I guess your coffee lesson will have to wait."

My head nodded, but my heart screamed no. “Maybe another time.”

“Can’t wait.” Alder leaned in and kissed me lightly on the lips.

I didn’t pull back, and he wrapped his arms around me. “I enjoyed this evening, Cece. But I better go before we put on an even better show for your neighbors.”

As much as I hated it, I gave him a gentle push in the direction of his car.

After Alder left, I checked my answering machine and found messages from Grant and Hazel. I ignored Hazel and called Grant. I wanted to thank him for sending Larry and Brad to help me at Delores’ house. Plus, I’d been too sharp with him the afternoon I’d found Lloyd’s body, and I wanted to apologize. Grant had been kind and caring, and I’d stomped off without even thanking him. Life seemed so complicated.

He brushed off my apology and said, “Good grief, woman. Don’t think a thing about it. You had quite a scare.”

I breathed a sigh of relief. Not only was he a good friend, he was also the only paying job I had. “Thanks for understanding. I don’t know when the police will let me get back to work. I’ll be at Hunter Springs bright and early tomorrow.”

“I hate to ask, but do you think Jessie can help? Sales have increased, and the agents are pushing to get the contracts closed.”

“I’ll check, but I can’t make any promises. It depends on her schedule,” I said.

When I called Jessie, she told me she had twelve-hour shifts the next three days, and there was no way she could help.

I thought about calling Beatrice but remembered she’d taken off for a wedding. Most of my so-called friends had snubbed me after Phillip left. They were wives of Phillip’s associates and had no loyalty to me. Besides, not a one of them would dream of lifting a finger to clean. They had maids for their dirty work. After Phillip left me, Hazel orchestrated my ouster from the country club and made sure the wives would turn their backs on me. Angie would help if she wasn't working, but she'd grumble the whole time.

I poured myself a glass of wine and sat down in my office with my cell phone. A few scrolls through my contact list left me disheartened. The calls I made resulted in either resounding *no's* or hemming and hawing, which I also took as *no*.

The more rejections I received, the more depressed I became. I refilled my wine and nuked a bag of popcorn to snack on while I pondered my situation. Grant had been great about giving me all the work I could handle. If I couldn't keep up, he'd hire an additional cleaner, but then I'd have to share the workload and the salary. I did have one more option though, and I couldn't believe I was even considering it.

~ ~ ~

I did the only thing I could. Trudging up the steps to the apartment, I repeated to myself, *it's your only option. It's your only option.* A temporary solution to a problem, nothing more.

Nancy answered the door after two knocks. "I know. I know. I'll stay out back when I smoke." She had changed out of her negligee and into a faded St. Louis University T-shirt with a pair of schnauzer-print boxer shorts. It made me wonder why she performed her little peep show on my front porch, unless she'd seen me leave with Alder and it was for his benefit. Who knew what went on in her head?

She'd placed a vase of flowers from my garden on the café table in the breakfast nook. I also noticed she'd propped a few photos on the coffee table—a lot of trouble for someone staying a couple of nights.

I'd only been in the apartment once after my previous housekeeper left, and I'd told Beatrice not to worry about cleaning it. In my absence, Nancy had been busy. The place sparkled, and I almost felt bad.

"Sit down," I ordered Nancy. "I have a proposition."

She dropped onto the sofa and pulled her legs under her. For once, she wasn't chewing gum. When she'd been at Bonafide, she'd been nasty to me every chance she got, and I'd been the desperate one. Now, I had the power. How the tables had turned. Bam!

I bit my tongue for what I was about to do and repeated to myself, *it's your only option*. "I have a job offer for you."

Nancy's eyes rounded, and she tilted her head. "Yes?" she asked, suspicion edging her voice.

"It's temporary," I said. "It's not glamorous. And you'll be working for me."

She leaned forward. "I'll do any—"

I cut her off. My proposition had conditions. "Don't agree until you've heard my terms." I took the chance that she might balk, but we needed to get some things straight.

"Okay?"

"No smoking. Period. It's a nasty habit, and it's not healthy. No sneaking around either, or you're gone."

"Anything else?" she asked.

"Yes. Get rid of the hooker outfits. You'll need comfy clothes. If you don't have any, you can borrow mine. We're about the same size." I had her attention and kept right on laying down the rules. "Be on time and work hard. Not a lot to ask."

"If I agree, what's in it for me?"

"I'll pay you a quarter of what I make, and you can stay here until you find a place."

"No rent?"

"No rent, but you're on your own for groceries. I'm not planning on raising you." I paused. "And no men sleeping over. I have a teenage daughter, and she gives me enough grief. I don't want to have to explain or justify your actions." With any luck, Nancy would be gone before Michelle returned.

Nancy thought for a minute. "What do I have to do? I'm not cleaning blood and guts."

"You'll be cleaning condos at Hunter Springs. It's easy work, but there's a lot of it and you have to keep up. No lolly-gagging around."

After a minute, she reached into her purse and pulled out a pack of cigarettes. "Can I have one last smoke?"

I shook my head and took the pack. "Cold turkey. It's the best way. And air this apartment out. It reeks. What made you think you could smoke in here?"

"Jeez, are you this bossy on the job too?" she asked.

"You have no idea." I pushed the cigarettes into my pocket. "If you want to ride with me in the morning, I leave at six."

Her cell phone rang, and she glanced its way.

"Go ahead. I'm leaving." I stopped at the door. "Don't be late, or the job offer goes away, and so does the apartment." I hoped I didn't have to honor my threat. I had no other options.

"I won't."

I lifted the top off the trash can at the bottom of the steps but thought twice. Nancy didn't need an excuse. I pulled the cigarettes out one by one and crushed them, sprinkling the remains on top of the garbage. If she had a relapse, it would be her fault, not mine.

I heard the phone ringing in my house, replaced the lid, and ran into the kitchen.

Alder's number appeared on the display.

"Hey," I said, trying for light and breezy, even though my knees went weak at the sound of his slow, southern drawl.

"Wanted to check in to make sure you didn't hurt her," Alder said with a laugh.

"Not yet, but she's trying my nerves." I carried the phone to the breakfast bar and sat down.

"Okay, well . . ."

"Yes?"

"Nothing, just like hearing you talk." Alder's voice deepened.

No, I thought. *Don't make me go all squishy inside.* "Space, remember? Space. No feelings," I said. "Don't talk like that, okay?"

When he didn't say anything, I said, "You still there?"

"Yes, keep talking."

"Stop it, now." The last thing I needed was more conflicted feelings, and Alder wasn't helping.

He laughed. "Okay."

"Good. Now can we hang up?"

"Not yet. I have something else to tell you," Alder said.

"This better be good."

"Oh, I think you'll like it."

"Now you're teasing. I'm hanging up." I walked over to the alcove desk.

"Wait. Don't hang up. I really do have something to tell you."

"Okay?"

"The investigation team finished up at the Redmond house," he said.

"Can we go back in?" I wondered if I should tell him I'd let the freezer detail slip when talking to Carla.

"Yes, we're done with everything we need to do. I still need to interview your friend Carla, so let her know. Will you?"

"As soon as she gets back to town," I said. "Oh, I have something to tell you too."

"Yes? We can talk all night, if you want."

"You aren't going to like what I have to say. I may have accidentally let it slip to Carla about finding Lloyd in the freezer." I paused. When he didn't say anything, I added, "I'm sorry. Really. It popped out. I didn't do it intentionally."

He let out a breath. "Okay, thanks for letting me know. Have you told anyone else?"

"Ugh, I may have told Angie, but she's a cop. She'd find out anyway. Right?"

Alder groaned. "Don't tell anyone else."

The minute I put the phone down it rang again.

"Hey, Cece." Carla's voice sounded chipper. "I'm flying back in the morning. Can you pick me up at the airport?"

Why? Why? Why? Of all days. Did I dare leave Nancy alone at Hunter Springs while I made the trip to the city?

"What time?" I asked.

"My flight lands at noon," Carla said.

I didn't have a choice. A taxi from the airport would cost her a mint. Angie was working. A rental car was overkill. She could use Delores' van once she arrived in Wickford.

"Yes," I said begrudgingly. "I have to rearrange some stuff, but I'll wait for you in the cell phone lot. Send me a text when you land, and I'll swing around to pick you up."

I hung up and wondered if Nancy could be trusted at Hunter Springs alone.

Chapter 9

"Working for her is going to be harder than I thought. She is sooo bossy. I mean, a girl has got to look good."
Nancy Lustbader

"Come in, it's open," I yelled when Nancy knocked on the door precisely at six the next morning. I grabbed a couple of apples and placed them in a cooler, along with several bottles of water.

Nancy wore a pair of too-tight jeans and a St. Louis Cardinals T-shirt which showed off her tanned and taut midriff. Her coral-colored toenails stuck out of a pair of sequin-covered sandals.

"This is all I had."

Better than her usual attire, but not appropriate for working.

She was smacking a wad of gum. If she stayed off the cigarettes, maybe I could ignore the gum popping. "Ummm, good try, but you're going to have trouble in those jeans. Check the laundry room around the corner for something more comfortable. Clean clothes are folded on the shelf."

She disappeared down the hall, and I ran upstairs to find her a pair of tennis shoes, hoping they'd fit. When I returned, she'd changed into a more suitable outfit. She'd also found a gray pullover. I handed her the shoes and said, "Trust me. After the first couple of days, my feet were killing me." I waited while she tried them on.

"They're perfect. Thanks for letting me stay here, and for the job." She sounded almost contrite, a big change from her usual snark. I wondered if her crankiness was a big show she put on to bolster her ego.

"Don't get comfortable. It's not permanent." I snapped the top on the cooler. "There's been a change of plans. I have to drop off supplies at another house I'm cleaning and pick up a friend from the airport. When we get to Hunter Springs, I'll have you shadow me at the first condo, then you can start the second condo by yourself while I'm gone."

Nancy's mouth popped open. "But—"

"No buts," I said. "You got this. Watch what I do, then do the same thing. You can always text me if you have a question."

"Okay, boss lady." Nancy blew out a bubble and put her hand up for a high five.

I ignored her.

~ ~ ~

The door to Delores' house was unlocked when I arrived. I made a mental note to tell Alder his investigators had not locked it when they'd finished. While I was in the kitchen unloading supplies, I heard the front door open and footsteps tramping across the living room. I froze and listened as they came closer.

"Who's there?" I called.

No answer.

Boxes still crowded the room, leaving no place to hide, just the open area I'd cleared the day before. Cursing myself for not being more careful, I slid into the pantry, closed the door, and held my breath.

"Who's in here?" Noah Feldman called.

I relaxed and poked my head out the door as he walked into the kitchen. "Noah, it's Cece."

"What are you doing here?" he asked.

"I'm dropping off some supplies for Carla." I walked out of the pantry and shut the door.

"Is she back in town?" he asked.

"I'm picking her up at the airport at noon. Unless you'd rather?" I was thinking an hour-long drive might give the two of them time to talk and sort out their issues. Carla would kill me, but she'd get over it.

"Absolutely not." He stood watching me, arms folded across his chest. "Looks like I have my work cut out for me here."

"We were making progress until we ran into Lloyd's body. Today's the first day the police have let us back in."

"I appreciate you pitching in, but I'll take it from here."

"I'd feel more comfortable if you and Carla work this out. I feel like a middleman in something not really my business," I said.

"She's going to have to face facts. The two of us are making the decisions." Noah clenched his hand and then relaxed it just as quickly. "I have a vested interest in what happens with my mother's care and her home."

"Like I said, you can talk it over with Carla. She'll be here in a couple of hours. I'll be happy to step aside."

"Don't worry. I'll smooth it over with Carla." He stepped around me and started rooting into the bag of supplies I'd brought in. "Mom's got a lot of personal things I want to take care of. You know, family mementos."

"Yeah, Carla is concerned about them too," I said. This sibling rivalry thing was getting old.

"I'll bet she is." He proceeded to unpack the cleaning supplies. "Thanks for dropping this stuff by. It'll come in handy. I've never seen Mother let her place go like this."

"It's sad. Being at Carla's may be the best thing for your mom. To get her back to her old self."

He slammed a bottle of window cleaner on the counter. "My mother isn't going anywhere. This is her home. She's lived in Wickford all her life. You, of all people, know how important this town is to her."

"Why don't you and Carla talk this out?" I squeezed his forearm. "Getting angry won't help."

He smiled. "I know. I get so aggravated with her. She takes everything on herself, and moans and groans and whines when things go south on her. Then she blames me for not being around to help. Like I have a choice."

The front door opened. "Mrs. Cavanaugh, are you here?" Brad called from the living room.

"Who's that?" Noah asked.

"Reinforcements," I said to Noah. "In the kitchen," I hollered to Brad.

When Brad came in, I introduced him to Noah. "Brad's been helping me. He was with me when we found Lloyd. I'm so thankful he was here. I don't know what I would've done without him."

Brad blushed, and the dimple appeared when he smiled. "Don't let her fool you. She's pretty tough."

"Brad, why don't you get started in the front bedroom? There are a ton more books in there that need to go to the dump." I gave him a gentle push to get him on his way.

Noah scowled. "I don't think it's a good idea to be hauling anything to the dump, or anywhere else, before we sort through it all."

"We're being careful." I decided to stand up to him, at least until Carla could get here and fend for herself. "My agreement is between me and Carla. Once you two talk it out, if she wants me to step back, I'll be glad to. In the meantime, Brad is the only one who has a truck and the means to haul this stuff away."

Brad hesitated in the hallway.

"Go ahead, Brad. Get started. We'll get this figured out, but for now I need your help," I said.

Brad shrugged. "Gotcha. If you need anything, I'll be in there," he said, pointing to the bedroom.

"Noah, why don't you wait until Carla gets here? You being here when I get back will just stir up a hornet's nest. If you want her cooperation, then come back later and work it out. Don't start off on a combative footing."

"You're right," he said.

"Let me give Brad some instructions, and then I'll walk out with you." I folded the canvas bag I'd brought the supplies in and put it under my arm, then went in to talk to Brad.

When I was in the bedroom, I said. "If you need anything, I'll be on my cell."

"I meant to tell you, I can only stay for an hour or two. Mr. Hunter has a project for me this afternoon, but I knew I could get at least one load to the dump for you. Hope it's okay." Brad wheeled a dolly under a stack of boxes.

"Works for me. I appreciate any help at all," I said.

Noah was waiting on the porch when I came out. "Thanks for everything you're doing, Cece. I mean it. Mom thinks the world of you."

"I'm happy to help."

We walked to my car, and he opened the door. Once I had strapped myself in and closed the door, he leaned against the car.

"It really is good to see you again," he said.

"Same here."

"Hey, you haven't run across any keys, have you?" Noah asked.

"What kind of keys?"

"Just a ring of keys. I keep a spare set here and want to make sure they don't get tossed in all the cleaning."

"I haven't noticed any, but I'll keep my eyes open and let you know if I find them," I said.

"Thanks." He slapped the car with his hands. "You better get to the airport to get my sister. Don't want to keep the queen bee waiting."

I put the key in the ignition and started the car. "Thanks, Noah."

"For what?"

"For understanding. For not putting me in the middle. I only want what's best for your mom. You and Carla fighting is not it," I said.

He smiled. "Go on, get out of here before I change my mind."

Noah followed my car out of the neighborhood. I turned left to go out to the highway, and he turned right toward the hotel.

~ ~ ~

By one o'clock, I had about given up on Carla. The flight board at the airport showed her flight had landed, but still no text. I circled around the arrival area and saw Carla standing at the curb.

"Sorry, we had a small delay. I tried to call, but my cell battery died, and you can't find a pay phone anywhere." She snapped her seat belt and leaned back in the seat.

"Max doing okay?" I asked.

"Yes." Carla rolled her shoulders. "He had me worried, but the doctor said he'd be fine. I can't wait until he sends this manuscript to his publisher. Then I'm putting my foot down. He needs to learn how to slow down before he *does* have a heart attack."

"It's going to be hard to get him to relax," I said.

"Tell me something I don't already know." Carla plugged her cell into the dash. "I better charge this up. Don't want Max going into a panic if he can't reach me. Hey, can you drop me off at Mom's? I need to get her van."

I pulled into traffic and exited the airport. "Alder called last night and said the investigators were finished at your mom's house." Her insistence about Delores' personal belongings still piqued my interest, but I didn't say anything.

"Did Noah call you?" she asked, digging into her purse.

"You haven't heard from him?" Traffic had picked up. It was a beautiful day, and trucks towing campers and trailers whizzed past us. I saw a motorcycle ahead and thought about Alder. Today was a perfect day for riding. I'd never had any desire get on a motorcycle, but one ride had convinced me. I resisted the urge to roll down the window and let the wind tousle my hair.

"He called last night." Carla's voice interrupted my musings.

"What?" I tucked away my daydreams of Alder and concentrated on driving and listening to Carla.

"He's not happy with my plans to take Mom to North Carolina. When I told him I wanted to sell her house, he blew a gasket." She twisted the air-conditioning vent. "Can you turn the air up? I'm melting."

I adjusted the fan. Thoughts of fresh air breezed out of my mind. The motorcycle weaved in front of me, and I caught myself speeding up to see if it was Alder.

"Well, you guys can hash it out while he's here." I pulled alongside the motorcycle and craned my head to see the driver.

"He's here? In Wickford?" Carla's voice rose an octave, and she turned in her seat to face me. "He never said a word about being in town. Why didn't you tell me?"

"Saw him at your Mom's this morning. I thought you knew. You said you talked to him last night." I clicked on the turn signal and moved into the passing lane.

"What was he doing at Mom's?" Carla asked, suspicion in her voice.

"I don't know. Looking around, I guess. Trying to get a fix on the situation. Figure out what he can do to help. He's your brother. Can't you keep tabs on him?"

"Not funny. He's done nothing to help her all these years and now—suddenly—he wants to swoop in and be the doting son." She fanned herself with a sheaf of papers she'd pulled from her purse. "He's going to have to stand in line. Mom gave me power of attorney, and I'm going to use it to take care of her, regardless of what he wants. We're going to finish cleaning her house. I want it on the market before I leave."

I let my mind drift back to Alder and left Carla stewing about her brother's arrival. All I would do by talking was flame her fury. It'd be best to let her calm down.

When we arrived in Wickford, I drove to Castleman Lane, located in an older section of town built back in the forties. The houses were the same type of little bungalows with one car, detached garages and postage stamp yards. The exteriors were asbestos-shingled in an array of colors. They reminded me of rows of Easter eggs. Not the fancy ones you see today, but the simple ones we used to dye with the cheap kits from Dingle's Market. When the girls were little, we'd dip one end of an egg in one color and the other in another. Delores' house had the bottom dipped in turquoise and the top in white.

Delores' van sat alone in the driveway. When we got to the front door, Carla turned over the fake rock, and the key was gone.

"Do you have it?" she asked.

"Not me. Maybe Noah took it." I checked the ledge over the door.

"Yoo-hoo, ladies." Mrs. Wafford headed across the street in full trot. "I've got fresh lemonade."

Carla sighed. "Hi, Mrs. Wafford. We don't have time right now, but we'll stop by later. I promise."

I lifted the rock. "You don't know what happened to the key, do you? I'm sure I left it here."

Mrs. Wafford put her hand on her chin and tilted her head. "Ummm. I don't recollect for sure, but it could come to me. Why don't you girls come over for some refreshments while I think on it?"

I looked at Carla and rolled my eyes. She nodded, and we followed Mrs. Wafford.

"You know the police were pokin' around here darn near all day yesterday and the day before. I counted five cop cars. A record for Castleman Lane, unless you count the time old man Farley ran off his good for nuthin' son-in-law with a shotgun and almost blasted the whole neighborhood to smithereens." Mrs. Wafford shook her finger all the way home, recounting each and every incident in the neighborhood requiring the use of law enforcement.

Her living room could have been decorated from a display at the Smithsonian. She instructed Carla and I to sit on a plastic-covered nylon sofa. The out-of-date avocado green sofa matched the twin chairs on the opposite side of the room. A metal TV tray with binoculars stood next to the picture window, along with a steno pad, ink pen, and an ancient wind-up clock. The window faced the street. Convenient.

On an ancient console TV, a much younger Angela Lansbury rifled a suspect's desk in a rerun of *Murder She Wrote*.

"Isn't Jessica Fletcher amazing? She always finds the bad guy." Mrs. Wafford set up two more TV trays and disappeared down the hall for the lemonade.

"How long do you think she'll make us stay?" Carla asked.

"Probably until we drink enough lemonade we see yellow." I glanced at my watch and prayed for a swift and painless extraction from Mrs. Wafford's 1950s living room. "If we try to rush her, we'll be here all day. She's wanting attention, and she wants to know what went on at your mom's house."

"She's holding us hostage for gossip?"

"Not gossip. She wants the real deal, so she can be the first in the neighborhood to spread the word." My mother-in-law was the country club version of Mrs. Wafford. When Hazel walked into a room, everyone gathered round, because she knew all the dirt worth knowing. Lately most of it had to do with me, and she had firsthand knowledge, thanks to her two-timing son.

From the first time she'd laid eyes on me, Hazel never felt I was good enough for Phillip and never let me live it down. Even with my membership in the club, she never missed the opportunity for a putdown at my expense. My only salvation would be if Phillip married his latest fling, Willow, after our divorce became final. I almost wished he would; then I could watch Hazel squirm. The old girl would be mortified when she met Willow. Especially if Hazel ever found out Phillip used Cavanaugh money to enhance Willow's bustline.

A car roared down the street, bass thumping loud enough to rattle the windows.

Mrs. Wafford rounded the corner carrying a plastic serving tray. It held three aluminum tumblers wrapped in knitted cozies, to catch the condensation, and a plate of chocolate chip cookies. She set the refreshments in front of me and peered out the drapes with her binoculars. "Those juvenile delinquents and their loud music. I've called their parents. I've called the police. No respect. Young'uns today got no respect for their elders. You practically have to kill someone to get the police to give a hoot." She made a note on the pad and returned it to the tray.

"About the key," I coaxed, hoping she'd divulge her secret.

"I thought about your key while I made our snack. Drink up first. I've got another pitcher chilling in the icebox." She took a tumbler and sat down with a *whoosh* on one of the twin chairs. "This is homemade. I squeezed the lemons myself. You don't find real lemonade these days. Most people use powdered drink mix. Not me. My Herbert, God rest his soul, always loved my lemonade. You girls haven't even tried it." She sipped and smacked her lips. "I use real sugar too. Not the artificial stuff. It'll rot your gizzard."

I lifted my lemonade. "Cheers."

Carla kicked me but lifted her glass and clanked it against mine. "Bottom's up."

I gagged down my lemonade and placed the empty on the tray. I took a cookie and had visions of the elderly ladies from the movie *Arsenic and Old Lace*. It took all I had to bite into it, but I ate it and helped myself to another one. Chocolate chip was my favorite.

"I'll get more lemonade." Mrs. Wafford pulled herself up.

"Don't go to any trouble. Finish yours," I said. Of all days to wear shorts. My legs stuck to the plastic. Every time I moved, I made little farting noises. If I wasn't exasperated, it would've been funny. Not to mention it hurt when I peeled my leg up to change positions.

Carla slammed her glass on the tray. "They carted Lloyd out. He was dead. Now tell us who took the key. We don't have all day."

Mrs. Wafford's knees buckled, and she fell back into her chair. "Lordy mercy, no. Lloyd Redmond can't be dead, he ran off with the neighbor woman." She leaned in, and her eyes glimmered with the possibility of a good dose of gossip. Gossip she would no doubt embellish when she passed it around the neighborhood. "He's dead? How did he die? On *Murder She Wrote* the other night, the wife did it. Oh, heaven help me, don't tell me Delores killed him. Did she kill the Bray woman too? Will Delores go to prison? I read a senior citizen can get pretty good treatment in prison. Three meals a day, medical care, and they have activities like in the nursing home."

Could Delores have murdered her husband? From all accounts, she'd been madly in love with him. And if she had, what about Rhonda Bray? If Delores had killed Lloyd, could she have killed Bray also?

Carla jumped in. "Stop it. You're letting your imagination run away with you. This isn't a TV show. There must be a perfectly logical explanation. Now tell me where the key is. We have work to do."

Mrs. Wafford took a long drink of her lemonade and smacked her lips. "Delores' boy stopped by this morning. He's grown into quite a looker, and polite too. Not like you. And not like your mother. Why the minute Delores married Lloyd, her world turned around Lloyd, Lloyd, and more Lloyd. Never had time for her friends anymore."

Carla gasped. "Noah came here? What did he want?"

"Well, I can tell you he liked my lemonade, and he wasn't nearly as rude as you are, young lady." She shot out of the chair, quite a feat considering her age, and carried the tray and cookies back to the kitchen. When she returned, she opened the front door. "I think it's time for you to get going."

Chapter 10

"Menopause has made Cece crazy. She needs to get a grip and face reality."
Phillip Cavanaugh

Mrs. Wafford practically pushed us out the door. All the way across the street, Carla cursed the old woman.

"Let it go," I said. "Sounds like she was jealous of Delores. At their age, it's not easy to find love again." I opened the car door and slid behind the wheel.

Carla stood in the yard with hands on hips. "Where are you going? I thought you were going to help, and if Noah was here, I want to see what the slimeball stole." She tried the front door. When it didn't budge, she trotted off around the side of the house. She didn't wait for me to tell her that Noah had left when I did, so unless he'd returned, he hadn't taken anything.

Like she'd know if anything disappeared out of Delores' house. With all the crap piled high inside, it would be a miracle. When I caught up with Carla, she'd already climbed the chain-link fence and was scanning the windows at the back of the house. I might still be in jogging shape, but I wasn't going to ruin a perfectly good pair of shorts trying to climb a fence. I went around to the other side of the house, where I'd seen a gate. The sight of the garage gave me the shivers when I remembered old Lloyd stuffed in the freezer.

Carla saw me and shouted, "I think the bedroom window is unlocked. We need to find something we can climb on."

"We? I don't think so. You scaled the fence like a pro, so you can go in the window. I'll stand guard," I said.

"It's too high. How about the trash can over there?" Carla asked.

The only trash can on the patio was a flimsy plastic one with a cracked lid. It wouldn't begin to hold my weight, much less the extra pounds Carla had packed on.

"No dice. It's wrecked. You'll kill yourself." I lifted the lid to show her the plastic flopping in the breeze.

"Keep looking." She jumped up and down trying to catch a glimpse in the window.

"How about you come help instead of disturbing the whole neighborhood? The sooner we find something, the sooner we can get you inside."

A yapping Pekingese in the neighboring yard raced up and down the length of the fence. A growling rag-mop dog in the back soon joined the chorus.

"Go check the garage." Carla knelt on the ground peering into the basement window.

Panic rose in my throat. "Ack! The last time I did I found Lloyd." I remembered my concern about Rhonda's whereabouts. *Nah, if she were in the other freezer, the cops would have found her. Wouldn't they?*

"Oh, you big baby. He's not in there anymore." Carla went to the garage and tried the doors. "Go ahead. I'll go around back to see if I can find anything in the old shed."

"Okay." Adrenaline flowed through my body. I had every intention of helping Carla get Delores' house ready, but I dreaded the garage.

I walked to the side door and flinched. *You can do this.* I had to do it. If only to prove to myself I could. I knew that I'd be cleaning crime scenes, once the victim was removed. In this case, I had found the body. Something like that scarred a person. I would forever see Lloyd frozen like a human ice cube.

Scrapping noises came from behind the garage. I held my breath and waited for Carla. Maybe she'd find something, and I wouldn't have to go in. When she didn't show, I slowly walked in the door. *Stop it.*

The police had removed the freezer. With it gone, my backbone grew stronger. I could do this. A large wooden stepladder sat wedged in between a workbench and a utility cabinet. I pulled aside three plastic totes of Christmas decorations, grabbed hold of the ladder, and pulled. Something was keeping it from sliding out. I put more muscle into it and gave it a good jerk. It came free, and three rungs fell off. Upon further inspection, I found more broken or mangled rungs. When I unfolded it, it listed to one side so badly I feared it would topple over on me. I shoved the ladder back into the space, but it caught on a shelf above. Trying a different angle, I wedged it beneath the shelf and gave it a good push. When I did, the shelf broke loose, and cans full of nuts and bolts and screws rained down on me.

After the dust settled, I brushed myself off and inspected the cuts and scrapes. Nothing serious, but it still smarted. I kicked one of the cans aside, to vent my frustration for whomever had left a rickety shelf filled with hardware, and a wallet flopped out. The exterior appeared to be a poor imitation of leather, all cracked with the finish rubbed bare in spots. I flipped it open, hoping to find a windfall to help Delores out of her mess. Instead, I found several credit cards and a pair of old California driver's licenses. I carried them over to the window to get a better view.

The first one had the name Frank Archer, and the second—

"Boo!" Carla raised up outside the window, and I screamed.

I shrugged off my discovery and stuffed them into a crack between the windowsill and a two-by-four for future prosperity, like a time capsule. No telling what other secrets a seventy-year-old house held.

"Are you trying to give me heart attack?" I yelled.

Carla laughed and said, "Seems like old times. You're scared of your shadow. Remember the time—"

"Stop." I waded through the mess, careful not to step on anything that might pierce my shoe, and met Carla outside.

"What happened to you?" she asked.

"Meh! I knocked a shelf loose trying to get a ladder. No big deal," I said.

"I heard the commotion. Glad you're okay. Did you find anything?" she asked.

"A ladder with half the rungs missing, the other half so broken and tipsy it looked drunk, and a hoard of killer hardware. How about you?"

Carla held up an aluminum lawn chair.

"Are you serious?" I asked. "The webbing is gone. It won't hold anything. Leave it there."

She threw it into an overgrown bush and stomped to the bedroom window. "Then I guess we do this the hard way. Come give me a boost," she hollered across the yard.

"Keep your voice down." I heard a car in the distance, and the neighborhood dogs increased their barking. "You're kidding? You outweigh me by twenty pounds." I had a bad feeling about this. It hadn't been too long ago I'd vowed to mind my own business—now Carla had me preparing to break and enter.

"Are you calling me fat?" Her mouth gaped open. "Because you aren't exactly skinny."

I trudged to the window, my heart not fully engaged in the activity. "Come on Carla, knock it off. Do you want in or not? If so, help me up."

The barking grew more insistent, and a car door slammed—nearby.

"Honest, I can't. I have a bad back. If my sciatica goes out, I'll be in bed for a month."

"Why don't you call a locksmith?" I asked. "Since the cops are done, you have every right to get in your mother's house."

"You big chicken. I'm not waiting around all day. I want to know what Noah was doing here. He's got no right to come snooping around after all these years. He's probably not even been to the hospital yet." Carla kicked off her shoes and wagged a finger at me. "If you stand right here, I think I can get hold of the windowsill."

"He left when I did. He didn't take anything," I said, wondering why Carla was being impossible. "And he has been to the hospital."

"How do you know he didn't come back?" Carla glared at me. "What else haven't you told me?"

"Oh, for Pete's sake. What is going on with you?" I asked. "He came by my house after he saw the condemned sign on your mom's front door, and I saw him this morning when I dropped off some cleaning supplies for you. I'm sure he didn't have anything sinister on his mind."

"You don't know him like I do," Carla replied. "My brother is interested in one thing—money."

"He's worried about Delores. And for your information, he even hired an attorney for her."

"Why?" Carla asked.

"Maybe because the husband who supposedly left her was dead in her garage? I'm sure Noah's watching out for her best interests."

"Humph. Noah only looks out for himself. Now boost me up."

Carla had always been bossy, but she was being beyond ridiculous. I positioned myself in the spot where she directed and made a cradle out of my hands. She hiked her leg and didn't get her foot even close. Another dog joined in the barking.

"Hurry up. I'm getting a cramp in my back," I said.

"Put your hands lower. How am I supposed to get my leg up there?"

I bent at the knees and did as she said. "Like this?"

Instead of easing her foot into my hand, Carla launched herself like a gymnast. I lost my balance and tumbled backward. She flopped forward and landed on top of me. We lay there stunned for a minute. Then we both started laughing.

She regained her composure first, rolled off, and pulled me up. "We'd make great cat burglars. How many old ladies do you suppose are spying on us through their blinds?"

I turned toward the Bray house. "Mr. Bray is probably having a good laugh. At least Mrs. Wafford can't see us."

"Don't bet on it. I don't think there's much she misses."

I brushed dirt off my shorts and repositioned myself. "Do you want to try again?"

She nodded. "Duh. I'm getting into this house even if I have to drive a car though the front door."

"Not my car." I planted my feet apart and bent at the knees. "Now take it easy this time. Once you get your footing, grab my shoulders and try to pull up. I can't support all your weight in my hands for long."

"There you go making fat jokes again."

"Shut up." I braced myself, interlacing my fingers and creating a cradle for Carla's foot.

She managed to get a good boost and grabbed hold of the windowsill. "I'm going to pull the screen. Watch out when it comes down." She pushed the window open and lifted her foot to my shoulder. "Stay where you are until I get inside."

I steadied myself. "Carla, there's a nightstand below the window. Be careful."

She gave one last push and disappeared into the bedroom. I heard a string of curse words. Finally, she stuck her head out the window and gave me a thumb's up. "Made it. But I think I broke my neck."

"Not funny. Go around and unlock the door." I picked up the screen and placed it against the house.

I waited for what seemed like forever. As small as the house was, and with the path I'd cleared, it shouldn't have taken her so long to make it down the hall and into the kitchen. Unless she stopped to pilfer the house. Did she know about the diamonds? No, if she knew about them, she would have taken them the first day she was here, not waited until now. But again, she didn't know she'd have to fly home because of Max. Given how weird Carla was acting, I needed to add her to my suspect list.

I climbed the steps, getting aggravated, and banged on the glass. "Carla, let me in." Nancy had been alone too long, and I needed to get back and check on her.

When Carla didn't answer, I went back under the window. "Carla, are you there? I've got to get back to work."

Dread clutched at my chest. What if she'd hurt herself? I ran back to the door and twisted the knob, but it wouldn't give. I was about to go around front when the door swung open.

I pushed in. "What took you so long? You scared me to—"

Alder stood inside the door, arms folded across his chest. "I could ask you the same thing."

Carla stood in the kitchen with a sheepish look on her face. "I tried telling him this is my mom's house. But he's not having any of it."

"What are you doing here? Why aren't you at work?" I asked, trying to figure out how to explain my involvement.

A muscle twitched near his right eye. "I am. Thanks to you and your partner in crime, dispatch got a call of breaking and entering. I was close by, and they knew I'd worked the case, so they asked if I'd check it out. Now I have to call in, or they'll send backup."

He stepped into the living room.

I rolled my eyes at Carla and mouthed, *Don't worry. I know him, remember?*

Alder came back into the kitchen. "Can I speak to you outside?" He turned to Carla. "Don't move. I'll be right back."

While we were standing on the porch, I noticed he was even more attractive when he was angry, but now wasn't the time to mention it. "I know how it seems," I started.

He rubbed his mustache, paying extra attention to the scar on his top lip. "It *seems* like you're doing something you're not supposed to be doing. Again."

I couldn't argue. "I know it seems weird putting Carla in a bedroom window and all, but there's a logical explanation." At least it had sounded believable when I'd let her rope me into it.

He leaned against the door. "I'm all ears."

"Delores leaves a key under a fake rock, but it's gone. Then Mrs. Wafford across the street made us come in for a glass of lemonade and held us hostage until Carla told her what happened here." I paused for a breath. "And this morning I found Carla's brother, Noah—you remember him from the hospital— had been snooping around. She wanted to make sure he hadn't taken anything." I hesitated and watched his face. "You believe me, don't you?"

He continued to stroke his mustache, but I could see a grin lifting his lips.

I pushed his arm. "You let me ramble on like a fool, and you knew the whole time."

"Go to breakfast with me in the morning, and I'll let you off easy. We can take my motorcycle out to the country for a ride. You could pack a lunch. I've got the day off, and we could spend it seeing the countryside."

My heart lurched. The thought of being close to him made me giddy. But was I treading on thin ice? I knew where Saturday evening would have wound up if it hadn't been for Nancy. Regardless of what my body said, my head screamed no. It would be too easy to let myself fall for him, and until my divorce was final, I couldn't afford to let my guard down.

"Detective, your proposition is a bit premature."

His laugh rumbled low and throaty. "Ma'am, I can assure you there is nothing premature about me."

I would have melted right there on the porch, except Carla stuck her head out the door, pushing Alder off balance. "Are you going to stand around and flirt, or are you going to let us go?"

Alder tipped a make-believe hat. "You ladies stay out of trouble. By the way, I had the key." Alder dropped it in Carla's hand, then got in his car and drove off.

"Oh, my heavens. You and the detective have a thing." Carla clicked her tongue like a mother hen. "I never dreamed when I met him that you two were—"

"We are not 'having a thing,'" I said and went back into the house. She followed close on my heels.

"Yeah, right. The electricity zapping between you created fireworks like the Fourth of July and New Year's Eve rolled into one." Carla pushed a pile of clothing aside and sat down on the couch. "Spill the beans. Have you slept with him? Of course, you haven't. The sparks are still flying. Once you sleep with him, it'll fizzle out."

"I'm not having this conversation with you. And no, I'm not sleeping with him. Now or ever."

"Ooooo, I smell scandal. Does Angie know? How about Witch Hazel? She'll make your life miserable." She rubbed her hands together in a conspiratorial way. "Is he the reason you're divorcing Phillip?"

I knew the more I denied an affair, the guiltier I'd sound. I hadn't done anything to feel guilty about, except for having impure thoughts, and I'd been having plenty of those lately.

"Discussion over! What's your plan? I can't stay here today. I have a condo to clean, and it's not getting done standing here listening to you speculate on my love life, or lack of one."

Carla stuck out her lower lip. "Hit a nerve? Since your cop friend, who you aren't—" she gave me a deadpan look and faked a cough, "—sleeping with, didn't run us off, I guess I'll stay here and get some work done. Don't worry about picking me up. I got Mom's van."

I handed her my extra garage door opener. "The inside door is unlocked. I left towels in the spare bedroom for you. Make yourself at home." As an afterthought I added, "If Noah comes back, play nice."

~ ~ ~

I'd left Nancy alone far too long. She couldn't get in trouble in an empty building, but with all the workers around, I didn't want to chance her sunbathing au naturel on the patio of one of the units, or otherwise making a spectacle of herself. Grant had been great about me bringing her on, I didn't want to screw up and give him a reason to be upset.

I hadn't packed anything but a snack for us, so I swung by my house to see what I could find for our lunch. My mind was wandering when I turned down my street. If I'd been paying attention, I would have seen the Cavanaugh Design truck idling in my driveway. I pulled in and parked before it even registered.

Phillip always started an argument about money or Michelle. Then he'd try to make amends by telling me he still loved me and wanted to start fresh. I almost fell for it a couple of times, but then I realized he couldn't care less about starting fresh. He wanted to come home and go back to the way it used to be: him fooling around and me blaming myself for his cheating—as if it were my fault he couldn't keep his pants zipped.

I had almost caved two months ago, but nearly getting myself killed put my life into perspective. Once I had time to reflect, I didn't like what I saw. My big revelation was I had to take care of myself. And the only way to do so was to declare my independence from Phillip Cavanaugh and the life I'd been sharing with him.

I knew what he wanted today. The court had ordered him to pay temporary maintenance until our court date. The payment was due today. If I were a betting person, I'd lay money he came to make an excuse.

My car had barely rolled to a stop when he came barreling out of my front door. From the look on his face, he'd either gotten a horrible sunburn or was about to burst a blood vessel.

As he approached the car, I held up my hand. "Don't even start, Phillip. Unless you have a check, get right back in your truck and leave." I'd learned the best way to deal with him was to meet him square on. If I didn't, he'd run me over every time.

"I'm not paying you a dime! You can work and support yourself," he shouted. "Michelle isn't even here. You've shipped her off. When she comes home you'll get money from me, and not until then."

"She's only been gone three weeks. Get over yourself. I have utilities and a house payment. Which, if you'll remember, you didn't pay for at least six months. Now I'm playing catch up to keep the bank off my back."

Sliding out of the car, I grabbed the keys and rushed up the sidewalk. My front door stood wide open with boxes piled on the porch.

"What are you doing?" I grabbed a box and carried it inside. My barstools were against one wall of the foyer.

Phillip's recliner and two lamps from the family room were in the hallway leading from the kitchen.

Our attorneys had barely begun negotiating our property settlement, and Phillip hadn't indicated what he wanted, nor had we agreed on what he could take. Mine suggested I change the locks after Phillip left, but I hadn't followed his advice. Now I was kicking myself. I'd been hopeful when Phillip first left that he'd come to his senses and return home. Funny, the difference two months makes.

He charged in the door after me. "I'm taking a few things. Don't get all twisted and irritable with me. I'm sure you'll get more than your fair share when your greedy lawyer is done." He snatched the box from me and took it back to the porch.

I sat down defiantly in his recliner and pulled one of the lamps into my lap. "You aren't taking these. Or my barstools. Those were birthday gifts. Mine, not yours."

"Yeah, in that case, get your butt out of my Father's Day present."

I crossed my legs and leaned back in his chair. "You can have your stupid chair, after I get my check." Phillip had never been physically abusive to me, and I wasn't worried now. He had nothing to gain. Besides, the front door stood open, and there was no telling who might be out jogging or walking a dog. Phillip would never put on a show for the neighbors for fear of it getting back to his mother.

He studied me for a minute then sat down on a barstool. "Why are we doing this?"

"Doing what?" I asked, drumming my fingers. "Fighting over a recliner?"

Phillip's mouth drew into a frown. "Why are we divorcing? Next year, Michelle will go off to college, and we could be traveling and having a good time, not living in separate houses."

I stared at him. How could he sit there and question the necessity of a divorce? He initiated it, and I intended to finish what he started. I'd finally seen the light after thirty years of being a doormat. It took everything I had not to burst out laughing. Crossing my arms over my chest, I continued to stare at the man with whom I had two children and had promised myself to for better or worse. Only, I never dreamed the worst would actually come true.

"Okay, I know I screwed up. Blame it all on me. I cheated. You want me to crawl on my knees and beg your forgiveness?" He was wheedling, a trait I'd become all too familiar with recently.

As much as the visual intrigued me, I knew the longer he stayed in the house, the more susceptible I'd be. I pulled myself out of his recliner. "Get out and take your ugly chair with you."

He grabbed my arm and pulled me onto his lap. "Whatever you want, name it. You want me to dump Willow? Done. You can't fool me, Cece. I know you still love me, or else you wouldn't have put up with me all these years."

I put my hands on his shoulders and looked him right in the eyes. "Whatever love I felt for you died a slow, agonizing death. The problem is, you love yourself more than you love anyone else. Otherwise, you'd think about other people's feelings and not your own selfish needs. If you had any respect for me or our marriage, we wouldn't even be having this discussion."

I pushed off his lap and held my hand out. "Do you want to give me my check now, or do I have to call my lawyer?"

Phillip stood and pulled a check from his shirt pocket. "You sure you don't want to go upstairs for a little while? I might be able to change your mind. Remember how good we are at make-up sex?" He winked.

I seized the check and stuffed it into my bra. "Not on your life, buster." My hormones might have been raging but hopping in the sack with him would spell disaster with a capital "D." I continued, "And if you ever lay a hand on me again, it will not bode well for your sex life, if you get my drift."

"Yeah, well, you'd better not forget the prenup you signed, and the fidelity clause. If you're sleeping with the cop, you're entitled to nothing. I'll take care of the girls, but you'll be on your own, Cece. Nothing! A big, blank check." Phillip smacked me on the butt and walked out.

"I'm not sleeping with anyone," I screamed and slammed the door behind him. "Especially not you!"

Chapter 11

"I need a day alone with Alder like I need another pair of holey socks. I want to keep my distance, yet I can't say no. What is wrong with me?"
Cece Cavanaugh

Carla sat at the breakfast bar with Nancy when I came down the next morning. I gave Nancy the evil eye and made myself a cup of tea. Beatrice had arrived and was dusting the great room, singing softly to herself.

I took my tea and followed the sound of her voice. "How was the wedding?"

"Beautiful. Made me tear up. Reminded me of my very own. Though, these days you gotta mortgage a house to pay for one. Best keep your two girls single." Beatrice laughed.

"Not sure I have much say in what they do. Especially my oldest. But I'm working on getting Jessie married. I want grandkids."

"You got a houseful living here. Do I have to tell The Barracuda you're so poor you're taking in boarders?" Beatrice asked.

"She'd split my head if she thought I was renting out rooms. Better leave it alone. She'd be over here before the words were out of your mouth." I sipped my tea, then squelched a chuckle. "No, don't even go there with her."

"You want me to clean the apartment?" Beatrice wrinkled her nose in displeasure.

"Nope. Nancy's staying there, she can keep it clean. Speaking of which, I better get back and see why she's even down here." I wiggled two fingers at Beatrice. "Glad you enjoyed the wedding."

"We've got bagels," Nancy said, holding up a sack from Café du Soleil. "Carla went to get them. She brought back the good coffee too."

"Obviously, the two of you have met?" I grumbled. After my run-in with Phillip yesterday, I'd gone back to Hunter Springs and had been impressed with Nancy's work. She'd caught on fast, and I let her know I appreciated it. What I didn't appreciate was her helping herself to my kitchen. I should have explained the situation to Carla. If she'd invited Nancy in, it was an honest mistake. Rather than make a scene, I said nothing.

Nancy had a newspaper spread out across the counter with ads circled in felt-tip marker.

"Do you have my paper?" I hated it when anyone messed up the newspaper before I had a chance to read it. Phillip had always left it a wreck, and it irked me to pieces if he got hold of it before me.

"Hope you don't mind. The quicker I find a job, the sooner I can get out of here." Nancy circled another prospect. "I appreciate your hospitality and all." The sassiness in her voice was as subtle as the flimsy negligee she'd strutted around in on my front porch.

I reached over and lifted the paper. The black ink had bled onto my granite counter.

"Oops. Did I do that?" Nancy gasped, but made no move to clean it up.

Before I could say anything, the doorbell rang. "I'll be right back. Please wipe it up before it leaves a stain, or Beatrice will kill you in your sleep."

Alder stood on my porch with a big grin on his face. "You ready?"

I stared around him at the motorcycle sitting in my driveway. Beyond it, I saw Angie, in her bathrobe, picking up her newspaper. She nodded and gave me the A-OK sign with her thumb and forefinger curved into a circle.

My mind blanked. "Ready for what?"

His smile faded. "Breakfast? Did you forget? You were going to pack a picnic lunch for our bike ride." He looked like a little boy who'd had recess canceled.

"Oh, I uh." *I what? I forgot? I thought you were messing with me. I can't be near you because I'll jump you so fast, we won't know what hit us.* "I didn't make a picnic lunch."

His mustache lifted slightly, parting at the scar. "No problem. We can pick up sandwiches along the way. Grab a coat and let's go."

"Hang on." I shut the door leaving him on the porch. Angie had already seen him. If I left, she and Carla would have their heads together swapping gossip. In high school, if one of us was missing from the equation, it was a safe bet the other two were talking about the absent person. The way Nancy and Carla were bonding, and the way Nancy and Angie had already bonded, did not bode well for me. Well, I didn't want to think about it. When I got home, I'd get the paper myself and find Nancy a job.

Nancy and Carla had vacated the kitchen and taken my newspaper to the patio, continuing to hit it off. They had their heads together acting like long-lost friends. And me, I might have been feeling a tad jealous.

I stuck my head out the door. "I'm taking the day off."

Carla looked up. "Good, Nancy can help me at Mom's today."

"What do you want me to do?" Nancy asked me.

"Condos," I said. "If you can do two today, then I'll see where we stand."

"If she gets done early, she can help me," Carla piped in.

"Doesn't matter to me, but I can only pay you for Hunter Springs," I said to Nancy.

Alder was sitting on his bike by the time I returned. I knew without even checking Angie was watching us through the two drapery panels in her living room. As soon as we left, she'd be at my house flapping her lips to Carla. And Nancy. My ears already burned, and I hadn't even left. Yeah, I was definitely jealous.

Pulling on the helmet Alder handed me, I hopped on behind him like an old pro. He told me to hold tight as we sailed off down my street. The smell of fresh air and summer filled my lungs. I laid my head against Alder's back and savored in a freedom I hadn't felt in months.

When he pulled into a spot in front of Elm Street Café, known for their oven-baked pancakes, my heart sank. A Lexus just like Hazel's sat front and center. If she saw me having breakfast with Alder, her evil mind would dive right into the gutter, dragging me along for the ride.

"Can we go someplace else?" I hoped he wouldn't think I was ashamed of being in public with him. It was just the opposite; he was so hot, I'd have been proud to walk in anywhere on his arm—as long as my mother-in-law and half of Wickford didn't have a ringside seat.

He swiveled his head around. "You don't like pancakes?"

"Umm, not so much. Not today," I said.

"How about an omelet?"

"Sure." I'd eat a pickled herring if it were anywhere else.

The front door swung open, and Hazel walked straight to Alder's bike with her best friend Bitsy Harris-Dodd, of the Harris and Dodd Wineries, in tow.

"Can we go?" I asked, but not before my mother-in-law had me in her sights.

"Bitsy said she saw you out here." Hazel gripped her Prada bag and glared first at me and then at Alder. "I told her it could not possibly be you, Cecelia. Considering . . ." She let her words trail off.

Bitsy pursed her blood-colored lips in a satisfying sneer. "It appears Phillip isn't the only one with fidelity issues."

Hazel swung around and screeched, "Do not talk about my son. This is what he had to put up with. Can you blame him?"

"I-I didn't mean it the way it sounded." Bitsy stepped back and caught her heel in a sidewalk crack. She went down with a *thud.*

I nudged Alder in the ribs. "Go now, while they're going at each other, or we'll never get out of here."

He started the bike, and we left the two biddies gaping. Alder drove to the old section of Wickford and parked in front of Café du Soleil. When Alder had mentioned omelet, I'd hoped he meant getting an omelet out of town, several counties over. The next state maybe. With only two places for breakfast in Wickford, the chances of running into someone you knew were always one hundred percent.

I had been to Grant's favorite hangout, Café du Soleil, several times with him. His truck was nowhere in sight, but it didn't comfort me, because another parking area sat out of sight behind the building. My stomach churned with anxiety, and I began to doubt if I'd be able to eat.

Alder stowed our helmets. "How's this?"

I smiled weakly. Running into Grant was not on my list of things to do today. I summoned my courage and walked in the front door, which Alder held open. I wasn't dating Grant, and I certainly wasn't dating Alder. If I wanted to have breakfast with a friend, then I could. Grant would understand. We were all grown-ups.

The hostess seated us at a table for two, across from one another, where I'd be staring into his distracting blue eyes. After the ride and being snuggled against him, it was a relief not to have to worry about accidently touching legs. Now I had to figure out a way to not drool into my omelet. My voltage meter hit the overload mark.

He reached for my hand. *Ah, why did he have to do that?* My knees quivered, but I pulled my hand back.

"We have to talk," I started. "What I said the other day about this being premature."

He waggled his eyebrows. "And you remember what I said?"

I felt a blush creep up my face. Oh boy, he wasn't going to make it easy. "You're not helping. Look, I like you."

"And I like you. We know we like each other; can we eat breakfast and enjoy the day? Or do I need to write you a note with little hearts on it and slip it across the table?"

He was right. Was I making something of nothing? What did it hurt to enjoy my day off?

After we placed our order, I changed the subject. "Any news about Lloyd's cause of death?"

Alder shifted in his seat. "I'm not talking business with you."

Sue me for being curious. "Come on. His wife is a friend. I'm not asking for military secrets."

He leaned across the table and whispered. "I'll tell you what I can, if you promise to keep your pretty little nose out of it. I saved your neck once. You might not be lucky the next time."

I shook my head eagerly. "Deal." I made a big show of crossing my heart.

"He's dead."

I sat and waited. "And?"

"And what. The guy is dead. Frozen like an ice cube."

"Funny!" I curled my lower lip. *Ah, now I'm acting like Nancy. Stop it.* I resumed normal lip position. "After all the help I gave you with Delores, the least you could do is tell me what's going on."

"I do have some news, but let's enjoy our day before we talk business." Alder pushed his coffee cup to the edge of the table and signaled a passing waitress to fill it up.

Our breakfast arrived, and Alder dove into his, adding a generous portion of hot sauce atop the heap of eggs. I narrowed my eyes and watched him eat. I sat back and ate mine, enjoying the savory flavors of the peppers and mushrooms mingled with ham and goat cheese.

Leaving the restaurant, we chatted about the prospect of wine-tasting. As we strapped on our helmets, Grant Hunter parked at the curb. I turned my back before he saw me. I hoped.

Alder tapped me on the shoulder. "There's your other boyfriend."

I closed my eyes and hoped the sidewalk would open and swallow me. It didn't. What were the chances of running into the two people I most wanted to avoid on my day off with Alder? Pretty darn good, when you live in a town the size of Wickford. And even better if you're Cece Cavanaugh. I had the rottenest luck. When I turned around, Grant had already gone into the café. I didn't know if he'd seen me, or if he'd even recognized Alder with his helmet on.

"Were you trying to hide?" Alder asked.

"It's complicated." I climbed on the bike behind him. "Can we go?"

"Complicated?" He pressed. "Complicated like you're involved, or complicated like he's stalking you? Cause if he's bothering you, I'll have a talk with him."

"No," I said too quickly. "I told you, I work for him, nothing else. Can we go?"

He shrugged and pulled into the street. We bumped down the cobblestones on Main Street then turned onto the highway, where we sped down the four-lane until it narrowed to two. The road dipped and rose as we skirted the Missouri River on our left. The morning sun glimmered through the trees, creating shadows and pools of light on the asphalt. One minute I shivered in the shade, and the next, the sun beat down, warming me.

Instead of relinquishing my cares and enjoying the day, I thought about Phillip's threat. If Hazel told him she saw me with Alder, and she would, he'd be fired up. Why did I ever agree to a prenuptial agreement? Or to a motorcycle ride with Alder?

Chapter 12

"Cece takes a while to get to know, but she's not half bad once you figure out she's a lot of talk."
Nancy Lustbader

An hour and a half later, we rode into the town of Hermann, known for wine, festivals, and German hospitality. We stopped at a winery and toured the cellar, participated in a grape pressing demonstration, and ended sampling regional wines in the tasting room.

When we left, Alder slipped his hand around mine. "You ready for a little sightseeing?"

I nodded. My hand felt warm and tingly in his. I resisted the urge to pull away. There would be time to talk about my misgivings later, when I wouldn't spoil our day out.

"Let's browse some of the stores, and then we'll grab some sandwiches and find a place to eat on the way back," Alder said.

Each time we entered a shop, I marveled at his ability to evaluate antiques. He readily spotted the reproductions and pointed out the authentic pieces. In the last shop, he expertly negotiated the purchase of an antique bud vase. The dealer wrapped it in several layers of paper and gave the package to Alder.

"It's for the lady," he said, handing the bag to me. "A remembrance of our trip."

I started to protest but decided to accept my gift with grace. "It's beautiful. I have the perfect spot for it."

Before leaving town, we stopped at a deli and selected a variety of cheeses, crackers, and fruit. We found a roadside park and set out our picnic. Alder had even thought to pack a blanket, wine glasses, and a corkscrew in the tote on the back of his bike.

At the park, he selected a towering oak tree and shook out the blanket in the shade, while I sliced wedges from a block of cheese and arranged them on a napkin. I added slices of apples, and he poured the wine and offered a toast. "To a magnificent day."

"Thank you again for the vase. I love it." I sipped my wine and settled back against the tree.

He bowed at the waist, and in a horrible John Wayne accent, said, "My pleasure, ma'am."

"Oh, sit down." I chose my next words carefully. "We always seem to talk about me. Tell me something about you."

He lowered himself to the ground. "Like what?"

"Well, I know you have a daughter, and you were in Afghanistan. But other than. . . ." I shrugged and let my words trail off.

"You're really asking what happened to Mrs. Alder," he said.

"Maybe." A ladybug landed on my leg, and I remembered as a child how I always thought they were a sign of good luck.

He took a deep breath and exhaled. "Joyce and I were married for four years and endured some torturous times dealing with infertility issues. While we were going through in vitro, I got called up for a second tour. I didn't know Joyce was pregnant. Five months later, she wrote me a 'Dear John' letter. By the time I got stateside, she'd taken off with my best friend Cal. She didn't bother to tell me about Becca until six years later. My daughter was six before I knew she existed. Cal had left by this time, and Joyce wanted us to get back together. I honestly tried, for Becca's sake, but I couldn't get past what Joyce had done."

A muscle twitched in his jaw. If I'd known the extent of his pain, I'd have left the subject alone. My timing had never been great. "I'm sorry. It's none of my business."

He stared into his wine and slowly swirled the glass. "Don't worry about it. I made peace with her a long time ago, for Becca's sake. Joyce is a museum curator. During Becca's senior year of high school, Joyce accepted a position at a museum in Belgium, and Becca came to live with me. Having her in my life has more than made up for what her mother did."

"Kids have a way of grounding us," I said. "Mine drive me crazy. Well, Michelle drives me crazy. Jessie is the mature, stable one. I don't know what I'd do without them."

Alder reached for my hand and gently kissed each of my fingertips. Before I could pull back, he pressed his lips against mine. I kissed back at first, but something stopped me. There was no question about the attraction I felt, but I didn't want to feel like I was getting even with Phillip, and I did.

Alder broke off the kiss and sat up. "I want you to know my baggage is all behind me."

Tears welled in my eyes, but I swiped them away. "I have so much baggage, I should own stock in Samsonite. My divorce isn't final yet. I—"

Before I could finish, he cut me off. "Cece, you can't deny there's something between us. Do I make you uncomfortable, or is it because you're still married? I would never knowingly go out with a married woman, but your marriage was on the skids long before I came along. I don't feel like we're doing anything wrong, unless you plan on going back to your husband."

I'd taken off my wedding ring months ago, but I still felt

the indent where it had been for almost thirty years. "It's not easy for me."

"Do you still love him?" Alder stroked my cheek with the back of his hand.

"It's kind of like an incurable illness. The result is always the same. My marriage was terminal from the beginning. I kept trying to administer first aid to a patient on life support, and it took me a long time to realize it."

"You have to mourn it before you can move on. I know. But we can deal with it."

"It's going to take me time," I said, praying he understood. How could he, when I didn't truly understand?

I knew I had to tell him about the prenup, but I held off. Part of me felt stupid for being strong-armed into signing the document in the first place. Phillip had waited until a week before the wedding to spring it on me. He'd claimed he believed he could change his mother's mind but hadn't been successful. Without it he wouldn't get his inheritance. Hazel assumed her maneuver would force me to call off the wedding. She had accused me of being a gold digger. What choice did I have? If I canceled the wedding, I would have played right into her hand.

Another part of me worried Alder would think I was more concerned with the money than I was in pursuing a relationship with him. Truth was, I may not have worked outside my home during my marriage, but half the assets Phillip and I had belonged to me, especially after setting aside my nursing career. I didn't care as much about the money as I did my independence. Throughout this ordeal, I'd learned not to rely on a man for my well-being. I couldn't get into a relationship with Alder or anyone until I had the wherewithal to support myself. It would not be fair to expect someone to take care of me.

Alder drained the last drop of wine into my glass. "We

probably don't need to get back on the bike for a while, since we drank the entire bottle."

He stretched out on the blanket and shaded his eyes from the sun. I collected the remains of our lunch and found a nearby garbage can for the trash.

"What were you going to tell me?" I asked, putting the prenup out of my mind for now. "About Lloyd's case?"

Alder sat up. "How well did you know Lloyd?"

I sank down cross-legged. "Well enough, I guess."

"You said he wasn't from Wickford, right?"

"Right. Delores said he came from California or Nevada. Out west somewhere," I said. "Why?"

Alder rubbed his chin between his thumb and forefinger. "Are you absolutely certain the man you identified was Lloyd Redmond?"

"Yes. Of course." I leaned forward. "Wait. Why are you asking?"

"We ran the fingerprints on the guy in the freezer, and they didn't belong to Lloyd Redmond. The identification on the body was fake. Lloyd Redmond didn't exist before he arrived in Wickford."

~ ~ ~

Alder's revelation about Lloyd made no sense. The photo of the dead man I had identified was Lloyd Redmond. I had thoughts of Lloyd on my mind when we pulled into my driveway. My garage door stood wide open—a violation of Harris Arbor's homeowner's association rules. Depending on how long the door had been open, I would hear about it from one of the board members. Nancy's Jeep was gone, but Carla had parked her mom's van in the spot behind my car.

I headed into the garage, and Alder followed. The door into my house gaped open too.

"They're air-conditioning the entire neighborhood." I rushed into the house and did a quick back step, bumping into Alder. My kitchen looked like a real Missouri tornado had touched down, paper strewn all over and the drawers pulled out and flung onto the floor.

Alder placed his hand on my shoulder. "Stay here and call 911 on your cell. Tell them to send a car. I'm going to check around."

I stared in disbelief as he pulled a small gun from a holster strapped to his ankle. "You've had a gun the whole day?"

"Shhh. Call the station."

I didn't stay put. My house had been ransacked. As soon as I'd made the call, I caught up with him. He checked the patio door and great room. If Phillip hadn't been here yesterday, I might have been more scared, but this looked like his handiwork. I did a quick glance around to see what he had taken this time.

Alder went up the stairs, and I followed behind, contemplating the fact he'd worn a gun the whole day and that I never even knew it was there. I didn't know how I felt about being with a man who carried a firearm. I told myself to get over it. It didn't bother me when he was on duty, and it shouldn't bother me when he was off duty. And it felt comforting in an odd way.

An eerie feeling passed over me as I stood in my bedroom watching Alder check the bathroom and closets. This was the first time a man other than Phillip had been in my bedroom. I feared Alder could see a whole new side of me, an intimate, personal side—one I'd been suppressing. If Nancy hadn't been strutting her stuff on my front porch when Alder brought me home . . . I shook off the thought and remembered Phillip's warning. Nancy being out there in her skimpy getup might have saved me from doing something stupid.

My underwear drawers had been dumped on my bed, for Pete's sake. My panties, bras, and nighties in plain view. And right on top lay a pair of my granny panties. Compared to the rest, they looked like a big, old pair of bloomers. I grabbed a pillow and tossed it on the pile. To Alder's credit, he didn't act like he'd seen them, but I noticed a wicked smile as he passed by to check the other bedrooms.

I returned to the hall and cursed my husband for his threat, for his manipulations, and mostly for existing at all.

"You okay?" Alder holstered his gun, took my hand, and led me down the stairs.

"Yeah. Phillip did this," I said. "I knew I should have changed the locks."

"Whoever did this didn't have a key. The glass in the patio door was broken," Alder said.

"Or wanted me to think they didn't have a key. This reeks of Phillip. I came home yesterday and caught him carrying stuff out." I headed out the patio door.

Alder called after me, "Where are you going?"

"To check the apartment. I don't know where Carla is. Her van's here, but she's not." I ran up the stairs to the garage apartment, where I found another open door.

Alder moved me to the side and pushed the door wider. "Your ex didn't do this."

The apartment looked as trashed as my place. Furniture turned over, drawers emptied. My anger turned to fear. Phillip had no reason to ransack the apartment. He didn't even know about Nancy. My burglar had been after diamonds.

"The diamonds . . . Do you think this is somehow connected to them?" I asked.

"My guess—it is. Who have you told?" Alder asked as we descended the stairs. No handholding like before.

"Now you're accusing me of being a blabbermouth. Nancy only knows because she's the one who broke all the elephants in the first place." I yanked open the patio door and stomped across the broken glass into the kitchen. I hadn't even noticed it before.

"It's not like it would be the first time you told something you weren't supposed to tell," Alder said.

"Funny!"

The sound of a car engine echoed through the open garage door. Then female laughter followed. Carla and Nancy walked into the kitchen and tripped over one another when they saw Alder, the mess, and me.

Carla spoke first. "Holy smokes!"

Nancy's eyes were as wide as my grandma's salad plates. She tried to suppress a giggle, but it came out as half snort and half hiccup.

"Someone broke in," I said, still not thoroughly convinced Phillip wasn't to blame. "Where have you two been?"

Carla swayed and bumped into the doorframe. "Nancy went with me to Mom's this afternoon, where we had another run-in with old lady Wafford."

Nancy wagged her head. "She is cray-cray. If I ever get like her, I hope someone shoots me."

"Are you drunk?" I asked, thinking I might take Alder's gun and fulfill her wish.

Carla answered for Nancy, "We stopped at Weezie's for dinner and had a couple of drinks."

Two officers arrived, and Alder went to meet them. While they did a walk-through and made a mess with their fingerprint kit, Alder secured my patio door with a piece of plywood he'd found in the garage. I stood in the kitchen with Carla and Nancy while he worked.

"I can't believe someone would do this," Carla said. "Did they take anything?"

I shrugged. "Who knows? I think Phillip did it, but Alder doesn't." My mind raced to the diamonds. Could Nancy have told Carla? Did someone think I had the diamonds? Other than Alder, only Nancy knew about them. Thank goodness,

Alder took them in as evidence. "How long have you two been gone?"

"We left not long after you, and we've been gone all day," Carla said. "She dropped me off at Mom's this morning. After lunch, she came back to help."

Nancy nodded and hiccupped.

"And you let her drive like this?" I shook my head.

"No, I drove home. What about Beatrice?" Carla asked. "She was still here when we left."

"She usually leaves at noon," I said.

When Nancy sobered up, she and I would have a talk. I didn't like her and Carla getting chummy. And I especially didn't like my suspicion that Nancy had something to do with the break-in.

After the police questioned Carla, Nancy, and me, Alder sent them on their way. He also told Carla to come to the station the next morning to answer questions about Lloyd. I walked him out to his motorcycle.

"Cece, if you find anything missing, let me know. I'll get it added to the report. In the meantime, don't take any chances. And get that door fixed." Alder straddled his bike and strapped on his helmet.

Still not convinced Phillip hadn't orchestrated the break-in, I said, "I'm not worried, but I'll be extra cautious."

After Alder left, Carla helped me straighten up a bit. We'd put Nancy to bed when she proved too drunk to be of any help. She could worry about the disaster in the apartment when she sobered up.

Nothing appeared to be missing, but I hadn't checked the safe. I waited until Carla had gone to bed, pulled open my closet doors, scooted a small chest out of my way, and lifted the piece of carpeting Phillip had cut to cover the floor safe. I spun the dial to the code, my anniversary date. What a kick in the teeth. If I could find the instructions, I'd change the code.

"A date we will never forget" was Phillip's joke when he set the combination.

Everything looked in order. We usually kept a couple hundred dollars for emergencies, but my whole life had been an emergency since Phillip left, and I had used those funds and never replaced them. We also had all the usual important papers. Not important enough for the safe-deposit box, but not ones you wanted in your desk drawer. Someday soon, my divorce decree would be in the safe as well. I closed it and replaced the carpet, smoothing down the seams like Phillip had shown me.

My mind whirled with questions. Who had been in my house? Would Phillip try to scare me into letting him come home? I also wondered if Carla and Nancy had really been together all day. Nancy could have slipped out long enough to come back here for the diamonds. Carla said they'd gone their separate ways in the morning. Nancy had her Jeep. If I had told her Alder had them, would it have prevented a break-in? Carla seemed concerned about what Noah might be taking from their mom's house, and I'd let it slip to him that I had some of the boxes here.

I called Beatrice, and she assured me she'd left at noon, and nothing had happened while she was here. At least I felt better knowing she hadn't been here when the house was broken into.

To put my mind at rest, I also called Phillip. He answered on the first ring.

"What did you take this time?" I asked.

"Cece?" he paused. Phillip must have covered the phone with his hand, but I still heard his muffled voice say, "It's nothing. Don't worry about her."

"Phillip! Tell Willow it is something, and you'd better worry," I said to draw his attention back. "I want to know what you took this afternoon."

"What are you talking about?" Phillip said to me.

"Were you or were you not in my house this afternoon?" I asked.

"Absolutely not. And it's my house too," he said. "Why?"

"Someone broke in." Even as I said it, I felt a chill surround me.

"And you think it was me? When I want in, I'll use my key like I always do." Phillip laughed. "Maybe you should call your cop and have him investigate."

I disconnected and slammed the phone into its cradle.

Instead of putting my mind at ease, the call only ratcheted my fear. If Phillip hadn't been here, who had? Did Lloyd's death have any connection? I pulled a note from my nightstand to start a list, but my phone rang.

The caller display showed Alder's number.

"Hello?"

"Checking in to make sure you're okay. You have everything locked tight?" he asked.

"Aye, aye, Captain. Everything is secure at 'Chateau Cavanaugh.'" I mentally smacked myself for using my family's nickname for our home.

"I had a good time today." I could hear the smile in Alder's voice.

Water running in the background made me imagine him standing at his kitchen sink, which led to a barrage of questions flashing through my mind. Where did he live? What did his bedroom look like? Did he have a manly home in need of a woman's touch, or did his daughter Becca decorate for him?

I capped those thoughts. "Me too." My insides went all gushy thinking about our talk at the roadside park.

"Hope it took your mind off everything you've been going through."

Umm, not so much. Instead, it highlighted my current issue with Phillip, the prenup, and how powerless I felt. "It did," I said, feeling inadequate.

"Tell Carla not to forget to come to the station in the morning."

"She'll be there," I said.

The sound of the water ceased, and I heard a cabinet door open and close.

"Are you washing dishes?" I asked, picturing him all domestic-like.

"Huh? No, I'm feeding Sam."

Sam, who is Sam? Did Becca have a son? I could picture Alder being a grandfather.

When I didn't say anything, Alder said, "My dog. Though, if it had been up to me we would have named him Satan."

"Cute," I said.

"Be sure to check your doors before you turn in," Alder warned and hung up.

"I will," I said to the dial tone. Now my mind conjured all sorts of scenarios about *his* dog. *Stop it*, I told myself. The dog probably belonged to Becca.

I ran downstairs and checked all the doors and windows. I would have set the alarm, but I'd canceled the service to save money after Phillip moved out. Then I came back up and started my list.

Lloyd Redmond:

Lloyd Redmond came to Wickford under an assumed name? Why?

Was he involved with the diamonds?

Rhonda Bray:

Motive: ???

Where is she?

Did Lloyd double-cross her?

Did she know about the diamonds? Are they the reason she's missing?

What is her background?

Did she kill Lloyd and then leave? But without the diamonds?

Peter Bray:

Motive: Lloyd was having an affair with Rhonda Bray.

Did he kill Lloyd?

If he killed Lloyd, why not take the diamonds then?

Noah:

Motive: He resented Lloyd marrying Delores, but enough to kill him? According to Carla, Noah and Lloyd had become friendly.

Did Noah know about the diamonds?

Why would he put the body in his mother's freezer?

Did he ship the diamonds to Lloyd? Diamond smuggling?

If so, why hadn't he taken the diamonds after he killed Lloyd? Or did he assume Lloyd had gotten rid of them?

What did he know about Rhonda Bray?

Delores:

Motive: Husband cheating with neighbor. Missing investments?

Did she know about the diamonds?

Did she know Lloyd had an assumed name? (Could be motive.)

Did she accidentally kill Lloyd?

As much as I didn't want to, I added Carla to my suspect list. She had as good a reason as anyone else.

Carla:

Motive: She didn't like Lloyd and resented him marrying Delores. The diamonds could be it, but why were they still in the house five years later? Wouldn't she have taken them? Unless, she didn't know where they were.

Did she find out Lloyd wasn't who he said he was?
Why would she put his body in her mother's freezer?
Did she know about the diamonds?
Where was she when Lloyd disappeared?

Making the list reminded me of the driver's licenses I'd found when I was in Delores' garage. Could they be connected? Alder had said Lloyd Redmond did not exist before he showed up in Wickford.

I went back downstairs and got my laptop. Time for a bit of bedtime investigation. I recalled the first name on one of the licenses, but the last name escaped me. I keyed in Frank and tried to recall the rest. The last name had started with an "A," maybe Albert or Alberts. No, it was Archer. I added Archer to the search and received over five hundred thousand results. Next, I added California. Two hundred thousand results came back.

If Lloyd was Frank Archer, maybe looking for something before he arrived in Wickford would help. I narrowed the search further by including the year before Lloyd had arrived in Wickford. Nothing. I continued changing the year, and finally, three years before Lloyd arrived in Wickford, I got a hit. My fingers trembled when I hit the enter key.

An article from a Cayton Bay, California, newspaper popped up. I clicked the link and a photo of the man I knew to be Lloyd Redmond displayed on my screen along with the article.

Local Con Artist Frank Archer Escapes
January 9, 2003 | Staff Writer | Cayton Bay News

Frank ("The Mooch") Archer, who was convicted of swindling widows out of more than $250,000, escaped from a minimum-security prison in Norval, Calif., on Tuesday.

Archer was sentenced in 2002 to fifteen years for cheating more than a half dozen widows out of their life savings.

Archer pleaded guilty to fraud. His wife, Katherine, was a suspect in the fraud but never convicted. Her whereabouts are unknown.

The two were known to target widows and widowers, reeling them in, quickly gaining their trust, and then making off with thousands of dollars.

Whoa! Whoa! Whoa!

I plugged in Katherine Archer's name and came up with a few articles about her suspected crimes, but no photos.

If Archer was after Delores' money, how did the diamonds come into play? I couldn't connect the dots. At this point, I couldn't tell Carla without giving away what Alder had told me about Lloyd not existing before he came to Wickford. And I couldn't tell Alder without drawing his wrath for snooping. Besides, if I had found the information so easily, Alder already had it. Alder had Archer's fingerprints.

My brain hurt. I went to bed with an unsettled feeling.

Chapter 13

"If more young folk were like that Cece Cavanaugh, we would not have all the bad goings on like we have here in Wickford. It's a disgrace."
Eleanor Wafford

"Did we have a party last night?" Nancy asked. "My apartment is trashed."

"No, we did not have a party. My house was burglarized."

Nancy yawned and headed to my refrigerator.

I beat a path to block her. "Were you too drunk to remember?"

"Ummm, oh yeah. I kind of remember your cop boyfriend being here." Nancy edged her way past me. "Do we have any tomato juice?"

"You don't have anything?" I reminded her. "And no, *I* do not have tomato juice."

"Oh, someone's a grouch this morning. Are you sure you're not hungover?" Nancy asked with sarcasm. "This is going to be a fun day."

I checked around to make sure we were alone and whispered, "Did you say anything to Carla or anyone else about the you-know-what?"

"Huh?" Nancy looked up at the ceiling.

"Remember what you broke and what came out?" My patience with Nancy teetered between angry and livid. If she had anything to do with the break-in, I'd haul her to jail myself. I didn't care how many condos Grant had ready. I'd tell Carla I couldn't help at her mom's, and I'd find someone else to assist me at Hunter Springs.

Recognition appeared in Nancy's eyes, and the light bulb in her brain snapped on. "Oh, the diamonds?" she said in a stage-whisper loud enough for the entire neighborhood to hear.

"Shhh! You don't have to announce it. Did you tell anyone? And more importantly, did you have anything to do with someone breaking in to my house?"

Nancy's face contorted into a panic-stricken mask. "Who would I tell? Why would I tell? No. I know you think you're better than me, but I need this job and a place to stay."

I pulled out a barstool and sat down. "Nancy, first, I don't think I'm better than you, and I resent you saying it. This is about trust. I need to know I can rely on you. Did you say anything to Carla?"

Nancy jerked her head in the direction of the hallway and bit her lip.

"What about me?" Carla rounded the corner in her bathrobe and socked feet.

"Cece wanted to know if I spilled the beans to you about her and the hottie cop." Nancy crossed her arms, satisfied with her bean-spilling self.

"Ha! I knew it." Carla hobbled into the kitchen. "But I need coffee first and something for a headache. If I'm getting questioned by the hunky detective this morning, I need to be on my A game."

"Oh, will you stop it? There's aspirin in my bathroom. Help yourself. There may be a bag of coffee in the cabinet next to the stove, but you're on your own," I said, pulling the coffee maker from the corner cabinet. "I can't stand the stuff."

Carla left in search of pain relief. I refilled my teacup and shot Nancy a sour look. "If you're satisfied with yourself, then I suggest we get to work."

~ ~ ~

Nancy slid into my car, rolled down the window, and stuck out her legs. I backed out of my driveway and headed to Hunter Springs. Before we'd reached the end of the block, Nancy turned the radio on to a popular oldie station. She launched into her own personal rendition of "this week in history's number one tune" at a decibel clearly intended to reach the masses.

I reached over and punched the radio off. "Please. Stop!"

She twisted her head my direction. "You got a headache too? Maybe you should have taken some of those aspirin."

I had an ache, but it wasn't in my head, and there wasn't a pill big enough to cure it. "Did you say anything to Carla about those diamonds?"

"No. Give it a rest, will you?" Her voice rose an octave.

"You have to admit, you and Carla were awfully chummy last night, and you'd been hitting the alcohol pretty hard." I made a right at the next intersection. "Maybe you said something while you were drinking."

"You asked me to keep quiet." She turned an imaginary key in her lips. "I've been around long enough to know how to keep a secret."

"Thanks, I think. My guess is those stones have something to do with Lloyd Redmond's death and the break-in at my house."

"Does your boyfriend know about them? Hey, will you stop at Café du Soleil? I could use some caffeine."

When we reached the café, I pulled into a parking space and turned to watch Nancy's face. "He's not my boyfriend. Will you put a plug in it? For your information, I gave him the diamonds."

Her expression didn't change. She pulled her feet in the window and unbuckled her seat belt. "Are they evidence?"

I nodded. "Yes, but Carla's my friend, and until I know if she's involved, it's between me and you. Understand?"

When she didn't get out of the car, I cleared my throat. "Thought you wanted coffee."

"Uh . . . Could I have an advance on my pay? I'm broke."

I handed her two dollars. She shook her head and said, "We're not at a fast food joint. This is the real deal designer java."

I dug out a five. "Will this do?"

"Yeah, unless you want something."

"Go, before I change my mind about giving you a loan."

While she spent my money, I thought about Lloyd Redmond and the day he disappeared. Delores hadn't remembered much, but I knew one person who didn't let anything slip by unnoticed.

Nancy returned a few minutes later, sipping the foam from a gigantic latte.

I rolled my eyes. "You couldn't get a smaller one?"

She glanced over her cup. "Sorry, but this is soooo good. I could never afford them when I worked for Fletcher. You want a taste?"

Yuck, not with the lipstick stains she'd left on the side of the cup. My stomach twisted. "No, thanks. And for your information, you won't be able to afford one working for me either. Consider this your lucky day."

I pulled out and made a U-turn at the stoplight, checking in the mirror to make sure no cops were lurking around waiting to give me a ticket. In Missouri, U-turns were illegal at intersections controlled by traffic signals.

"Hey, you're going the wrong way. Did you forget something?" Nancy asked between slurps of her designer java.

"No, I have an errand. We're making a little detour." I drove to Castleman Lane. I didn't want Nancy going with me, but I'd have to go out of my way to drop her off at Hunter Springs and then circle back. When I pulled into Eleanor

Wafford's driveway, Nancy blew out a breath. "What are we doing at this old bag's house?"

"She's the neighborhood snoop. If anyone knows what happened the day Lloyd disappeared, I bet she can tell us." I put the car in park and opened my door.

Nancy slouched down and put her feet on the dash. "You, not us. I'm staying here. The old bat doesn't like me. She made me and Carla drink her horrible lemonade. If I have to drink another glass, I'll gag. The stuff tasted like dirty socks."

"Speaking of dirty socks, get your nasty feet off my dash." I reached in and swatted her leg.

Across the street, a car I didn't recognize pulled into Delores' driveway. I waited a minute. When the driver didn't exit, I shrugged it off. It wasn't Noah's rental. Probably someone turning around. I steeled myself for another encounter with Mrs. Wafford and jogged to her door.

When I rang the bell, Mrs. Wafford peeked out the front window with her binoculars. She answered the door with notebook in hand. Her eyes remained glued to the vehicle across the street. "What do you want? I'm busy," she said.

"What do you remember about the day Lloyd Redmond disappeared?"

She set the binoculars on the metal tray and gave a last glance across the street. "That was years ago. My memory's good, but what makes you think I'd remember happenings from way back then?"

Because you're a nosy old biddy who has nothing better to do than spy on neighbors almost came out of my mouth, but I suspected she wouldn't be forthcoming with information if I told her my true thoughts. Instead, I said, "I can tell you're concerned about the neighborhood. I bet there's not a lot happens around here you don't know. You seem well informed."

She stood straighter. "I reckon I am. Some people don't 'preciate how hard I try to keep up with the doings around here. Folks 'round here are too lazy to care what goes on right on their own street." She peeked outside. "Is the smart aleck staying in the car?"

I nodded.

"Good. I can't abide rude people. She came here yesterday with Delores' rude daughter, and I threw them out. Makes me want to slap some sense into them. How about I get us a glass of lemonade, dear? I'll have to check my books and see what I can recollect. It might take me a while. You know, Delores didn't do herself no favors when she married Lloyd Redmond." Mrs. Wafford stood aside and let me enter. "Why, me, I would never besmirch my Herbert's name by marrying some ne'er-do-well and turning my back on lifelong friends, like Delores did." She walked out of the room tsking to herself.

I called it right. Mrs. Wafford had a touch of the green-eyed monster—jealousy. She moved up a notch on my list of suspects. Maybe she killed Lloyd, hoping to regain her friendship with Delores. Or she wanted to pin the murder on Delores in retaliation for snubbing their lifelong friendship.

A car door slammed somewhere in the neighborhood, and I thought how disappointed Mrs. Wafford would be to have missed it.

It took forever for her to return, but when she did, she not only had lemonade and cookies but also three notebooks neatly labeled with years and dates. Thank goodness she was organized. I had wisely sat in the only chair without a plastic cover. Mrs. Wafford frowned when she saw me but didn't say anything. She slowly sat on the sofa, probably so it wouldn't whoosh out a blast of air.

The lemonade tasted as revolting as it had the last time I visited. I gagged it down with a couple of cookies while my hostess thumbed through her books. I did have to admit, she baked a fine cookie.

"I'm pretty sure Lloyd disappeared in 2013, but it could have been 2014." She stopped turning pages and looked up. "If Lloyd didn't leave, what do you reckon happened to the neighbor he ran off with? Rhonda Bray? What a piece of work, I tell you. Flitting around the neighborhood showing off her assets, if you know what I mean. Trying to get the men all riled up. Thank goodness my Herbert wasn't around to witness her spectacle. Her own husband turned a blind eye. No wonder she ran off. Unless Delores caught them. You don't think Delores killed her too, do you?" She covered her mouth with her hands in exaggerated shock.

"I don't think Delores killed anybody." I had suspected Phillip of cheating, but I'd never walked in on him. No telling what I would have done in a similar situation. I couldn't say for sure. Thinking he cheated hurt, but catching him? At least I had something to be thankful for.

An anniversary clock on Mrs. Wafford's console TV chimed seven times. I had four condos to clean today, and my patience grew thinner the longer she prattled. Grant gave me plenty of leeway in my schedule, but I didn't want to take advantage of his good nature. "Have you found anything yet?"

"I'm thinking." She flipped through the book, running her finger down the page as she went. "Yes, here it is, I think." She skipped ahead, read a few entries, and then turned it back to the first page. "The Bray woman left July 15, in a cab with three suitcases. I never saw Lloyd Redmond come out of the house after July 17, 2013."

My mouth dropped at her record keeping. If she had this right, Lloyd could have died after Rhonda Bray left town. "You saw Lloyd on the fifteenth and sixteenth?"

"Yes," she said.

She clicked her tongue as she scanned the page. "Delores' daughter arrived July 19 and the son visited on July 21."

"Carla and Noah were both here around the time Lloyd disappeared?" I asked.

"Isn't that what I said?" Mrs. Wafford shut the book and took a long drink of her lemonade.

Was she good or what? I wondered if she had other spies in the neighborhood, or if this was all her handiwork. I almost giggled aloud at the thought of a band of old women relaying gossip down the street. I could almost visualize them, in camouflage robes with dried twigs and leaves poking out of their sponge curlers. *Eleanor, this is Velma. The Curry kid spit on the sidewalk. Make sure you write it down. Next time you talk to his lazy mother, be sure to tell her how disgusting her brat is.* What every neighborhood needed—commando grannies.

Carla hadn't said anything about visiting her mom around the time Lloyd disappeared. Five years was a long time, it could have slipped her mind. But still, Lloyd disappearing? Surely Carla would remember such a catastrophic event in her mother's life. And why had Noah been there around the same time?

Just because Mrs. Wafford didn't see Lloyd after the seventeenth didn't mean he was killed on the seventeenth. It could have easily been the nineteenth or the twenty-first. Carla needed to stay on my suspect list, right next to Noah. And what about Mrs. Wafford's elaborate notes? Could she have fabricated all this to make herself appear innocent?

Another car door slammed, and an engine roared to life. Eleanor Wafford dropped the book and tottered to the window. "The smart aleck left in your car." She made a notation in the current book.

"What?" I ran outside in time to see my car disappear around the corner.

Chapter 14

"Attitude is going to be the death of me. I figured when Michelle went on vacation I'd have a month free of attitude. But no!"

Cece Cavanaugh

Mrs. Wafford let me take the books with the promise to return them and come back for more lemonade. I waited twenty minutes for Nancy, to no avail, and I didn't have her cell number. I called my house, and no one answered. When the answering machine came on, I yelled, "Nancy, Carla, if you're there, pick up the phone. Now!"

No one answered.

Carla hadn't arrived at her mother's yet, but I didn't want to call her. She'd give me the third degree about my visit to Mrs. Wafford, and Alder would kill me for *interfering*. I definitely couldn't call him. I chose Grant instead.

The minute he arrived, I knew he'd seen me with Alder at Café du Soleil.

"Thanks for coming," I said as I crawled into his truck. "Nancy stole my car, and I don't have a clue where the dumbbell went. At this point, I don't know what to do."

"No problem." He focused on backing out of the driveway. No small talk, no smile. Just a somber expression.

I wanted to reach out and punch him. What right did he have to be angry or hurt? We were friends. I'd told him not to have any expectations of a relationship, and he said he understood. Me having breakfast with Alder was no different than me having coffee with him. Okay, there were feelings mashed into the middle of my day with Alder, but I had them under control. I had no choice after Phillip's threat.

"Grant, I—"

"You don't owe me an explanation," he said.

"You're right. I don't," I said. "When I told you I needed time, I meant it. You acting jealous or aggravated or whatever it is, is a waste of time."

"Where do you want me to take you?" He stared straight ahead.

"To Hunter Springs, I guess. Maybe Nancy's there. Or maybe she stole my car and took off for parts unknown."

Instead of taking me to the condos, he drove to Main Street and stopped near the river. He didn't say anything, parked, slammed the door, and walked down to the water.

"Grant," I yelled out the window. "What are you doing?"

He stooped, picked up a rock, and threw it in. Several rocks later, he got back in the truck.

"Did throwing rocks in the river make you feel better?" I said, hoping my attitude got his attention.

"Yes."

Men!

When we arrived at Hunter Springs, Nancy and my car were nowhere to be found. "I'm going to kill her." I pounded my fist on the dash. "I don't know where she is, but when I catch up with her she'll be sorry. I'm going to yank every frizzy hair out of her head and then slap her into the next county!"

"Well, I can't leave you out here without a car," Grant said. "Do you want me to take you home?"

"I need to finish these units, but I don't even have my supplies. Everything I use is in my car. Yes, take me home. Please. At least until I can figure out where Nancy went."

"Can do," Grant said.

I touched his arm, expecting him to draw back, but he didn't. "Grant, I'm not ready to date anyone. I can't talk about it. Please don't put me in an awkward position. You have to drop the attitude."

He placed his hand on mine. "Okay."

Grant was one of those people you wanted in your life. He cared and understood to a fault, but the jealousy had to stop.

He put the truck in gear and raced out of the parking lot. "Before we head to your house, let's see if we can find Nancy. A yellow Mustang shouldn't be too hard to locate."

"What? Are you serious?" I bumped my head on the window as he made a U-turn and sped up Main Street.

~ ~ ~

Grant drove around for more than an hour but couldn't find my car. In a town the size of Wickford, it should have been easy to spot. We finally gave up, and he drove me home. My car sat in the driveway, unaffected by Nancy's joyride.

Grant came around and opened my door. Two men in one week had opened doors for me. I liked it. Even though I had mixed feelings about Grant and Alder, the respect they showed toward me didn't go unnoticed.

"Do you want me to go in with you?" Grant lagged behind as I rushed up the sidewalk.

I started to dismiss his offer, but I remembered the break-in and decided I needed a male presence to bolster my confidence. "Would you mind?"

The bud vase Alder had bought for me at the antique store stood on the porch with a single red rose. In all the excitement yesterday, he'd forgotten to take it out of the storage compartment on his bike.

"Looks like the cop left his calling card," Grant said. "The guy is serious."

I gouged him in the ribs with an elbow. "We had a deal."

"You're right. I'm sorry." He threw an arm around my shoulder and led me in the front door.

When we got to the kitchen, Grant whistled. "Wow. What happened in here?"

Carla and I had closed the cabinets and put the drawers back in place after the police left, but we didn't get around to doing much more than scooping the mess of papers into a big pile on the kitchen table.

Not wanting to alarm him, I brushed it off. "I suspect Phillip tried to scare me. He stopped by earlier in the week to get his recliner."

"Why didn't you say something?"

"What's to say? I told you my life bordered on disaster." I spotted Nancy outside, through the undamaged side of the patio door. "Thanks for bringing me home and for understanding and for—being you." I hugged him.

He wrapped his arms around me in a protective embrace and kissed the top of my head. "I only want what's best for you."

I backed away and pushed him toward the living room. "You'd better go."

"Can I at least send one of my guys over to fix your patio door?" Grant asked.

I hesitated, but finally said, "Yes, that would be appreciated."

After I saw Grant out, I charged outside. "Where have you been? You've got a lot of nerve, leaving me stranded. I had to call Grant Hunter to come get me."

"Worked out pretty good for you. I never dreamed you were doing the boss too." Nancy had my newspaper and a giant glass of iced tea in front of her.

I jerked the paper out of her hand. "You want a paper, buy your own. And for your information, I am not *doing* anyone. And don't be spreading rumors about me."

Nancy shaded her eyes from the sun and squinted at me. "Probably why you're getting a divorce. You gotta do the hubby once in a while, or he'll find someone who will."

She had a lot of nerve, coming into my home, making accusations she knew nothing about. As soon as I caught up at Hunter Springs, she'd be history. "Let's go."

When she didn't make an effort to move, I stormed back inside. I could do this with or without her. She finally sauntered in.

"For your information, I came back to get you, and you were already gone. I talked to the old battle-ax and knew you had a ride." Nancy followed me to my car.

"Well, now I feel comforted. At least you didn't *plan* to strand me. But you did," I yelled as I slid behind the wheel to start the car. "Where are my keys?"

"I put them on the kitchen counter."

"Are you kidding? You don't have them?"

"I told you, they're on the counter. Did you lock the door?" Nancy asked.

"Of course. My house was broken into yesterday. Do you think I'm an idiot?" I got out of the car, slammed the door, and stomped over to Angie and Dave's for my spare key.

~ ~ ~

When we were almost at Hunter Springs, Nancy finally broke the silence. "Aren't you going to ask where I went?"

Not wanting to give her the satisfaction of begging, I said, "No." I could tell she couldn't wait to tell me. It would only be a matter of time before she came clean. In the meantime, I could wait.

Grant had purchased five hundred acres on a bluff outside of town, overlooking the river. From what he'd told me, the development contained three phases. The condominiums I was currently cleaning were phase one. Town homes would come next, and the last section consisted of single-family homes. When completed, the development would have recreational areas as well as shopping and entertainment.

When Grant started the extravagant single-family homes, it wouldn't surprise me one bit for the country club set to make the move to Hunter Springs. Several trendy boutiques had already signed leases for the upscale shopping area.

Nancy fidgeted in her seat. "Okay, I'll tell you."

I ignored her and pulled into the driveway of one of the units. The workers had moved down the street. We'd had rain a few days ago. Landscaping hadn't been installed—resulting in mud—and the workers tracked it everywhere.

"I followed the car," Nancy said.

"What car?" I removed our supplies from the trunk and sidestepped the muddy globs on the sidewalk.

"The one in Carla's mom's driveway."

"Why?" I unlocked the door with the master key Grant had given me and dropped off half the supplies. At the next unit, I did the same. To save time, Nancy would clean one while I did the other. Then we'd move down the line until we finished.

Nancy pulled a handful of rags from the trash bag she'd brought in. "I figured you'd want to know what the woman was doing."

"What woman?" I put a broom and mop in the kitchen while Nancy trailed after me. "Why would you chase after that car?"

Nancy rested her hands on her hips. "I saw a woman inside. She left the front door open, and I went in. She was rummaging through drawers in the nightstand in the back bedroom. When she saw me, she took off. Practically knocked me over on her way out." Nancy's breath hitched. "She had something in her hand."

Nancy had my attention. "What?"

"I don't know. Why do you think I followed her?" She headed out the door.

"Wait, where are you going?" I grabbed her arm.

"I've got work to do. You said so yourself." She trotted off down the sidewalk, and I gave chase.

"Where did the woman go?" I shouted after her.

Nancy entered the other condo and slammed the door. Now she wanted me to beg her for the information. I wished I'd never let her into my house, much less agreed to give her a job. She was worse than having another kid around. If I groveled to Fletcher, he might invite her to Florida to take care of him. No, he was probably sicker of her than me. Could she be the real reason he relocated to Florida, leaving her homeless?

I wasn't about to plead with Nancy. She'd tell me in her own good time. I went back into my condo and started cleaning. What did I care if some woman rummaged around in Delores' house? Carla could figure it out. The only person I cared about in the equation was Delores. If Carla carted her off to North Carolina, Delores' hoarding days were over. Carla would relegate her mom to the guest bedroom with a twin bed, nightstand, and dresser. Delores would be hoarding spare time and nothing else.

I stepped out to the car to get another roll of paper towels and saw Grant's workers going into the condo next door—the unit assigned to Nancy. A short while later, music blared through an open window. Being the suspicious type, I walked next door and peeked inside. Nancy lounged on the breakfast bar, swinging her feet to the beat of the music. Grant's men were mopping, cleaning windows, and wiping down the walls. If Brad was in on this, I would rescind my invite to dinner, and he would *not* be meeting Jessie.

I threw open the front door. "What in the world are you doing?" I asked. "You're supposed to be working."

"Come on in. The guys got it covered." Nancy swept a glance around the room.

The men waved and continued working. I breathed a

sigh of relief upon seeing that Brad and Larry were not part of the crew here.

"You." I pointed to Nancy. "Get down. Are you trying to get me fired? Or them? Grant will have all our heads if he finds out about this."

The men looked from Nancy to me and back "Stop! All of you." I grabbed a sponge and threw it at Nancy. "Tell them to leave."

Nancy hopped off the counter and turned down the music. "Sorry, guys. Guess the party's over."

I should have threatened to rat them out to Grant but doing so could backfire on me. From now on, they wouldn't be shirking their duties to cater to Nancy. I'd make sure of it.

After they left, Nancy picked up a broom and pushed it around the floor, scattering more dirt than she collected. "You are no fun at all. When I worked here the other day, they asked if they could help. It's not like I made them."

"You had them cleaning the other day?" I sank to the floor. No wonder she'd gotten so much done. "Do you have any idea how much money they get paid an hour? And you had them in here washing windows?" Grant might have a soft spot for me, but he wouldn't appreciate paying his carpenters to do work he paid me to do.

"I don't know why you're upset. You said the boss sent a crew to help you clean out the hoarder's house. You didn't have a problem with his guys helping then."

"Forget it. If you want to clean, fine. If you don't, then I'll find someone who will. You decide."

At quitting time, Nancy stuck her head in the door. "Is it safe to come in, or are you still in a cranky mood?"

"Funny," I said. "This might be a game to you, but it's the only job I have right now. If I blow this, I might as well forget about my business. No one will hire me without references."

"If you're done chewing me out, I have something to show you." Nancy had already packed her supplies and helped me carry mine to the car. "Give me your keys."

I eyed her. "Where are we going? I don't trust you after today's escapades."

"Oh, get over yourself and hop in," she said. "Give me your keys. You have to trust someone once in a while, or else you won't have any friends."

Chapter 15

"Cece's starting to grow on me. At least her friends are cool. So, she must be okay for them to hang around." Nancy Lustbader

Nancy drove to a storage facility in an older part of Wickford. A six-foot chain-link fence surrounded the place. She pulled the car into an alley and motioned for me to get out and be quiet. I followed her to a trash bin at the end of the alley.

Before I could ask questions, I received my answer. The car I saw at Delores Redmond's sat in front of one of the units, trunk open.

Nancy pushed on my shoulder and dropped to her knees. "Get down, so she doesn't see us."

"She, who?" I asked, straining to get a better view.

"Beats me."

I eyeballed the oily puddles next to the trash bin. Nancy grabbed my hand and pulled me down. "And you worry about me being stupid. You can always wash your fancy designer clothes later. Haven't you ever followed anyone?"

"No, as a matter of fact, I haven't." I found out about Phillip and Willow the day he walked out on me. Following him seemed to be a moot point, since I didn't know about his affair. Not much intrigue there. I wasn't sure in this case. I didn't even know who we were following. Someone had murdered Lloyd, it could easily have been this person.

"This is where you went today?" I observed a woman coming out of the locker.

Nancy nodded. "Yep, she stopped by a creepy motel in town and then came out here."

"Anyone else with her?" I asked.

"No." Nancy crawled around the edge of the bin, craned her head around, and held her fingers to her lips. "Stay down and be still."

"What did she do?" I asked.

"Who knows? She never went inside. I think maybe she didn't have the right key. She kept messing with the lock and finally gave up."

I followed, keeping my eyes on the woman. A loud crash echoed in the alley near the vicinity of my car. Nancy grabbed my wrist. "Stay still."

The woman froze.

An engine revved down the way.

"Let's go," I said.

"Just a sec," Nancy said. "Let's wait and see what she does!"

"Um, no." I ran to the car, leaving Nancy behind. If the boogeyman got her, one less worry off my mind.

Nancy came running to the car. "She's got someone!"

"What?" I peered out the window. "Who?"

"I don't know. You ran off, and I lost my concentration, but I saw her drag someone out of the trunk. She pushed them in the locker." Nancy's breath hitched as she relayed her sighting.

"Oh, seriously. She dragged someone out of the car? Now you sound like Mrs. Wafford and her TV shows. It makes no sense."

"Get down, here she comes," Nancy said.

We both sank down in our seats. I peeked over the dash and watched the woman key in the access code to open the gate. She was alone. I slid back down and waited until I no longer heard her car.

"Let's go," I said to Nancy. "This is ridiculous."

~ ~ ~

Carla hadn't returned by the time we came home. I tried her cell phone all afternoon and left numerous messages. I didn't know what time she'd arranged to meet Alder, but I knew she'd be at her Mom's the rest of the day. Her thirty days were ticking away, so she didn't have time to waste. Noah had probably shown up and thrown a major roadblock in her way.

After dinner, Carla still hadn't called. I tried her cell again with no response.

"Are you sure you saw two people go into the locker?" I asked Nancy.

"Yes. Pretty sure. It could have been a shadow, but . . . I don't know, maybe." Nancy hemming and hawing didn't make me feel any better. "Call your cop friend and have him check it out."

"Oh, right. Have him chew me out for interfering. And you don't even know for sure if you saw someone. If I send him out there for nothing, I'll never hear the end of it." Doubt lingered in my head. Nancy certainly fit the profile of a flake, especially with all the crazy antics she'd been pulling. Did I dare trust her on this? I only saw one person in the car when it left the lot. And I'd only seen one person at the locker.

"What if the woman you saw went back to Delores' house, and Carla interrupted her?" I tried Carla's number again, and it went to voice mail.

"We could go check ourselves," Nancy said. "I have a plan, but we have to wait until dark."

I paced around waiting for Carla to return my call. By nightfall, I'd come to accept Nancy might be right about what she saw. The good Cece wanted to call Alder and have him swoop in and rescue Carla, thereby saving me the danger. If Carla wasn't in the storage locker, I'd look like a dope, and

Alder would know I was snooping. The bad Cece loved the intrigue and mystery, thoroughly aware of the risk. Nancy didn't seem the least bit fazed. She ran up to the apartment to make plans for our big night. It made me wonder what she did before she worked for Fletcher. She was way too ditzy for law enforcement. Though, it wouldn't have surprised me to find out she had a habit of sneaking around. I had to give the bimbo credit for intestinal fortitude.

Pulling on a black turtleneck and workout pants, like Nancy suggested, I tried to decide how to conceal my blonde hair. It's not like I owned a black ski mask. I found a suitable hoodie in Michelle's closet which would have to do. With my tendency to hot flash and the current temperature of eighty degrees, I'd likely melt. Nancy had been adamant about concealing my hair. I smeared on deodorant and tugged the sweatshirt over my head. We'd have to blast the air-conditioner all the way to the storage facility.

When I got to the kitchen, Nancy's black ensemble consisted of a scoop-neck tee with rhinestones spelling out *Baby Doll* across her ample chest and tight black pants. A wad of black knee-high nylons lay on the counter.

"You're kidding with the rhinestones?" I asked. "If I have to wear this sweatshirt to cover my hair you better do something to cover those. You jiggle those babies, and they'll see you from the space shuttle. It'll look like Big Al's Autorama when he's got his 'once in a lifetime annual huge not-very-used car sale' complete with searchlights."

She pulled off the shirt, flashing her near-nothing bra, and turned it inside out. "Is this better?"

If we got caught, it wouldn't be the rhinestones that did us in. It would be because I was scared out of my mind or crazy. Or both, considering I'd let her talk me into this.

"When we get there, I've got stockings for us to disguise our faces." She shoved them in her pocket.

"Tell me you're joking. I'm about to self-combust, and you want me wear a nylon on my head." Beads of perspiration had already formed at my neck.

While we were discussing the need for me to go up in flames, the doorbell rang.

"For the love of Pete, you've got to be kidding me." I pulled off the sweatshirt and untucked the turtleneck, hoping to achieve a casual beatnik appearance. "Get out of here until I get rid of whoever it is."

Nancy dashed out the door, I didn't move until I heard her footsteps on the apartment stairs.

I flipped on the outside light and peered out the peephole. Noah stood on my porch. Crap! Crap! Double crap! Why had I turned on the light? Now he knew I was home. I wondered what Miss Manners would say about this situation. Are there times when rudeness is acceptable? Such as when you're getting ready to pull a caper and your wannabe boyfriend from high school shows up. Could you forgo courtesy in the event he might be a murderer or at best, a diamond thief?

Why had I made Nancy leave?

Noah rang the bell again, then knocked.

I took a deep breath and opened the door. "Oh, hi Noah," I said, feigning disinterest.

"You're home. I almost gave up. Thought maybe you had one of those motion lights." His eyes roamed over my attire, and he smirked. "Got your comfy clothes on, I see."

I yawned. "Fell asleep on the couch. Fighting off a headache. What can I do for you?"

"Checking in on my invite for dinner. Didn't think to get your number. I drove by your neighborhood and decided to swing by and see when you had an opening on your calendar." Noah's smile cut into my heart. The same sweet smile he'd flashed at eighteen, only to other girls—not me.

"Now. Tonight?" My mind raced with ways to get rid of him. Or I could level with him about my fears that Carla had gotten kidnapped. But would he care? Jeez, the life of a sneak never proved easy.

"No, just wanted to see you again." He shoved his hands in his pockets with a shrug to his shoulders. "How does tomorrow sound?"

"Yeah, sure, that works," I said. "I'd invite you in, but I'm going to take some aspirin and go to bed." After Nancy and I checked out the storage locker, I'd probably have a headache, and I'd definitely go to bed.

"Okay, I'll pick you up tomorrow at six." He stole another glance at my outfit. "Wear something a little sexier. Those gym clothes don't do you justice." He winked and strolled to his car.

Of all the times for Noah Feldman to notice me. Why hadn't this happened in tenth grade? I slammed the door and headed to the kitchen, ready to get this escapade over. Nancy scampered in the side door.

"I've got something you might be interested in," she said.

I sincerely doubt it. "What?"

She pulled a tin of black shoe polish out of her pocket. "You like this better than a knee-high?"

I shook my head. "Where do you come up with this stuff?"

"My old boyfriend was ex-military. Once he got home, he liked to play war games. Maybe if you and the mister had tried it once in a while, he might still want to fondle your bazookas." She looked down at my less-than-endowed chest. "Naw, probably not."

"My personal life is none of your business."

She smirked. "Yeah, it's not like you don't flaunt it. How you got the cop and the boss man after you, I'll never know. You must be good at *something*."

I gave her a famous Cavanaugh eye roll and stuck my finger in the shoe polish.

She jerked the tin away. “Not now. You want to get stopped by the cops for a burned-out taillight or something and have to explain why you’re dressed for a Halloween party in June?”

Good point.

Chapter 16

“My very own three-ring circus. Complete with clowns, lots of clowns. That’s how I characterized my home these days.”
Cece Cavanaugh

We crouched behind the trash bin watching to make sure there was no activity in the storage facility compound. The still air amplified all the neighborhood sounds in the darkness.

“Something crawled across my foot,” Nancy shrieked.

“Shhh.” I put my hand over her mouth. “Pretend it’s a cat.”

“Cats don’t like me, and they make me sneeze. It wasn’t a cat,” she said. “I’m not even sneezing.”

Shuffling noises came from inside the bin. I bit down on my hand to keep from squealing. If something came out and landed on me, I’d pee my pants and then drop dead. I couldn’t think of a worse way to be found, especially since we’d smeared shoe polish on our faces. The streetlight glared down on the front row of storage lockers where we intended to break-in.

We’d driven Nancy’s black Jeep since concealing a yellow Mustang would have been more difficult than smearing my face with shoe polish. Nancy had circled the facility twice to make sure there were no vehicles making late-night deliveries and to scout for the mysterious woman. The front gate had one of those touch pad security devices where you punch in a code. A code we did not have.

Satisfied no one saw us, I gave Nancy a thumbs up and ran across the grassy area separating the alley from the storage facility. Nancy climbed the fence like a commando on a mission, surprising the heck out of me. Once over, she jerked her head in my direction.

I hesitated, attempting to figure out the mechanics of getting my butt over the fence without ripping my pants. Or worse, like slicing off a finger on the pointy parts where the fence met the top post. Nancy motioned for me to hurry.

"Give me a minute, okay. I haven't climbed a fence in . . . . Ever! I'm a virgin fence-climber," I whispered. Somewhere down the alley, a dog barked. Maybe it could eat the non-cat thing that had slithered across Nancy's foot.

Nancy placed a finger to her lip and shushed me.

I tried to stick my foot in the fence, but it wouldn't fit. My shoes were too fat. Where were the skinny, pointy-toed witch shoes when you needed them? Nancy saw my quandary and threw hers over the fence. Who knew hooker shoes would come in handy?

I cringed at the idea of putting my feet in someone else's shoes. Okay, Michelle and I shared shoes occasionally, but I gave birth to her. A little foot sweat from my daughter wouldn't kill me. What did I know about Nancy? She could be on a bowling league for all I knew. Or have athlete's foot or toe fungus. Or warts.

Nancy glared at me.

I tossed my shoes over the top, slid my feet into Nancy's, and stuck my toe through the chain-link. Perfect fit. Now I wished I'd paid more attention when she scaled the fence. I grabbed on with both hands and put my other toe in a hole. My butt stuck out. Not a flattering pose. I pulled myself up and managed to get hold of the top rail without getting maimed. It was a long way to the ground, and I faced down. I twisted around and threw my legs over, struggling until I got a toehold.

On my next step, I missed and slid down the fence, landing in the gravel. Nancy shook her head and helped me to my feet. We crept along the row of lockers, until I stopped and stared at the doors.

"What's the matter?" Nancy whispered.

"Which locker is it?" I asked.

Earlier when the mystery woman's car was parked outside, it was obvious. Now, in the dark, all the lockers looked alike.

"I don't know," Nancy said.

"Didn't you see the number? You've been here twice."

"It's not like we were that close to it." She pointed to a door. "Those numbers are tiny. I can barely make them out from here."

I studied the doors. "I think it's this one. What do you think?"

She shrugged. "You're the boss."

"Now what?" I asked.

She pulled two paper clips from her pocket and twisted them open.

"What are you doing?"

"Picking the lock, silly." She stuck them into the lock and began to turn them.

"Oh, right. I have to see this," I said. "Maybe you and Mrs. Wafford should team up. Is this something you saw on TV?"

"Don't even ask."

What kind of woman knows how to pick a lock? I pushed my thoughts aside and sent good vibes for it to work. What choice did I have? If Carla was in there, I didn't care what we had to do to get her out.

Minutes ticked by, but eventually Nancy removed the padlock and pushed up the garage door. I marveled at her skill.

"You did it," I said.

"Never doubt me when I put my mind to something," Nancy said.

"Enough patting yourself on the back, get inside."

Tires crunching gravel interrupted the silence. I pulled down the garage door, plunging the room into darkness.

"Did you bring a flashlight?" Nancy asked.

"No, I figured you'd bring one. This was your big plan, Einstein." I slid one foot in front of me and held my arms out searching for anything to guide my way.

The car passed by our unit. The driver cut the engine. A couple seconds later, a garage door opened down the way.

We both froze. I heard a muffled sound at the back of the room and tapped Nancy on the shoulder. "Hear that?"

"Shhh."

When the door slid down, and the car drove off, we both exhaled.

"I'll push the door open a crack," Nancy said.

"Are you nuts? The streetlight will be a dead giveaway."

Nancy had the tools, but she still lacked the smarts to be an effective burglar. I shuffled until I ran into a row of boxes and then began feeling my way toward the back of the locker.

"Carla, are you in here?" I called.

The noise grew louder.

I bumped into something big and solid. I felt around and realized it was a file cabinet.

"I can't see anything," Nancy squeaked. "I hate the dark."

"It was your big idea to leave our cell phones in the car," I said. "I think Carla's in the back. Carla, keep making noise."

The shuffling grew more frantic.

I slid my hand along the side of the wall to guide myself. "Oopf." I tripped over something and fell to my knees.

"What?" Nancy called. "What happened?"

"Broke my kneecap. No biggie." I pushed myself up and felt my left knee. It didn't feel warm and gushy, so I assumed I wasn't bleeding. I waited a minute for the throbbing to subside.

"Seriously?" Nancy asked.

"No, I was being sarcastic," I said.

"She's here," Nancy called. I followed her voice. "She's tied up. Come help me get the ropes off her."

I dropped and crawled toward Nancy's voice, wincing when my knee made contact with the concrete floor. When I got to Nancy, I felt around until I found Carla's head. She had her mouth taped shut.

"This is going to hurt," I told her and then ripped it off.

"Owww," Carla yelped.

"It's okay. Let's get you out of here." I talked to her in low tones. "Can you walk?"

"My hands and feet are numb."

I reached down and rubbed Carla's legs. "This will help you get the feeling back. Once the blood starts flowing, they're going to hurt like crazy." I helped her stand.

"Think you can climb a fence?" Nancy asked.

Carla nodded. "If it's the only way out, I guess I don't have a choice."

"Don't let her kid you," I said. "She's an expert fence climber."

They formed a line behind me and followed, each holding the shirttail of the one in front, leaving me to navigate on my own. Nancy snapped the lock back on the door.

When we got to the fence, I gave Nancy her shoes, and she scaled the fence with as much ease as before. She threw her shoes back to me.

"Carla, you go next. Cece, give her a boost," Nancy said.

"Why do I always have to give the boost?" I was the smallest person out here, yet they treated me like a pack mule. Life was so not fair in the criminal world.

Nancy glared at me. Carla struggled up the fence with as much grace as I had. She blamed it on her numb legs. I didn't do much better, but at least I didn't fall this time.

I gave Nancy her shoes and realized I'd left mine on the other side of the fence.

"Leave 'em," Nancy said, when she saw me eyeing my only pair of trail shoes.

"But I love them. They're comfy," I said.

"Then hike your butt back over there and get them," Nancy replied.

I hobbled to the car, squealing every time I stepped on a rock.

Carla climbed in the seat behind me, and Nancy ran back, scrambled over the fence, and retrieved my shoes. She returned before I'd buckled my seat belt.

"There! Don't say I never did anything for you." Nancy slammed the Jeep in drive and squealed down the street.

"Thanks for rescuing me," Carla said, once Nancy had slowed the Jeep to a normal speed. "How'd you even know where to look?"

"We were at Mrs. Wafford's house this morning, and Nancy chased away a woman who was ransacking your mother's house." I brushed the gravel off my feet and slid them into my shoes, wiggling my toes in the comfort.

"That woman was Rhonda Bray," Carla said.

~ ~ ~

Carla had quit complaining about her arms and legs and started shrieking about Rhonda by the time we got to my house. She went upstairs to soak in a hot bath while I wrestled with my conscience about the diamonds.

Nancy had changed from her cat burglar costume and donned leopard-skin skinny pants and an off-the-shoulder black peasant blouse—à la Heidi meets Jungle Jane. She leaned against my kitchen sink mixing a batch of margaritas. "So, you gonna tell her about the diamonds? Seeing as how they probably got her kidnapped?" Nancy asked.

I'd opted for pajama pants and a T-shirt. Comfort mattered, and my rear still smarted from my tumble over the fence. I'd slathered a soothing body cream on my feet, after cleaning them with anti-bacterial soap to kill the foot germs and stuffed them into my favorite house slippers.

"I don't know. Something still bothers me about this whole thing. All along I've been thinking Noah could be involved in Lloyd's death, and it had to do with the diamonds. Maybe Lloyd found the diamonds. Or maybe they were Lloyd's, and Noah found out and killed him. And he's been sitting on them all these years. But why not take them after he killed Lloyd?" I shifted in my seat and licked my lips while Nancy poured the icy concoctions into frosted glasses. I hadn't said a word to Nancy or Carla about Lloyd not being Lloyd—or rather, being pretend Lloyd. Alder would hang me out to dry. "But if Rhonda Bray murdered Lloyd, why did she tie Carla up instead of kill her? Or was Carla somehow involved? I don't know if I'm ready to tell Carla."

"Tell me what?" Carla stood in the doorway, a towel wrapped around her hair.

Nancy startled and missed the glass. "You have to stop sneaking in on us." She scooped up the mess with a spoon and dumped it into her glass. "Hate to waste the good stuff."

I weighed how much Carla had heard. Nancy handed me a margarita, and I took a big drink. "You know those boxes I brought from your Mom's house?"

"What about them?" Carla asked.

"Detective Alder took them as evidence," I said.

"Evidence of what?" Carla pulled out a stool at the breakfast bar and sat down. "Why would he take Mom's stuff?"

I hesitated and watched Nancy dig through my pantry.

"I found pretzels and chips," Nancy yelled, holding two bags. "Who wants a snack to go with the margaritas?"

I gave Nancy the side-eye and hoped she'd follow my lead and keep her mouth shut. I had made her promise to keep quiet about the diamonds. I only hoped she remembered.

"They came from the scene of a crime," I said. "I suppose they have to consider all angles during the investigation."

"All angles of what? My mother's personal mementos?" Carla slid off her stool. "I'm going to call Angie. This is ridiculous."

"Leave her alone. You know she can't influence an investigation." Sweltering heat seared my skin as a hot flash enveloped me. "You'll get everything back as soon as the investigation is over." I remembered the box of cookbooks I'd rescued. "Hey, I do have your mom's cookbooks. Alder didn't take them."

"Why would he leave those, when he took everything else?" Carla asked.

"Beats me." I downed my margarita and held my glass out to Nancy for another. "You want a refill, Carla?"

She nodded. "What was in the boxes he took?"

Nancy filled our glasses and dumped chips and pretzels into bowls and handed one to Carla.

Carla pushed it away.

"Figurines and stuff," I said.

"Junk Noah sent?" Carla asked. "What does that have to do with Lloyd?"

"I don't know. Alder said he had to take them into evidence. I had forgotten about the cookbooks, or he probably would have taken those too."

"On another note," Nancy interrupted. "He asked Cece to go to dinner."

"Who did?" Carla and I said at the same time.

"Your brother." Nancy chugged down half a glass of margarita. Why she didn't get brain freeze amazed me. It confirmed she didn't have a brain to freeze.

I rolled my eyes. "Thanks, Nancy," I said it sarcastically, but hoped it would distract Carla enough to change the subject.

"Oh, good. Stab me in the back. Again!" Carla picked up the bowl of chips Nancy had offered. "You'd think your schoolgirl crush would be over by now."

"You're jealous. You were then, and you are now," I said. "What is it with you two? You never see each other, yet the hostility is madly intense."

Nancy's headed twisted back and forth as she followed the volley of words between Carla and me.

"There's no dealing with him. Since I took control of Mom's affairs, he's been second-guessing every decision I make. He thinks he should get a say in every part of her business, yet he's unreachable most of the time. I need to decide, like right now, and move on. As often as he's gone, I can't sit around waiting for him to call me back in two weeks, or a month, or whenever he has cell service and time on his hands," Carla said.

"The more he fights me, the angrier I get. He's not happy about the attorney I used to make her estate plan. He's not happy with her living will. If I put everything in his name and washed my hands of it, he wouldn't be happy either." Carla tugged the belt of her robe tighter. "He'd blow a gasket if he knew her investments were gone."

"He doesn't know? Carla, he deserves to know about your mom's finances. Let's go in the great room. It's more comfortable," I said. My feet started for Phillip's recliner before I remembered he'd taken it. I detoured and curled up on the love seat, leaving the sofa for Nancy and Carla.

"No, he doesn't. This is between me and Mom, and you better not tell him. I can take care of it. Please Cece, I'm begging you, don't say anything." Carla paced the room before finally settling on the sofa.

"When I saw Rhonda's car at Mom's today, at first I thought she was Noah. He hasn't bothered to get in touch since I came back," Carla said.

"How'd you wind up at the locker?" Nancy asked.

Bless her heart. It had been bugging me how Rhonda had gotten Carla to the storage facility. Maybe Carla and Rhonda were in cahoots, and Rhonda had turned on Carla. Conflicting scenarios battled in my mind.

"How do you think I did?" Carla demanded. "I went to Mom's to clean and saw someone in the garage pilfering one of Lloyd's toolboxes. I went in expecting to confront Noah, only it was a woman—Rhonda. She'd found a set of keys. It took me a minute to recognize her. She had her car backed up to the door, lunged at me, and knocked me off balance. Before I could get my bearings, she pushed me in the trunk and took off."

"She couldn't get into the locker earlier because she didn't have keys." I noted to myself that Noah had asked me about keys too. It hadn't stuck me as odd at the time, but now that I thought about it, it did. Noah didn't own a home or a car. What spare keys did he keep at his mom's?

If the keys Rhonda found were the same ones Noah wanted, then it meant Noah knew about the locker too. "If they were in the toolbox, then the storage locker must have been Lloyd's. We have to call Alder and tell him," I said.

"Tell him what? My stepfather's ex-lover stole some keys from his toolbox. Don't you dare. I don't want Alder taking any more of my mother's stuff into evidence. At least not yet. I want to know what Rhonda's doing and what's in there."

"Say what?" Nancy's eyes bulged.

"It's awfully coincidental Lloyd is found dead, and now Rhonda shows up, of all people." Carla ran her finger around the rim of her glass and licked off the salt. "How did she know about the storage locker, and if she wasn't with Lloyd, where's she been all these years?"

"And we know for sure she wasn't with Lloyd." Nancy cackled.

Carla got a wicked glint in her eyes. "I'll tell you what I'm going to do. I'm going to turn the tables on that witch, then the cops can have her. She messed with the wrong person when she locked me up. Something is not clicking, and I aim to find out what it is."

"Wait. We need to let the police do their jobs." I had a bad feeling about this.

"Cece, this is my mother. Her life savings is gone. She may be a suspect in a murder. Now her former neighbor and husband-stealer is robbing her blind. And my brother is lurking around with who knows what in mind," Carla pleaded.

"She has a point," Nancy said. "And if we don't get anywhere, we can tell your detective."

"We? When did we become a *we*?" I asked. "And he's not *my* detective."

Nancy set her drink on my coffee table, on a coaster no less. Had to give her credit, she could be trained.

"If we have a plan and execute it, we can find out what's going on. If there's nothing to it, my mom stays out of it, and the cops don't have to be involved. They're going to continue to investigate anyway." Carla paused. "All we have to do is keep out of their way. We're not impeding their investigation."

"I don't like it, but I'm willing to hear you out," I said. "What's your plan?"

"Two parts. The first is I want to talk to Mom to see if I can get any information out of her about Rhonda or Lloyd. And second, I intend to find out what's in the locker. I didn't get a good look before she whacked me, and tonight it was too dark. Plus, I was too scared to hang around."

Nancy jumped up. "Goody! We get to go back. I love spy stuff."

Perfect!

Chapter 17

"If Cece thought her crush on Noah didn't go so well in high school, she'd better buckle up. He hasn't changed."
Carla Edison

Before going back to the storage locker, Carla convinced me, at least for Delores' sake, to do a bit of investigating on our own. Delores couldn't take care of herself, much less defend herself against the possibility of criminal charges being filed. Alder might not want me to get involved, but tough toenails. I didn't want to see Delores charged with murder. The next morning, Nancy headed to Hunter Springs to clean with explicit orders to leave the workers alone or I would fire her. Carla and I went to the hospital.

Beatrice had instructions to call Jimmy Keefur, the locksmith, and schedule an appointment to have the locks changed. I needed to know Phillip would not be pilfering my house while I was out. Before I left, I changed the code on the garage door opener too.

Delores was sleeping when we walked into her room. For someone who might be in trouble with the law, she looked peaceful. Carla and I pulled chairs next to her bed. I watched the gentle rise and fall of the blanket covering her meager form. Could she have put Lloyd in the freezer? She hadn't always been tiny and frail, but I couldn't remember when she started to decline. As a librarian, she'd pushed and pulled her share of carts through the stacks—not to mention loading and unloading boxes of books—like the ones in her house.

The last time I visited was when Alder and I came to tell her about Lloyd. It had been late in the evening, and she had seemed unusually disoriented. I hoped morning would find her in a better frame of mind, or at least more settled. When Carla touched her mom's hand, she stirred a bit.

"I'm glad you're back," Delores said, her voice low and soft. "How's Max?"

Carla fluffed Delores' pillow and rearranged her blanket. "He's fine. Had a panic attack. He's under a great deal of pressure, but he's okay. Your color is good today. Are you eating?"

"They always bring too much food." Delores' eyes clouded over. "I'm glad you called Noah. I don't like seeing you two at each other all the time."

"Don't worry about us, Mom," Carla said.

"Cece, you were here the other day, but you weren't with Phillip." Delores frowned.

"No, I came with Detective Alder." I looked to Carla.

"Mom, she and the detective brought you news about Lloyd."

Delores gripped the edge of her blanket. "You said Lloyd was dead."

"Yes, I'm sorry."

"Lloyd didn't leave with Rhonda?" Delores asked, her face brightening.

"It appears not," I said.

"Mom, do you remember why you thought Lloyd left with Rhonda? Did he tell you? Or did you have an argument?" Carla prodded.

"I'll never forget. They'd been carrying on, you know—Lloyd and Rhonda. Peter finally put his foot down. He gave her an ultimatum: stop seeing Lloyd, or he'd file for divorce and put her out on the street," Delores said. "I was gone to a Friends of the Library meeting. When I came back, Lloyd was gone. He'd left a note on the table saying he was leaving with her. He didn't even said goodbye."

"Would you mind if I checked the cards he sent you?" I asked.

"What cards?" Delores and Carla asked at the same time.

"The ones from Lloyd you have in your purse," I said to Delores.

"How do you know about them?" she asked.

"You showed me the other day when I stopped by with the detective. With the ribbon tied around them."

Delores' breath hitched. "No, those aren't from Lloyd. They're from my first husband, Carla's dad."

Now I was confused. Carla's dad died years ago.

"What are you talking about, Mom?" Carla asked. "You have cards from Dad in your purse?"

Delores pointed an arthritic finger to the closet built into the wall. "Get it, please."

I retrieved the purse and handed it to Delores.

She pulled the bundle out and released the ribbon, letting it fall onto her blanket. "Your father wrote beautiful letters. Every birthday, anniversary, even when you kids were born, he'd write me a letter."

"Oh, Mom, I never knew Dad wrote you letters. What a great memory to have," Carla said.

"When I'm gone I want you to have them, but not before then. There are days when your father's memory is all I have." Delores thumbed through the letters, and tears sprang to her eyes. "He always provided for us, you know."

"Mom, I talked to your financial planner," Carla said. "He said you withdrew all your money. Did you reinvest it? I've checked all your papers and can't find anything."

"You're going through my business?" Delores retied the ribbon and pushed the letters into her purse. "Just because I'm not home, doesn't mean you can snoop."

"I'm not being nosy. With your insurance and Medicare, I need to have everything organized. Your mail was piling up. I found several bills you hadn't told me about." Carla pulled her chair closer to Delores' bed. "Mom, you're going to have to face the fact that you may not be able to live alone anymore."

Delores snapped her purse closed and pushed it toward me. "Put this away for me."

I returned it to the closet and edged myself closer to the door to keep from distracting Delores.

"I take care of my own business. I don't need you doing my bill-paying. From now on, when the mail comes you bring it to me—unopened." Delores motioned to a water pitcher on her bedside table. "I need a drink."

I poured a tumbler of water and held the straw to Delores' lips.

"I always do your bills, remember? We set it up last year. I can do everything online. And you have a log-in. You can see what I'm doing."

Carla had her hands full. I wasn't sure how she was going to deal with Delores in the future. It sounded more and more like Delores was exhibiting signs of dementia. I wondered how a murder investigation would go when a suspect had memory loss.

Delores took several sips, then closed her eyes.

We waited several minutes. It wasn't unusual for an elderly person to nod off, especially given everything Delores had been through recently.

"Is she asleep?" I asked.

Delores' eyelids fluttered open. "Carla, you came. I'm glad you made it."

"Mom, I've been here. You just dozed off," Carla said.

"You were here?"

"Yes, Cece and I have been here for a while."

"Good. I need a favor. I want you to make a buttermilk pie. It's Lloyd's favorite. The recipe is in my library cookbook. You know the one? All my important recipes are in that book. All your dad's favorites. I had to hide them from Lloyd, or he'd give them away. He hated when I cooked, you know? Don't let him give my recipes to that woman."

"Mom, what are you talking about? Lloyd is dead," Carla said, her voice quivering.

I jerked my head up.

"You remember about Lloyd, right?" Carla asked, tears starting to gather in her eyes.

I placed a hand on Carla's shoulder. "Do you want me to step outside?"

"No, stay. Please," Carla said.

"He's not," Delores screamed. "He's in cahoots with Rhonda, and they're trying to rob me blind."

Carla ran her hand down Delores' arm. "Mom, calm down. No one is stealing anything. Lloyd died."

"Go home and hide my recipes," Delores shouted. "Do not let Lloyd and Rhonda near my recipes!"

A nurse heard the commotion, gave Delores something to calm her down, and asked Carla and me to leave.

~ ~ ~

We walked into my kitchen, and I came to a stop when I noticed a vase of roses on my counter.

Beatrice had her back to me, loading the dishwasher.

"Where did these come from?" I asked.

"Florist delivered them a few minutes ago. Someone has nice taste." Beatrice pulled a jug of detergent from under the sink and squirted the dispenser full. "There's a card."

Indeed, there was a card, which I could tell had been read. "What's it say?" I asked.

"Says that he 'enjoys spending time with you but fully understands your need for space,'" Beatrice said with a joyful tone. "I already like him, and I've never even met him. I can tell they aren't from the cop. This guy has expensive taste. You need space? How come you need space?"

Carla grabbed the card and pulled it from the envelope. "Are these from Noah?"

I snatched it back. "No, nosy. They are not. They're from my boss."

"Some boss," Beatrice said. "You never send me flowers."

"Yeah, and I never give you a paycheck." I read the card and put it beside the vase. "Talk to The Barracuda if you want roses."

Beatrice snorted. "I prefer tulips. If you need me, I'll be cleaning the guest bathroom. Oh, the locksmith had a cancellation and was able to change your locks already. Your new keys and the bill are on your desk. And if you haven't already noticed, the patio door is fixed. Good-looking man stopped by to replace it."

I hadn't noticed, but now I did. I'd have to call Grant and thank him.

"Who's 'The Barracuda'?" Carla asked.

"Hazel," I said. "It's a long story. Remind me to tell you sometime."

Carla, Nancy, and I planned to rendezvous at my house to plot our strategy for going to the storage locker.

When Beatrice was out of earshot, Carla said, "I've never seen Mom as confused as she was this morning. It's like her mind has completely gone haywire."

"This is a repeat of the night when Alder and I went to talk to her. She kept talking like those letters were from Lloyd. And how she'd been getting them all along." I thought back to when we initially went into her room and how lucid she seemed, then in an instant a switch flipped, and confusion set in.

"I need to talk to her doctor. With the hoarding and how confused she is, there's more going on than I've been privy to. With her age, I'm scared it's Alzheimer's." Carla pulled a tissue from the box I kept on the counter. "All her talk about recipes and keeping them from Lloyd and Rhonda. Crazy talk."

"She insisted you make the buttermilk pie," I said, remembering all the times Delores had brought her specialty pie to the library bake sales. "My mouth is watering thinking about it. Speaking of her cooking. I found Lloyd underneath a mountain of frozen TV dinners and desserts. Why would Delores have a freezer filled with store-bought stuff?"

"Blame it on Lloyd. He hated Mom spending all her time in the kitchen. Once they married, he did all the grocery shopping and budgeted her to the last penny. He'd wait until Dingle's Market had a sale, and then he stocked up. Kind of 'just desserts' you found him buried underneath it all." Carla chuckled at her joke. "And probably why Mother didn't discover him. Once he left, she went back to her old ways."

"I wondered," I said. "It seemed out of character for her. With all the clutter, she didn't have much room to be cooking in her kitchen."

"She didn't cook much for herself before she married Lloyd, said it didn't make sense to go to all the effort for one. She ate at the seniors' center most of the time. When she married Lloyd, she started baking and cooking again, but he put a stop to it. He said it was frivolous and a waste of money. I miss her homemade meals. Our kitchen always smelled so heavenly," Carla mused. "You know, I don't even have any of her recipes. Max loves her cooking. Who am I kidding? Max loves food, homemade or store-bought."

"I have her cookbooks. Remember? It's the only box Alder didn't take." The minute I said it, I wanted to kick myself. Carla had dropped all the talk about the stuff I'd taken from her Mom's, and I hadn't brought it up again.

Until now. Lucky for me, the doorbell rang. “Be right back,” I said, scooting out of the kitchen.

At this point, I didn’t care who was at my door; I was just thankful for an opportunity to escape Carla’s interrogation about why Alder had taken her mom’s stuff into evidence.

When I opened the door, I changed my mind. Interrogation and waterboarding might have been more pleasant than staring at my mother-in-law.

Hazel pushed by me and made a straight line to my living room. She dropped her handbag on my sofa and assumed her battle stance—one hand on her hip and her petal pink pumps planted firmly in my carpet. “We need to talk about this degrading idea of yours to clean houses. Phillip told me about your preposterous plan, and I want you to put an end to it, immediately.”

I followed her, picked up her purse, and shoved it toward her. “The only plans I have which might concern you are the girls. Otherwise, my affairs are off limits.” Wrong, wrong, wrong word choice. I realized it one second too late.

“And here’s another thing,” Hazel said, pointing a lacquered fingernail at me. “You do understand your affair with this detective will trigger the morals clause in your prenup.”

“I’m not having this conversation with you.” I saw no point in arguing with her. If I denied an affair with Alder, Hazel wouldn’t let it go. She would pick it like a scab. I figured I’d look guilty if I tried to defend myself. Hazel had a one-track mind. Once she latched onto your weakness, she went for blood.

“Think about Michelle. You continue this nonsense, and you’ll make her life difficult at Lakeview Academy,” Hazel said. “Think how demeaning it is to have your friends talking about your mother like a common laborer.”

“Spare me your snobbery.”

"Cecelia, I won't allow it." Hazel pulled her checkbook from her purse. "How much do you want to end this nonsense?"

Talk about striking a nerve. For Hazel to whip out the checkbook meant I must have been getting under her skin. I liked the feeling. But as much I needed money, taking a handout from the devil did not fit into my agenda. "Put your checkbook away, Hazel. I don't want your money."

"You never seemed to have a problem spending it in the past. Now how much will it take?" Hazel stood her ground, pen poised atop the check. "Ten thousand? Twenty?"

"Get out!" I said.

Hazel shoved her checkbook in her bag and glided to the door. "You'll be sorry, Cecelia. When Phillip is done with you, you'll be right back where you started. Destitute. You better hope your detective makes enough to support you, because you won't see another penny of Cavanaugh money." Hazel slammed the door on her way out.

My hands clenched at my sides. I waited a minute for my pulse to return to normal. More like five.

When I walked back into my kitchen, Carla had cookbooks and a pile of cash spread out on the breakfast bar. She was flipping through one of the books, pulling out money as fast as she could turn the pages.

"What are you doing?" I took a handful of bills and fanned them out, revealing crisp Benjamin Franklins.

"Check this out." Carla opened a battered copy of *The Joy of Cooking* and plucked out more hundred-dollar bills. "I've opened seven books and found forty bills in each one. All hundreds."

I did a quick calculation. "Twenty-eight thousand dollars."

"Yeah, and there's thirteen more books," Carla said. "If they all have the same amount there's—"

This one took longer. Math and I do not get along. "Another fifty-two thousand. Holy schnikeys. Eighty-thousand bucks."

"Mom wasn't worried about Lloyd and Rhonda getting her recipes. She was worried about them getting her money." Carla pulled another stack of books from the box. "My mother was hoarding money. Do you think this is what Rhonda was after today?"

"How would she even know about it?" I asked.

"Lloyd had to have told her," Carla said. "Do you think this is what got Lloyd killed?"

"Why would she wait until now. Why not after Lloyd. . . ." My words trailed off as another idea surfaced. "Carla, when Brad and Larry helped me at your mother's house, I had them haul a truckload of books to the dump. You don't suppose she hid money in those books too?"

"What? Jeez, you're making me sick. This is all my fault. I should never have trusted anyone to do this." Carla sank onto a barstool.

"I'm sorry. We should have checked those boxes, but you said—"

"I'm not blaming you. This is all on me," Carla said. "I'm so confused. My mother's broke, but she has piles of money stashed in books. What was going on in her head? Where did it come from?"

"Do you think she converted her investments into cash to keep it away from Lloyd?" I shook my head. "Why not get a safe-deposit box at the bank? Or, I don't know. Anything other than hiding it away."

"What if her house caught on fire?" Carla moaned. "Not too far-fetched, considering what a mess her house is."

My mind went to the diamonds. What did the money have to do with the diamonds I gave to Alder? He would rupture a blood vessel if he knew about the cash.

"We need to call Alder," I said.

"Oh, no we don't. Not until I get to the bottom of this. My mom's life savings are missing, and if she's hidden it around her house, it has nothing to do with Lloyd. I'm not giving Alder this cash."

"But—"

Carla shook a cookbook at me. "Make yourself useful. Call those guys and find out where they dropped those boxes. We're going to the dump tonight."

"Well, it's going to have to be later, because—and you aren't going to like it—I'm having dinner with Noah," I said.

"Seriously? Why would you even consider it?" Carla asked. "You know he's using you to piss me off. Noah has nothing on his mind but getting into my mother's business, and he's using you to find out about it. I'll lay you odds that all he'll do is pump you for information."

"What's wrong with you? It's dinner, for crying out loud. I'm not going to confess state secrets." I gathered up the books and shoved them back in the box.

"You better not spill the beans about finding this money. That's exactly the sort of thing Noah is looking for. He's sniffing around acting all concerned, and you should know better." Carla stacked the bills on top of the others. "Cece, he never looked twice at you in school. Why do you think he's so interested now?"

"Whoa, give me some credit, will you?" I went to my desk and brought back a manila envelope for the cash. "I'm putting it in my safe until we get to the bottom of this. There's no reason to have it lying around." I shoved the bills in, sealed the envelope, and put the dollar amount on the front.

"But—" Carla started to protest.

"My house has already been broken into. The money goes in the safe until we figure out what's going on. Either that, or you're own your own tonight. I won't call Brad, and you can hunt around out there by yourself." I pulled out a stool and sat down next to Carla. "Come on. Chill about Noah. He may show his hand to me, and then we'll know what he's after. If he's after anything."

"Okay. But I don't like it, and the only reason I'm agreeing is because I don't want to go to the dump by myself," Carla said.

I leaned over and hugged her. "It's going to be fine, you'll see."

~ ~ ~

But it wasn't fine. Noah and I never made it to dinner.

I convinced Carla not to engage Noah when he arrived, so she excused herself to the guest room to read.

Noah had other plans. He walked in ready for a quarrel. "Is Carla here? I saw Mom's van out front. Tell her I want to talk to her," Noah demanded.

"Don't do this," I said. "Let's go have dinner." I knew Carla wouldn't back down either, so the best plan was to keep them apart. If they wanted to duke it out, they could go to Delores' house. My walls had witnessed too much arguing. I'd finally settled into a peaceful existence with Phillip gone, and I intended to keep it that way.

"No, you're the one who said to talk it out with her. Go get her. I'm tired of dancing around Her Highness. This won't take long. All I want is some stuff she took out of Mom's house. I don't give a rip about the rest of it." Sweat glistened on Noah's forehead.

"It's about time you showed your face," Carla said as she came down the stairs.

"Where'd you take them?" Noah moved closer to Carla.

"Take what?" Carla asked.

"The souvenirs you took out of Mom's house. You have no right getting rid of stuff."

"There's plenty of that crap left over there. Have at it. You want the magnets? Or maybe the hula girl lamp? Whatever, feel free. Because I'm not hauling it to North Carolina when I take Mom back with me." Carla walked right up to Noah and shook her finger in his face. "You come in here all full of bluster and acting like you're put out with me. I got news for you. I've had it with you too. Either get on board with the program or get out of my way and let me handle it, because I'm tired of your bullying."

I backed into the kitchen, giving them space. But I kept them within hearing distance.

They continued to argue another fifteen minutes, then I heard the front door slam. When I walked into the foyer, Carla was sitting on the bottom step, crying.

"What's gotten into him?" I asked. "He acted half-crazed."

"Beats me, he was carrying on about elephants, and he mentioned keys. Cece, I think he was after the keys Rhonda got from the garage. If so, then he knows about the locker too."

"Carla, what do you remember about the time frame of Lloyd's disappearance?" I waited for her reaction, and if she would tell me the truth about her visit.

She stood up and paced the foyer. "Mom was beside herself. She called me when she found his note, and I came out to check on her, but I was still working at the time and couldn't stay long. It was a tough time. I think in her heart Mom knew about Lloyd and Rhonda, but when she thought he had actually left, she couldn't deal with it."

"Did you know Noah came after you left?"

Carla stopped. "No, he didn't. I tried calling. Mom tried calling. He was off somewhere. I never even got through to him."

"He was here a couple of days after you," I said.

"How would you know that?"

"Mrs. Wafford. She keeps scrupulous notes about everything going on in the neighborhood. Remember when we were there, she had the little table and binoculars by the window? She has years of notes."

"Are you serious?" She resumed her spot on the bottom step, putting her elbows on her knees.

"Yup, she said a day or two after you left, Noah showed up." I wasn't ready to share the journal with Carla, so I didn't mention I had it.

"Then he must have shown up looking for something. And that something is probably in the locker," Carla said.

"It also means he's not in this with Rhonda, or else he'd know she had the key. Unless she's going to double-cross him. Or it could mean we're jumping to conclusions."

"What in the world is he mixed up in?" Carla asked.

I sat down next to her and put my arm around her. "I don't know, but we're going to find out."

Chapter 18

"I'm beginning to regret agreeing to meet Mrs. Cavanaugh's daughter. I'm not a blind date kind of guy." Brad James

"How long are we going to wait on her?" Carla asked.

"Let's give her a few more minutes." I could tell Carla was still miffed at me because of the blowup with Noah. He really had shown his hand, and it had shaken her. I now knew why she'd been wise to steer clear of him. He had issues, big time. But at least I knew he had a connection to the diamonds, and I had a pretty good idea who had broken into my house.

Nancy said she'd meet us in the commuter parking lot across from the county dump at eight-thirty. It was eight-forty and almost dark. I'd also called Brad and asked him to meet us here. Carla and I had parked next to his truck, but he was already searching for the boxes. He had sent me a text when he arrived, saying he'd go ahead and see if he could locate the area they'd made the dump.

I sat drumming my fingers on the steering wheel. When I gave Nancy the address, I'd offered directions, but she said she wouldn't have a problem. Only now did I realize my mistake. I should have given them to her regardless of what she said. It took me a while to catch on to Nancy's imperfections.

"Let's give her a few more minutes." I checked my cell for messages, but nothing new was there. I'd almost given up on her when she wheeled in next to my car and parked.

My eyes about bugged out of my head when she jumped out dressed like a nine-dollar hooker and tottered across the parking lot in spiky heels. Her eyes darted wildly, checking out the surroundings.

"Are you freaking serious?" Carla asked. "Get a load of her. Our very own porn star."

"Why are we out in the middle of nowhere?" Nancy asked when she neared my car.

She didn't have a clue what we were going to do. The lines of communications had definitely closed down on this one. From now on, I'd have to be more explicit in my directions.

"This is the dump," I said, pointing to the gigantic sign on the other side the road which read COUNTY DUMP in enormous letters.

"I don't get it. Where are all the cars?" Nancy asked.

"What are you talking about, and why are you dressed . . . like you normally do?" I climbed out of my car and slammed the door.

"It's what I wear to go clubbing." She twirled on her heels to give us the full effect. "I didn't know you were dragging me out to some hole in the wall. Come to think of it, I don't even see a building. Where's the band going to play? And you two could have dressed up."

Carla groaned and burst out laughing.

"You thought we were . . . . Oh, never mind." I raised my arms in front of me. "This is the county dump. A landfill. A place where trash trucks bring garbage to rot. This is great. You thought the county dump was a nightclub?" I shook my head and scolded myself for having asked for her help in the first place. "Remember the boxes Detective Alder took?"

She nodded. "Oh, the ones with the diamonds?"

"What diamonds?" Carla asked. "You never said anything about diamonds."

"We'll talk about it later," I said to Carla. "Now let's get in there and see if we can find those boxes."

"No, tell me what she's talking about." Carla nodded to Nancy.

"Please, Carla. Can we not talk about this now?" I pleaded. "I promise I'll tell you everything, but we need to get out there before Brad starts opening boxes."

"I swear, you better tell me everything. Let's go," Carla said.

"Oh boy, did I mess up?" Nancy shrugged. "Sorry."

Carla leaned in and whispered, "Why did you ask her to come out here? This is a humongous train wreck."

I nodded and gave Carla a playful nudge.

Nancy followed me to the back of my car. "Do you think there are diamonds out here?"

"Shut up." I clicked the remote and popped the trunk.

"What did she say?" Carla turned around and demanded.

"Nothing. Don't worry about it. We have more important things to do," I said to Carla.

To Nancy, I said, "No. Carla found cash, a lot of cash, in the box Alder didn't take. I had Grant's guys bring a truckload out here. If Carla's mom had a stash, we may have brought it out here and dumped it."

Nancy's eyes grew wide. "You think you threw away money?"

I touched a finger to my nose. "Bingo. Now come on. We've got work to do."

She shook her head and backed up. "No way. If you think I'm going to go digging through a dump, you are wacko. I am *not* crawling around in garbage."

I shook a finger at her. "If you don't need a place to sleep, then don't worry about helping us. But if we find out the money was stolen, and there's a reward, don't go expecting to share it either."

"Reward?"

Now I had her attention. I laid out my plan. My first big job for Fletcher had been cleaning a crime scene. It paid well. Anyway, I'd purchased a case of protective coveralls, and I had plenty of leftovers. I'd brought three along for our trek into the trash. I handed one to Carla and one to Nancy. "Put these on."

Nancy unbuttoned her blouse and slipped it off.

I stopped unfolding my coverall and stared in disbelief. "You wear it on top of your clothes." *Bwa haa haa!*

Carla snorted and fell against the car roaring with laughter. "Oh, my gawd, I have never."

"No way. I'm not about to ruin this outfit." Nancy stripped down to her underwear and wiggled into the suit I'd given her.

I stuck one foot in the leg of the coverall and toppled over. "Stop it, I'm going to pee my pants, if you don't quit."

"What?" Nancy asked.

I pushed myself up. "Nothing. Just put it on."

Carla held her stomach and between giggles, managed to get herself dressed.

Ten minutes later, flashlights in hand, we walked along the edge of the dump.

"Omigod. This seriously stinks. I think I'm going to throw up." Nancy held her nose and made gulping noises.

"Will you be quiet? And stop complaining." I scanned the dump for anything familiar. Brad was sorting through a pile of trash near a towering pile of wooden pallets, and I waved my flashlight.

"I can't walk in this stuff. My feet are getting all icky," Nancy wailed. "This is gross. You better let me stay forever for doing this. Omigod, I can't believe I'm knee-deep in garbage."

I cringed at the sound of her voice. Did she always sound this whiny?

Brad shook his head. His face had a *why did you bring the bimbo?* look.

Sorry, I mouthed. My flashlight died, and I slapped it, trying to get it to come back on. When it didn't, I stumbled and fell. I felt a searing pain in my arm. "Owwww."

Brad swung his light around. "What happened?" He reached down and offered his hand.

"Tripped over something, I'm okay. Keep looking. We've got to find those boxes," I said.

"I know they're around here somewhere, I remember the pallets. But during the day, this place is totally different." Brad handed me his flashlight. "Here, now you can see where you're going."

"Omigod, something crawled across my foot." Nancy shook her feet, alternating one then the other. She lost her balance and fell butt-first onto a pile of garbage bags. "Ewwww, get me up. There's something gooey on me. Ick. Help me up."

Carla made a gagging sound but kept her thoughts to herself.

I grabbed Nancy's hand and pulled her to her feet. "Just stand still and hold the stupid flashlight for us."

Brad continued digging, tossing bags and boxes aside. "This is about where we threw all the stuff, but someone else has been dumping. I haven't found anything like what we brought."

"Can you guys hurry up? I have to pee." Nancy jumped up and down, crossing and uncrossing her legs while the beam of light from her flashlight zigzagged across the dump.

"Go behind something and have a squat." I slapped my flashlight against my thigh and it flickered back to life. "Take the flashlight Brad gave me. And for goodness sake, be careful."

She gasped. "You want me to pee here? Are you serious?"

Brad got to his feet and jerked the flashlight out of her hand. "It's a dump. No one is going to care if you pee."

I knew I liked him. He had a no-nonsense attitude. A *don't give me any crap* kind of philosophy I found irresistible. I could see him with Jessie. And their babies would be adorable. I almost swooned thinking about grandbabies.

"Who made you the boss?" Nancy asked Brad. "You don't have to be so hateful."

"Just go do your business and hurry up." I knew without even looking that she had her lower lip stuck out. I barely knew the woman and already recognized her tells.

"Well, he still doesn't have to be so mean." She squatted behind a rusted-out washing machine.

She'd only been gone a minute when she hollered out, "Do you have a tissue in your purse?"

"No," I yelled. "I'm not a freaking mini-mart. Why would I even drag my purse out here?"

Brad stopped digging and pointed to a bouncing light coming toward us. "I think we have company."

"Crap." Just what we needed, a nosy night watchman. "Keep digging. The worst that can happen is we have to leave."

I was *so* wrong.

The person carrying the flashlight pointed it directly into my eyes, temporarily blinding me. I blinked several times. "Will you get your freaking light out of my eyes?"

The light swung down to the ground. "Sure thing. Now you give me one good reason why you're here."

I froze. "Uh, Alder. What are you doing here?"

Nancy made a noise from behind the washer, and Alder flashed his light her way. She screamed and stood up, giving all of us a good view, the coverall still down around her ankles.

Alder frowned. "I think I have a bunch of dump rats here. Now you had all better start explaining."

Nancy put her hands on her head and walked toward us, dragging her coveralls behind her.

Alder pointed his light to the ground. "Would you mind pulling your clothes up? I'm not even going to ask what you were doing."

"But you three." He turned back to Brad, Carla, and me. "I want you to tell me everything and start at the beginning."

I stood taller. "They don't have anything to do with this. Let them go."

Alder scratched his chin.

"Come on Alder," I begged. I couldn't have my future son-in-law going to jail. If he did, I could never introduce him to Jessie. *Errr, Jessie, this is Brad. I got him arrested, but he's a nice young man. I think the two of you would hit it off. What am I thinking? I'll be in jail, and Brad, Carla, and the bimbo will be off scot-free.* The things mothers do for their kids.

"Okay, you three get out of here before I arrest you. I'll bring Cece home after she explains your outing."

"Do you want me to call Mr. Hunter?" Brad asked.

"No, she does not want you to call Mr. Hunter. Now get out of here before I change my mind."

Nancy took off as fast as her pointy heels would carry her. Periodically, we heard her yelp as she ran across the gravel.

I tossed my car keys to Carla. She and Brad followed behind Nancy, but I could tell by the sag in his shoulders Brad's heart wasn't in leaving me behind. Yeah, he would make good son-in-law material. He barely knew me, yet he displayed a loyalty which endeared me to him. I wouldn't have to worry about him telling mother-in-law jokes to his buddies on poker night. Would Jessie even let him play poker? I'd have to remember to tell Jessie he deserved to have a poker night occasionally—after they were married.

When Brad, Carla, and Nancy pulled out of the parking lot, Alder turned to me. "What's the story?"

I gritted my teeth and wondered where to start or how much to tell him. By the set of his jaw, I knew he wouldn't be sympathetic to my situation. "You know all the stuff I've been hauling out of Delores Redmond's house?"

He crossed his arms, a mask of exasperation on his face.

"I accidentally threw out several boxes containing sentimental items." I hadn't lied. Money was sentimental—to the person who lost it. And it wasn't like I planned to keep it. I had every intention of finding out who it belonged to, but I didn't want anyone getting hold of it until we figured out if it belonged to Delores.

"What kind of sentimental items?" he asked.

Why did he have to be so nosy? "Books, antiques, family photo albums. Yes, there were several photo albums missing. I figured we'd brought them here. Brad and Larry delivered a truckload from the house, the morning I found Lloyd in the freezer."

He shook his head. "Sure, you did. Let's get out of here. It stinks. But I'm not done with you."

"Are you going to arrest me?" I stopped. "Wait, this isn't even in the city. You aren't even in your jurisdiction. How'd you find me?"

"Dicky invited me to a poker game, remember? I saw your car when I passed by. It doesn't exactly blend in when you park a yellow Mustang in a commuter lot with two other cars in the middle of the night. I ran the plates on the other two. When they came back to your tenant and Brad James, I knew you were involved in something."

Alder led the way with his flashlight. He opened the passenger door of his car and helped me in. "Crikey, you stink. I was going to ask you to go to Dicky's, but honestly I don't think I could sit next to you."

I don't know if he believed my story, but at least I didn't have to worry about going to jail. Not tonight anyway. "Who said I would want to go anyway?" I started to fluff my hair, but my hands were grungy. I feigned a disinterested look instead.

Before he shut the door, he stuck his head in the window. "I know there's more to this than you said. I'm not sure what. But you can bet, I'll find out." He held his nose and kissed me on the cheek. "Now let's get out of here, before I change my mind."

As he walked around the car, I heard him say, "Now I'm going to have to fumigate the car."

~ ~ ~

Nancy's car and mine were parked in my driveway when we pulled in. I wanted to talk to Carla and Nancy about our next steps, but I wouldn't be able to think straight until I showered and changed clothes. Those boxes were still in the dump, and we needed to figure out a way to get them. But first I had to get rid of Alder.

Before he could get out, I turned to him. "I have to take a shower. I can't even stand myself. Nancy and Carla are here, or else I'd ask you in."

He reached across the seat and took my hand. "Please, whatever it is you're doing, stop. I can't do my job *and* watch out for you at the same time."

I pulled my hand back. "No one asked you to watch out for me. Do not feel obligated. I can take care of myself."

Alder laughed. "How did it work out the last time you stuck your nose in one of my cases? Let me see." He tapped his finger against his forehead. "As I remember, you almost got yourself killed and at the very least kidnapped. Don't do this to me, Cece. You know I care about you, and I can't be worrying about what you're going to get yourself involved in. If you got hurt, I would never forgive myself."

His words both pleased and infuriated me. I knew he cared about me, and I wanted to let myself fall for him, but at the same time, I needed to stay focused on my divorce. And I'd promised Carla we'd get to the bottom of what was going on with her mom. I wouldn't let my feelings deter me, regardless of what Alder said.

"Alder, I'm a grown woman, and believe it or not, I've raised two children and lived with a jerk who cheated on me. I've fended off my tyrannical mother-in-law and have emerged otherwise unscathed. I can take care of myself without you watching my every move. Now if you'll excuse me, a hot shower and a glass of wine are calling my name." I opened the car door and stepped out.

He reached across the seat for the door handle and said, "You might want to burn those coveralls, there's a pretty toxic-looking stain on your rear-end."

I turned around and slammed the door in his face.

"I'll show you my rear-end," I muttered, marching up the sidewalk and giving him a good view of my backside.

~ ~ ~

After my shower, I pulled a bottle of my best wine from the rack and started slicing some cheese and fruit. Carla was nowhere to be found. I assumed she and Nancy were in the apartment. Nancy might be a flake, but she did get us into the storage locker the first time, and we'd need her assistance again.

As I climbed the stairs, I heard strains of Elvis coming from the apartment. His heyday was before my time, but I had a weak spot for his music. My DVD collection contained every movie he'd ever starred in, and I went weak in the knees watching him gyrate around a stage. When Angie's husband left to go to medical conventions, Angie and I hunkered down in my great room for Elvis marathons complete with popcorn, gallons of iced tea, and enough chocolate to keep gyms across the country in business forever.

I set the tray on the railing and knocked.

Angie opened the door. “Omigod, Nancy and Carla were telling me about your adventure at the dump. Did Alder have a stroke?”

I peered around her shoulder. Nancy sat cross-legged on the couch with a huge bowl of popcorn in her lap, and Carla lay sprawled on the settee with a giant box of chocolate-covered peanuts. Elvis was frozen in mid-gyrate on the television screen.

“No, Alder did not have a stroke.” *Well, almost.* “What’s going on in here?” I asked.

Angie’s smile faded. “Uh. I was sitting on the porch when they came home. Nancy hauled this out of her trunk.” She pointed to a scruffy velvet painting of Elvis. “I came to see if I could help and found out she loves Elvis as much as we do.”

The painting hung above the kitchen table, replacing the scenic landscape I had matched to the decor.

“Where did you get this?” I walked over for a closer inspection. In several places, the fabric appeared worn and shiny. The gold-colored frame had big chunks missing.

Nancy jumped off the couch, scattering popcorn on the carpeting. “Oops. Sorry. I’ll clean it up.”

Angie beat her to the floor and began scooping up the buttery mess. “I’ve got it. Don’t worry.”

“Don’t you love it?” Nancy asked, pointing to the picture. “I’ve always wanted one. It’ll need a new frame, and maybe I could touch-up some of the paint. But isn’t it the best?”

“It stinks,” Carla said around of mouthful of chocolate-covered peanuts.

It did have a familiar odor. The same smell I’d washed

down my shower drain. "You didn't drag this home from the dump, did you?"

Angie stopped collecting popcorn and reared back on her heels. "Ah, gross. How disgusting? Why would anyone throw The King in the trash? So cruel."

"Yep, as we were hightailing it to our cars, she found this lovely piece of art. The only way Brad and I got her to leave was to help her load it in her Jeep." Carla wandered to the table and refilled her iced tea from a pitcher on the table. My pitcher. The one from my fridge downstairs.

"Listen you guys," Nancy started. "It's not bad, really. I can get some fabric spray stuff to make it smell better. Besides, it'll clean up good."

"Nancy, you don't even know where the thing has been." My nurse training kicked in and the lecture poured out. "Do you know how many germs are crawling on it? It's a bacteria factory. They're multiplying even as we speak. *Salmonella*, *Shigella*, and *E. coli*. Those are only a few. You might even have botulinum toxin on there."

Nancy stuck out her lip. She lifted Elvis off the wall and ran her fingers across his face. "I'll throw it away. But can I keep it until we finish the movie? Please?"

I looked over my shoulder at Angie, who had resumed popcorn cleanup.

"Don't be such a poop! It is Elvis, after all. How often do you see The King immortalized in velvet?" Angie asked. "Get her some sanitizer. She can spray the thing down. You three were in the dump, and we're not going to throw you away."

"Yeah, what she said," Carla chimed in.

I relented. Nancy slapped the painting on the wall and gave me a big hug. I cringed and pulled away.

"Oh, sorry. I'll go wash my hands. You wanna stay and watch the movie with us? We'll start it from the beginning."

What could I do? “I brought wine. You can keep the painting, but only if you sanitize it. I don’t want a bunch of germs crawling around. And if you start breaking out with boils or your flesh starts rotting, you’re out of here.”

Chapter 19

"I need to start listening to my intuition instead of my friends. They mean well, I suppose."
Cece Cavanaugh

After a late night of Elvis, I had trouble pulling myself out of bed. We'd sat up until almost two in the morning watching movies, eating popcorn, and having a good time. It had been good for Carla to get her mind off her mother and for me to stop thinking about my stupid divorce.

But back to reality. I flipped the covers off and slid my feet around on the floor searching for my slippers, my mind still struggling with Lloyd's—or rather, Frank Archer's—murder. I had yet to ask Noah why he'd been at Delores' house so close to Lloyd's disappearance. I pulled Mrs. Wafford's notebooks from my nightstand and flipped to the entry on July 15, the day Rhonda Bray left. Mrs. Wafford really could use a lesson in penmanship.

July 15, 2013

8:30 a.m. Peter Bray left. Probably going to gas station for newspaper and a pack of smokes

8:45 a.m. Gus Guffey's cab arrived at Bray's house. And the Bray woman got in the cab with 3 suitcases. Ha! She'll be late wherever she's going. Old Gus will get a ticket for sure

9:17 a.m. Bray returned. Funny, he didn't say goodbye to his wife. She's probably running home to her mama

10:00 a.m. Delivery to the Redmond house

10:37 a.m. Redmond put a box in his trunk and left

11:38 a.m. Redmond returned. Needs to mow his grass. If his dandelions go to seed, Bray will have a fit

1:20 p.m. Bray got his mail

3:05 p.m. Delores got her mail

5:17 p.m. Bray went to the Redmond's

5:26 p.m. Bray returned home

Notations about various neighbors filled the page, but nothing more about the Redmonds, the Brays, or Carla and Noah. I flipped to the next entry.

July 16, 2013

7:30 a.m. Bryce let his dog crap on the sidewalk and didn't pick it up

8:30 a.m. Peter Bray left. Probably going to gas station

9:14 a.m. Bray returned

10:03 a.m. Delores and Lloyd left

10:31 a.m. Bray went to the Redmond's and sprayed something on their front lawn (Probably weed killer. Lloyd has ferocious dandelions)

12:36 p.m. Delores and Lloyd returned

2:00 p.m. Bryce let his dog pee on Bray's front lawn

2:01 p.m. Bray came out with a bucket of water, yelled at Bryce, and poured the water on the lawn where the dog peed

3:00 p.m. Bray got his mail

4:03 p.m. Lloyd got his mail

I stopped and flipped back several pages. Mrs. Wafford noted the daily comings and goings of every neighbor on Castleman Lane within eyesight of her front window. Talk about someone who had no life. Apparently, she didn't care too much for Bryce, whoever he was.

The rest of July 16 looked uneventful. Kids speeding down the street. One of them had the audacity to throw a soda can out the car window. Wow. I was barreling toward my senior years, and if spying on my neighbors was all I had to look forward to, I needed to find a hobby. If lonely old ladies naturally turned into nosy nellies, what hope did I have? Maybe by then I'd be back in good graces at the country club and be able to renew my membership. I already missed my tennis lessons.

July 17, 2013
8:30 a.m. Peter Bray left. Probably going to gas station
9:05 a.m. Bray returned
10:17 a.m. Delores left
10:45 a.m. Bray went over to the Redmond's
11:55 a.m. Bray went home
1:31 p.m. Delores returned
2:28 p.m. Bray got his mail
2:47 p.m. Delores went over to Bray's
3:15 p.m. Delores went home

The rest of the day had many more entries concerning other residents.

July 18, 2013
8:30 a.m. Peter Bray left. Probably going to gas station
9:20 a.m. Bray returned
10:15 a.m. Bray sprayed his front lawn
2:10 p.m. Bray got his mail

July 19, 2013
7:10 a.m. Bryce let his dog poop in my yard
7:15 a.m. Bryce picked up the poop with the bag I gave him, IDIOT!
8:30 a.m. Peter Bray left. Probably going to gas station
9:11 a.m. Bray returned
2.45 p.m. Bray got his mail
3:10 p.m. Delores' daughter arrived. Smart aleck!
7:21 p.m. Delores' daughter got the mail

July 20, 2013

6:31 a.m. Found a bag of poop on my porch

6:45 a.m. Delivered poop to Bryce's car (underneath the front seat. That'll teach him to lock his car doors. IDIOT!)

8:30 a.m. Peter Bray left. Probably going to gas station

9:16 a.m. Bray returned

3:11 p.m. Bray got his mail

4:15 p.m. Delores' daughter got the mail

6:17 p.m. Delores' daughter left

July 21, 2013

7:03 a.m. Bryce walked his dog on other side of street

8:30 a.m. Peter Bray left. Probably going to gas station

9:16 a.m. Bray returned

12:18 p.m. Delores' son arrived. Nice boy!

2:17 p.m. Delores' son went to Bray's house

2:55 p.m. Delores' son returned to Delores' house

4:01 p.m. Bray got his mail

4:32 p.m. Delores' son got her mail

7:47 p.m. Delores' son left

What an incredible waste of time! I threw the book down, got dressed, and joined the bleary-eyed duo sitting in my great room. Carla and Nancy were nursing coffees, and I had my usual hot tea.

"Before we go back to the dump, we need to get in the locker and see what's in there," Carla said.

"Who said anything about going back to the dump?" I asked. "You didn't have to deal with Alder. I'm lucky I didn't spend the night in jail."

"Right! Like he'd throw you in jail. He's so hot for you, you could probably get him to go to the dump and load the boxes into his cop car," Nancy said.

"We'll never know, because I'm not asking, and I'm definitely not going back. Not even with a gun to my head."

I pulled the tea bag from my cup and dropped it in the saucer. "And please, stop making remarks about him being hot for me. My mother-in-law and Phillip are waiting for me to mess up, so they can screw me over in the divorce. Phillip and I had a prenup with a morals clause. If I cheat on him, I get nothing. I don't even need a whiff of anything going on between me and Alder."

Carla scoffed. "From the sound of it, you have nothing to worry about. Look at Phillip's record in the sleeping-around department."

"Not the way it works," I said. "Call me young, dumb, and in love. The prenup only worked one way. In Phillip's favor."

"Honey, it's not your fault he cheated. He's a piece of crap," Carla replied, patting my hand. "Now, let's figure out how to get back into the locker. We'll talk about the dump later."

"I've got a plan," Nancy said.

Carla looked at me with big, round eyes and mouthed, *no way.*

"Stop it and listen." Nancy punched her arm. "I have good ideas. It's not like your dump idea ended so great."

"Okay, lay it on us," I said. "But I want you to know, I am *not* dressing like a commando. I am *not* wearing a stocking on my face or smearing it with shoe polish. I am *not* hiding out behind a trash bin, and I don't have all day. Michelle will be home this evening, and Jessie's coming for dinner." I left out the part about inviting Brad.

"We'll be in and out in no time," Carla said.

Nancy had concocted a scheme to get us back into the storage locker during the day. It involved Carla and me going to the locker while Nancy stalled Rhonda to make sure she didn't catch us.

"It all sounds good except for one tiny flaw," I said.

"How are we going to get back in? You snapped the lock back on when we left."

Nancy whipped out a padlock and her paper clips. "I'm going to show you. It's easy. If I can learn it, you should be able to pick it up in no time."

An hour later, Carla and I were sitting at my kitchen table practicing lock picking with paper clips. Nancy had tried to show us several times but had eventually given up and found a video on the Internet. After forty-umpteen tries and four hours, I had managed to open it once. Carla refused to try because of her arthritis. Said it would make her fingers hurt. *Boo-hoo.*

"Do we have to climb the fence again?" Carla asked. "If we find anything, how are we going to get it over the fence? Plus, our chances of getting caught increase tremendously."

Nancy scoffed and dangled a slip of paper from her apricot nails. "I got the security code for the gate."

I snatched the paper from her fingers and read it. "Way to go! How'd you get it?"

"When you two decided we had to go back to the locker, I knew we couldn't drive a car through the locked gate. Why do you think it took me so long to get to the dump last night? I stopped by the office at the storage place." Nancy adjusted her cleavage until it spilled out of her scoop-neck tee. "My girls have a way of convincing even the most honest attendant. I told him I'd lost the code and asked if he could help me get to my locker. Then I wiggled the girls a little, and ta-da! I'm having dinner with him, but it'll be nice. Nerdy guys kind of turn me on."

One of these days, I needed to talk to Nancy about her extracurricular activities, but for now, she kept bailing us out with resources. No complaints from me.

"We're going to need a truck," Nancy said.

"Why do we need a truck?" I asked.

"Who knows what we'll find. We have to be ready for anything," Carla said.

"Where do you suggest we find one? I sure can't afford to rent one," I said.

Nancy cut a glance at my chest and shook her head. She batted her eyelashes. "How about the boss man? Being in construction, he's got a bunch of trucks. Surely, he has one itty-bitty truck sitting around he'd let you borrow. He's knows you're still working at Carla's mom's house. As a matter of fact, I'd lay odds he'd do anything for you."

Grant always seemed to come to my rescue, and I knew he'd come through this time, but I hesitated to ask another favor."

"Wait," Carla said. "We can use my mom's van."

"Good idea. How are you going to stall Rhonda?" I was afraid to ask; worried Nancy might take on more than she could handle.

"I have my ways." She winked. "The main thing is you need to get to the storage locker as fast as you can. I don't want to be fussing around with her all afternoon."

"Wiggling your *girls* won't help with Rhonda. I think she's into guys. And old ones at that," I said, trying not to laugh.

I had been practicing all afternoon with the paper clips and a padlock, but I worried I'd get to the locker and not be able to do it without Nancy there to coach me along. I picked up the lock and inserted the paper clips like the video instructed. "What if the lock is different? It was dark, how do you know this one is the same?" Nancy had bought my practice lock at the hardware store and swore it matched the one she'd picked.

She sighed. "It is. Don't worry. You don't have to be in a hurry. Take your time with the lock, but don't dawdle either. I've got my cell, and I'll call if there's a problem. Now get back to work. We're not doing this until you can open it with your eyes closed."

I went back to my lock picking duty, and Carla cheered me on until her cell rang.

She peered down at the screen and frowned. "I'll be right back. I need to take this."

"What's your plan with Rhonda?" I asked after Carla left the room.

"Don't worry," Nancy said. "You keep at it."

Not worry? How could I not worry? Why did I not get a warm, fuzzy feeling? This was Nancy we were talking about. The woman who thought the county dump was a nightclub. The woman who wore pointy-toed shoes to climb a fence at the storage locker. Well, that one worked out okay, but the rhinestone-embellished T-shirt? Not so smart.

Carla came back to the kitchen with a long face. "We have to postpone. Mom's having some difficulty breathing, and the hospital wants me to come as soon as I can. I don't know how long I'll be, but it sounds serious."

"We got this," Nancy said. "It will probably be better if Cece goes alone anyway. Draws less attention."

"Have you lost your mind?" I asked, working the paper clips into the lock. "Eureka, I opened it four times in a row! No, we'll wait until Carla gets back." I snapped the hasp back in place and inserted the paper clips again.

"Please, Cece. I have to know what Rhonda is doing. You've practiced, and you're ready to do this," Carla pleaded.

"But it hinges on having your van," I said.

"She can take your car, you take her van, and I'll take my Jeep. It all works," Nancy said. "Then we'll meet here afterward."

I knew I'd regret it, but I said, "Okay, let's roll."

~ ~ ~

Carla, Nancy, and I parted ways after lunch. Carla headed to the hospital. Nancy went to distract Rhonda, and I waited outside the fence at the storage facility for the all-clear. Nancy would text me when she had located Rhonda.

I had my target—the locker—in sight and startled when the first text sounded.

Nancy: her car @motel

Me: Good. Is she there?

Nancy: unless on foot yes

Me: Knock on her door.

Nancy: c movement in window

Me: Is it her?

Nancy: who else would it be

Me: Good point. Okay, I'm going in. Text me if she comes out the door.

Nancy: LMK when ur done

Me: Huh?

Nancy: Let me know when you're done

Me: Okay.

I pulled next to the fence and punched in the security code. The gate slid open, and I drove around to the first row of lockers and parked the van.

My hands dripped with sweat. I could barely hold on to the paper clips. I had practiced most of the day with the lock and opened it about half the time. To be successful now, I had to remember to get the ends of the paper clips into the proper position. My heart sank when I saw the lock. Nancy had been right about the style of lock. It matched the one I'd been practicing on, but that one hadn't been clipped to a storage locker. Sure, the practice one was locked, but I could position it however I needed. This one had a short shank, and the hole for the key faced the ground. I could barely move it around, much less turn it upright to have better control.

I had pulled the van close to the door and squatted behind it to work. At least I'd be hidden. I twisted the lock around as best I could and inserted the first paper clip, then promptly dropped the second one. After digging through the gravel to retrieve it, I slid it in the lock and twisted it around, feeling for the pins like the video had instructed. After five tries, frustration set in. The paper clips kept sliding around, and I had to keep stopping to dry my hands on my pants. I'd feel the first paper clip slide into place only to drop the second one.

"How in the world do criminals do this?" I muttered to myself.

I stopped and checked my phone.

Nancy: u in

Me: What?

Nancy: Are you inside yet

Me: No. My hands are sweating. Everything okay there?

Nancy: BN

Me: Stop it with the abbreviations.

I cursed Nancy, slid the phone back into my pocket, and took a deep breath. *Relax.* I raised and lowered my shoulders and flexed my fingers before lowering myself in front of the lock. Finally, on my next attempt, it slid open.

Furniture was piled on either side of the locker, but an open space in the center provided ample space to park the van. I decided to back in, easier to load, and easier to make a fast getaway. I backed in, left the headlights on, and pulled down the overhead door. No need to advertise my presence, and parking the van inside allowed me to load it with no witnesses. This time, I'd brought a flashlight.

When my eyes adjusted, I saw a column of boxes along the back wall next to a workbench and file cabinet. Several bookcases, a sofa, end tables, and a bed were stacked along the sidewalls. I pulled the top carton, slid it onto the workbench, and lifted the lid. My mouth fell open. I reached in and pulled out eight plastic-wrapped blobs. Inside were exact replicas of the jade elephants I'd brought home from

Delores' house. The second box yielded the same treasure. I continued to open boxes, and before long had rows and rows of elephants.

My phone vibrated in my pocket. I yanked it out and checked the screen.

There were three text messages in a row from Nancy.

Nancy: BN means BAD NEWS

Nancy: She's leaving

My breath caught.

Nancy: LOL nvr mind opposite direction I'll follow keep wrkng

"I know where you sleep at night," I shouted at the phone. My voice ricocheted off the walls like a belch in a five-star restaurant.

Before I could slide my phone back into my pocket, it rang. Dread rose in my throat, and I froze. I held it below the flashlight beam, praying it wasn't Nancy. Michelle's number displayed on the screen. Great, she hadn't called in at least a week, and she picked now of all times.

I hesitated, but let it go to voice mail.

When it rang a second time, my mother instinct took hold. Michelle was on the road with Delia's family. What if they had been in an accident or worse?

"Hi honey," I answered, sounding more chipper than I felt.

"Mom, we stopped for a bathroom break. We're in Illinois. We should be home in a couple of hours."

"Okay, sounds good," I choked out. "We'll talk when you get home."

"Delia's dad let us rent mopeds at the cottage. We could come and go anytime we wanted." Michelle continued to extol the virtues of her beach vacation.

"I gotta go, Michelle," I said.

She ignored me and continued to talk. I held the phone

to my ear and listened while I loaded the elephants back into boxes. Multitasking at its finest.

"Mom. Are you listening?" Michelle asked.

"Yes, you rented mopeds. Great idea. I better get back to work."

"Mother, you weren't listening to a thing I said. I asked if you'd heard from Daddy. He hasn't called me since I've been gone."

Michelle hadn't given up hope that Phillip and I would get back together. We'd both talked to her about the divorce, but she continued to act like everything could go back to normal. Even after she'd seen Phillip and Willow together. It had broken her heart when she learned her father had a girlfriend. I had kept Philip's affairs hidden from the girls. Heck, I'd denied them myself. When Phillip had his midlife crisis and left with Willow, it came as quite a shock to Michelle.

Phillip hadn't helped. He'd initially filed for divorce, and then when I turned the tables and agreed to the divorce, he'd changed his tune. Suddenly he acted like the doting husband who'd been done wrong. Michelle and I had been walking on tenuous ground. After I'd gotten kidnapped by the lunatic co-owner of Harmony Inn during Wickford's first murder investigation a few months ago, Michelle and I made headway in the relationship department.

"Yes, Michelle, he stopped by the other day to pick up some of his things." In the beginning I had tried to protect the relationship between Phillip and the girls. But I'd run out of energy trying to cover for him. At this point, he could defend himself. I wouldn't bad-mouth him in front of the girls, but I certainly wouldn't lie to protect his image.

"Oh." Her voice fell, and I could hear the disappointment.

I wanted to get these boxes out of here in the worst way, but my daughter's feelings came first. "Why don't you give him a call? The phone works both ways, you know."

"I know. I hoped he'd call me once in a while." Again, the tone of her voice went straight to my heart.

"Call him or send him a text."

"Okay. How's Jess?" she asked.

"She's been working overtime, so I haven't seen much of her. But she's coming to dinner tonight. Don't tell her, but I found a nice guy to introduce her to." I lifted the hatch of the van and started piling the boxes in.

Michelle groaned. "Mother, when will you learn? She's going to flip."

Tires crunching on gravel outside forced me to cut my call short. "Hey sweetie, I got to go. I'll see you in a couple of hours. Love you." I hung up and listened. Nancy hadn't texted, or had she? I'd been so busy talking to Michelle I hadn't paid attention to my phone.

I pulled up my text message screen.

Nancy: BN! BN!

Nancy: Bad News

Me: What? What's going on?

No response.

I threw the last couple boxes into the van and shut the hatch. A car door slammed—close by. I flicked off my flashlight and raced around the van to cut the headlights and tripped. My phone sailed out of my hand, slid across the floor, and stopped when it hit the wall. Before I could get to my phone, the garage door flew up. Peter Bray stood in the opening with Nancy, a woman I presumed to be his wife, Rhonda, and a gun.

Chapter 20

"I feel sorry for Jessie, but I'm glad my mother isn't always trying to find me blind dates. That is seriously messed up. Who wants to date a guy your mother likes? Yuck!"

Michelle Cavanaugh

The duct tape on Nancy's mouth did not bode well. The woman was Rhonda Bray. I'd seen her photo the first time I visited her husband.

I did a double take. "Mr-Mr. Bray, what are you doing here?" I sputtered.

"I'll ask the questions," Bray said.

Rhonda flicked a light switch on the wall and pulled the door down behind her. She had obviously been here before. Who knew there was a light switch? In addition to the duct tape on Nancy's mouth, which really wasn't such a bad idea given her penchant for snark, her hands were bound together. Bray pushed her forward. She stumbled on her heels and fell to her knees, banging her head on the van's bumper. When she hit the ground, she grunted and rolled onto her side.

I ran to her and bent down. "Are you okay?" Putting my arm on her elbow, I helped her to feet. "Sorry I got you into this."

"*Mwa dwa nwi*," she mumbled through the tape.

"Get in the corner." Bray shoved the gun into his waistband and pulled a roll of tape from his fanny pack. "My dear wife spent her years sitting in California waiting for a man who never showed because he was dead. Then the minute she hears he's dead, she shows up snooping around his house with this bimbo following her like some R-rated sleuth."

Nancy moaned and kicked her foot. I knew what was going on in her head.

"Watch it," I said. "She's not a bimbo."

"You're as mouthy as she is. It's not an attractive quality." Bray ripped a piece of tape from the roll and started for me.

"If you think you're going to tape me up, you better think again." I ran for my phone, but he tackled me and pushed me to the ground. I tried to get in a position to give him a good swift kick, but he straddled me and held me down.

He pushed my hair aside and leaned into my ear, his breath hot on my neck. "You listen to me, sweetheart. I'm not playing games."

Both times I'd talked to him at his house, I'd felt sorry for him. And I thought he was nice. Well, other than screaming at Mrs. Wafford, he'd seemed like an okay guy.

"Get off me!" I screamed. I bucked and tried to knock him off.

He jerked me up and shoved me into the corner next to Nancy. "You stand there with the bimbo and be good, while I see what we've got here." Bray pocketed my phone, then hauled the boxes from the van to the workbench.

"Now what's this?" he asked as he unwrapped an elephant.

"Diamonds, baby, like I told you. Every one is chock-full. Lloyd and Noah had quite the racket going on." Rhonda slammed an elephant against the workbench, revealing the same sparkling gems I'd seen at my house. So, Peter didn't know about the diamonds, but she did. After Carla's screaming match with Noah, I'd placed him higher on my suspect list, making him my number one bad guy. Partially anyway. If what Rhonda said was true, so was Lloyd. Instead of two villains, we had three bad guys and a bad gal.

After Rhonda counted the elephants, she searched the file cabinet, pulling files and examining the papers inside.

I tried to signal to Nancy with my eyes but couldn't get her attention. Blood oozed from the gash at her hairline, and tears streamed down her cheeks. Bray had his back to me. If we rushed him and Rhonda, we might be able to get them on the ground, but I couldn't do it by myself.

Rhonda spun around, "Is someone holding out on us? There's twenty elephants here. Noah's shipping documents says he shipped thirty-two. Twelve are missing."

What the what? Noah and Lloyd were in on the diamond elephant deal, but how did she fit into this whole scheme?

Mr. Bray leveled his gaze on me. "Did you take the other diamonds?"

I squared my shoulders and stared back.

"Or did you, bimbo? What about all the stuff you've been hauling out of Delores' house? Did you help yourself to some diamonds? Or maybe my faithful wife made off with the jewels?" Bray pushed Rhonda out of his way and slammed the file drawer shut.

"You'd better start talking." He pushed her against the wall.

"Peter, don't be ridiculous. I told you about them, didn't I? And there's money," she said. "Lots of money. The old woman had a ton of it."

"What are you talking about?" Bray shouted. "What money? Why did you call and beg for money every chance you got?"

"I know how it seems. But I did this for us, me and you. The only way was to go along with Lloyd. Once I got my share, I would have left him. Delores unloaded all her investments before he could get his name on them, then she hid the cash. He found her hiding place. That's when he decided we were leaving. We were supposed to meet up and when he didn't show, I figured he'd taken the money, and the diamonds, and ditched me." Rhonda started to cry. "Don't you see, I couldn't come back."

Hold the phone! Mrs. Wafford's journal flashed in my mind. I thought it was just the gibberish of a lonely old woman. It all made sense. How had I overlooked the obvious?

"How much money?" Bray asked.

I nodded my head at Nancy trying to get her attention.

While Bray and Rhonda were arguing, if there was ever a time to get away, it was now. Nancy's headed bobbed back and forth between Bray and his wife, paying me no mind at all.

"A couple hundred thousand. Lloyd couldn't wait to get his hands on it. Please, let's just take these diamonds and go. I swear I didn't know he was dead."

"But you did," I said to Bray. "Because you killed him."

He stiffened.

OMG, did I say that out loud? Nancy moaned and shook her head vigorously. Now, she looked at me. As did Bray and Rhonda.

Jeez.

I couldn't let it go. Nope, I had to keeping yanking the chain. "Only you didn't know about the diamonds or the money, did you? You killed him to keep him from leaving town with your wife. Too bad Rhonda had already left. Mrs. Wafford had a notation in her book that you went to Lloyd's while Delores was at a meeting. That's when you killed him. And you knew he was found in the freezer, even though the police didn't release that detail."

"You killed Lloyd?" Rhonda wailed and kicked at him.

"You tramp!" He turned around to face her, and I saw the gun again. He punched Rhonda, smashing her head against the wall, and she went down.

I gasped and stepped back.

Bray swiveled and moved in so close I could smell his breath when he spoke. "You shut up."

The knots in my stomach tightened.

He slapped a piece of tape over my mouth and used another to bind my wrists together. "Now you'll keep your trap shut too."

My knees went weak. It would have been easy to give up, but I knew if we were going to get out of here, it would be up to me. Nancy and Rhonda were useless. I had to make a plan to distract Bray until we could get help. Or get myself killed in the process. And that prospect did not appeal to me.

Three months ago, I would have been a sniveling mess, but I'd learned I'm not as helpless as I'd always thought. But he did have a gun. *Time to pull on my big girl panties.* I wracked my brain for a way to divert attention and an idea materialized. One I hoped would keep me from getting shot.

"*M meel umthinf,*" I said, nodding to a jumble of boxes strewn across the floor.

"You got something to say?" Bray asked.

"*Umf ivf,*" I said.

He lifted a corner of the duct tape on my mouth and tugged it real slow. "What? It better be good, because you're getting on my nerves."

I could feel the skin on my lips tearing as he pulled. I bit back tears and willed myself not to show emotion.

My mouth ached, but I held myself in check. "We'll show you where the money is."

"Yeah right. I'm not falling for your trick," Bray said. "Where is it?"

"At the county dump," I said.

Nancy's head jerked around. Finally, I had her attention. She nodded, her eyes wide.

"We took a truckload of trash to the dump, I swear. You can ask Nancy. Delores had the money hidden in old books. We didn't realize what we'd thrown away until afterward.

We went back last night searching but couldn't find anything in the dark." I could tell the wheels in his brain were turning, weighing whether it'd be better to believe me or not. "We'll take you there."

Nancy's head bobbed up and down. She had stopped crying, but I worried about her head. She had a nasty gash.

"Let me check Nancy before we go," I said. "I'm a nurse, and she's hurt bad."

When he didn't say anything, I asked again. "Come on. There's a first aid kit in the van. I saw it in the back when I opened the hatch. Then we'll go to the landfill and show you where the boxes were dumped."

Bray lifted the hatch and retrieved the kit. He pushed Nancy to the floor and taped my legs together, before removing the tape from my hands.

"If you try anything, neither of you are leaving here alive."

Nancy's head wasn't as bad as I originally thought after seeing all the blood, but I cleaned the wound and put on a bandage. Once we got out of this mess, if we got out of it, she'd need stitches. I dawdled long enough to develop a strategy for when we got to the dump.

When I finished, Bray undid my legs and taped my arms. He started to tape my mouth.

"Don't. I'll keep my mouth shut, besides I can't tell you how to get there if I can't talk," I said.

"Tough. I'll pull it off when we get in the car. I'm not going to take a chance you'll yell your fool head off when we get outside."

He opened the passenger door of Delores' van and motioned for Nancy to get in. She did, and he fastened the seat belt around her.

"You." He pointed to Rhonda. "Get in the back seat."

Rhonda still lay facedown on the floor. Bray jerked her to her feet.

"Peter," she cried. "Don't do this. I came back to tell you about the money and the diamonds."

"What do you know about these books she's talking about?" Bray asked.

"That's where Lloyd found it. All those hundred-dollar bills, hidden in her stupid books. If I had known he was dead, and that the loot was still there, I would have come back sooner."

"Liar. I know all about you and Frank, Katherine," Bray yelled.

My ears perked. *Frank? Katherine?* Alder's revelation about Lloyd Redmond not existing before he came to Wickford and the news article all made sense. Lloyd was Frank Archer. Bray had called Rhonda by the name Katherine, and the news story said Archer's wife's name was Katherine.

Holy cannoli!

Rhonda went still. "How?"

"After you started messing around with Lloyd, I did a little snooping. I found the marriage license in your things. Then I called in some favors and figured out Lloyd Redmond wasn't Lloyd Redmond.

"When you left, I confronted him. And you see how it turned out. Only I didn't know about any money or diamonds, because you weren't just scamming Delores, you were scamming me, weren't you?" He covered Rhonda's mouth and wrists in tape. "I didn't have any money, but you used me to get close to Delores. Go after the widows, isn't that what the two of you did?" He pushed her into the van and fastened her seat belt.

I headed around to the driver's side, but he cut me off.

"We're not taking the van." He opened the driver's door and started the ignition. "Just a little insurance. You double-cross me, and these two are going to nod off to dreamland. Carbon monoxide is a beautiful thing. It shouldn't take long in this locker. So, don't dawdle. You show me where the money is, and we'll come back and get them."

Nancy stiffened and flung herself against the door.

"If your friend here doesn't cooperate," he said to Nancy, "you'll go to sleep and never know the difference."

I didn't have to think about what he'd do. If I didn't find a way to escape soon, Nancy and Rhonda were goners. I'd be one too. When he figured out I didn't have a clue where the boxes were, or even if we found the boxes and there was no money, he'd leave me at the dump. Dead.

Nancy continued to struggle as Bray closed the garage door. He pushed me into his car and ran a length of duct tape around my legs. Once we were out of the lot, he yanked the tape off my mouth.

~ ~ ~

"Turn left and head out to Old Quarry Road, near the county line." My breath hitched as I swallowed my fear.

"I know where I'm going," Bray said.

I didn't know how long Nancy and Rhonda had. "Go faster." The county always targeted speeders on Old Quarry Road, and I counted on Bray getting caught.

"Ha! Do I look stupid? I know all about the speed traps. The county deputies still have quotas to meet, and I don't aim to help them, so shut up or I'll put the tape back on," Bray said.

He could care less what happened to Nancy and Rhonda. The only thing on his mind was money. He had nothing to lose. He'd murdered once and wouldn't hesitate to do it again.

I glanced at the clock on the dash. Time was ticking away. It had been ten minutes since we'd left Nancy and Rhonda back at the locker. "Mr. Bray, let's go back and get them and the diamonds. Nancy can help find the money, so you can leave. The police have no idea you killed Lloyd. Don't make it worse."

"Shut up! The diamonds mean nothing to me. I don't have a way to get rid of them. The money is another story." Bray turned the radio on and tuned me out.

When we got to the dump, it had already closed. The barricade was down, and the attendant booth was empty. Bray threw the keys in the console, jerked me out of the car, and unwrapped my legs. He left the tape around my arms.

"You run, and I'll use this." He pulled the gun from the waistband of his pants and waved it at me.

"You don't need that." I blinked, said a prayer, and ducked underneath the barrier with Bray right behind me. The dump looked different, now that I was scared out of my mind. I struggled to retrace my steps. Nancy had peed by a rusted-out washing machine, but when I looked around, I saw all sorts of washers in varying degrees of decay scattered around the lot. I turned and scanned the road, trying to figure out the distance.

"Get moving and quit stalling." Bray secured the gun back into his waistband and shoved me forward.

I stumbled and without having my arms free to brace myself, I fell against a roll of old fencing. "Owww."

"Quit jacking around and help me find those boxes. The longer you screw around, the worse it's going to get for your friend and my dear wife." He grabbed me by the arm and yanked me to my feet.

My arm throbbed, and when I checked, blood leaked from a ragged slash above my elbow. I thought about the lecture I'd given Nancy about bacteria and winced. No telling what I'd pick up out here. But right now, bacteria seemed like such a minor concern.

I had almost lost hope when I saw the stack of wooden pallets. "This is it. Somebody's been here and dumped, but this is the place." My hopes soared for a moment, then plummeted. Now what?

The smell of garbage rotting in seventy-five-degree temperatures made my stomach lurch. For some reason, it hadn't seemed as bad last night, but between the icy fear and apprehension, my stomach acids churned in my gut.

"Sit down and don't move." Bray pointed to a rusted-out water heater rolled over on its side.

I carefully lowered myself, while he flung trash bags every which way, frantically searching for books containing Delores' life savings. The situation might have been funny, but since I had no clue if the books were in the dump, I saw nothing humorous about my predicament.

If I could get him closer to the pallets, I might have a chance to tip them on top of him. If I did it right, he wouldn't be able to get to the gun at his back, but if I missed—I couldn't miss. This was a one shot—poor choice of words—deal. My life, and Nancy's, and Rhonda's, literally hinged on me making a split-second decision and making it count. Bray continued digging and cursing the filth. The deeper he walked into the garbage, the more he cursed.

"Over there." I raised my arms and pointed. "I think I see something."

"Get in here and help," he said.

I took a deep breath and waded in. As I approached him, I held out my arms. "You're going to have to take this tape off, or I can't dig." If he freed my arms, maybe I had a chance at getting the gun, while he was digging in the garbage. But could I pull the trigger? I'd never fired a gun. Could I hurt another human being?

"No way. Watch where I'm searching and tell me when you see something familiar."

I inched a few steps back. "This way."

He followed, oblivious to the pallets looming above him.

Perspiration beaded on my forehead and dripped into my eyes. I raised my arms and rubbed my face against my sleeve. Patience had never been one of my virtues, but I had to time this perfectly or else. I couldn't think about that.

"You better not be jerking me around," he said. "If we don't find those boxes soon, I'll put a bullet in your pretty little head."

I sucked in a breath and choked on the bile rising in my throat. I took another step back.

Bray did the same. When he neared the pallets, I hollered, "Here, here they are."

He bent and pulled a trash bag out of the way.

I planted my feet, squared my shoulders, and ran against the stack. When I smashed into it, my breath left my body in a giant *whoosh*. The stack teetered and wobbled. My head spun from the impact. Bray jumped up and turned at the sound. The stack fell like a giant tower of dominos. One pallet slid off, then the next and the next, pinning him underneath.

"*Oopf!*" He screamed a string of curse words.

This only thing sticking out of the pile was his head. I ran all the way to the road. My hands and arms were useless, flopping in front of me. If I could flag down a passing car, I could get back to Nancy. How long had it been? How much time did she have left? I prayed I wouldn't be too late. If she survived, I'd owe her big time for getting her into this mess.

When I got to the street, it was deserted. No cars in the commuter lot except Bray's. He had left the keys in the console. Using my fingertips, I opened the door and slid in. Starting the car seemed hopeless, I had to lie on the seat and force my arms under the steering wheel. An edge of the tape had lifted, and I used my teeth to tear it back. When the end was long enough, I pressed it into the steering wheel and pulled until the tape came free. The sticky mess had managed to glom onto my hair and face, but my hands were free, allowing me to pull the rest of the tape away and start the car.

Which direction should I go? I was twenty minutes from the storage facility, but only a few minutes the other direction, in Ferris, was Dicky's—the place Alder had taken me a few nights ago. Dicky's seemed the logical choice, considering I didn't know how long Nancy had before the carbon monoxide killed her. Once at Dicky's, I could call 911 or Alder or Alder and 911. I'd call everybody I could think of.

I locked the doors, because in all the scary movies the bad guy appeared just when the good guy made a break for it. Bray wouldn't be showing up, unless he could push all those pallets off himself, but I wasn't taking any chances. I backed out of the lot and turned the car in the direction of Dicky's.

~ ~ ~

The purple neon sign flashing "icky's" looked a hundred times better than it did when I came with Alder. Only one car sat in the lot tonight. I pulled all the way to the front door and ran inside. Dicky stood behind the bar wiping down glasses. When he saw me, he waved and said, "Hey, what brings you in? Is Alder with . . . Whoa! What's happened?"

I ran to the counter screaming, "Peter . . ." *Gulp.* "Bray." I couldn't catch my breath. "Call Alder. Emergency." Nausea squeezed my stomach along with a sensation of dizziness. I blinked trying to clear the fog from my brain.

Dicky came around the bar. "You're bleeding. Let's get you settled down."

"No!" I screamed. "Nancy needs help. Carbon monox . . ." The room spun around me, and I grabbed onto the bar.

"What?" Dicky gently turned me around. "What is it?"

I had to hang on for Nancy. "Help . . . " was all I squeaked out before I went down.

~ ~ ~

Something cold lay across my forehead. I opened my eyes, looked up, and saw Alder staring down at me.

"Take it easy," he said. "You passed out."

I tried to sit up and got dizzy. "Help Nancy!"

Alder patted my arm which had a towel wrapped around it. "Everything's okay."

"Everything's not okay. We have to get Nancy." This time I fought the dizziness and sat up. "And Rhonda Bray. He left them in the locker with the car running."

"Mary Grace, bring her a hot tea." Alder grasped my elbow and helped me to a booth. "You have a nasty laceration. Dicky's wife cleaned it up while you were out, but you're going to need stitches. Nancy and the other woman are at the hospital. There's nothing to worry about. Except maybe your arm."

"What?" I asked. "They're okay? Both of them?"

"They're fine," Alder said.

A woman about my age brought four cups and sat down across from me. "Hun', it's going to be okay," she said, pushing one of the cups in front of me.

Dicky slid in beside her and kissed her cheek. "Thanks, babe."

"Cece, can you . . ." Alder choked on his words. "Can you tell me what happened?"

Tears brimmed in my eyes, and my lips began to quiver. All the feelings and emotions which had been building the past few days spilled out. Alder scooted closer and took me in his arms, stroking my hair, "Shhh, you're all right."

Dicky and Mary Grace carried their cups to the bar, leaving us alone.

"Is Nancy really okay?" I asked.

"Yes," he said. "I put them in an ambulance and then headed out to find you. Lucky for them, the van ran out of gas. Nancy said right after you left, it started sputtering and died."

"How'd you find her?" I asked.

"A neighbor across the street got suspicious when she saw Nancy and the Bray's at the Redmond house and called 911. A squad car followed them to the storage locker, but they were diverted to a multi-car accident and had to pull off. Dispatch called me. By the time I got there, you and Bray were gone. He'd left the door unlocked. I let myself in and found Nancy and Rhonda Bray. Nancy said Peter Bray had taken you to the dump."

"Mrs. Wafford!" I blew out a sigh of relief. "I've never been so scared."

"We better get you to the hospital and have them check your arm. Dicky said you did a number on it." Alder helped me out of the booth and led me to the door. "Thanks, Dicky," Alder called over his shoulder. "I owe ya, man."

"How did you get away from Bray?" Alder asked once we were in the car.

"I pushed a stack of pallets on top of him. Oh, Alder, he's hurt bad." I hugged my arms around me to keep from shivering.

"You cold?" Alder asked. "I can turn the heat on."

"No, relieved is all, and it's starting to sink in," I said.

"Nancy told me about the landfill. Dispatch sent a couple of county boys out to find you guys. When they didn't, I went out of my mind worrying. I was only a couple of minutes from the dump when Dicky called and said you were at his place."

"Is Bray going to be okay?" I still couldn't wrap my head around Noah and Lloyd smuggling diamonds. I'd known Noah most of my life, though I hadn't heard much from or about him in recent years. I realized Carla had every reason to distrust her brother. Poor Delores, she'd always doted on

Noah. This news would certainly break her heart.

"Physically, yes. Legally, no," Alder said. "And I'm sorry to tell you, we arrested your friend, Noah Feldman. Once we get you taken care of, we need to talk."

Chapter 21

“Not only has my mother moved outside her comfort zone since my dad left, she hasn’t even left a forwarding address. I’m glad to see her exerting her independence.”
Jessie Cavanaugh

Jessie was waiting in the emergency room when Alder brought me in. When she saw him, she shot me a look. “What did you get involved in this time?”

I waved her off. “Nothing. We had some excitement. We can talk at dinner tonight. You haven’t forgotten, have you?”

Jessie shook her head. “No mother, I haven’t forgotten. I was leaving when they told me you were on your way in. Right now, we need to get a doc to look at you. The woman they brought in earlier is in Treatment Room 4,” she said, pointing to a curtained off area. “You might as well go down there, and the doc can take care of you too. I’ll get you signed in.”

On the way back, I passed an officer leading a handcuffed Rhonda out. She glared at me but didn’t stop. I overheard Alder give him instructions to take her to the station. I continued down the hall to the only treatment room with a closed curtain.

I knocked on the wall and stuck my head in. Nancy sat on the gurney with an oxygen cannula stuck in her nostrils, chewing her gum rapid-fire and flirting with the young, male doctor mindlessly dressing her wound. I guess the shock from thinking she might die had Nancy in overdrive. Lucky for her, the van had run out of gas, or else her gum-smacking, man-chasing days might have ended in the front seat of a van.

She batted her lashes endlessly. “Is it going to leave a scar?”

The young intern gulped, and his Adam’s apple bobbed up and down. “Maybe, but it should fade with time.”

I’d have some tall apologizing to do. Nancy had been an innocent bystander in this whole mess. Though, she seemed more than willing to go along with the whole shebang.

The doc kept his head down, not making eye contact with her.

I cleared my throat. “Next,” I said and sat down beside Nancy.

A nurse came in with forms. The doctor signed them and said with a bit too much enthusiasm in his voice, “Nancy, you’re good to go. Check back with your own physician in a week to have the stitches removed.”

He turned to me, and I smiled.

“Two for the price of one?” I asked.

After the area around the wound had been sufficiently numbed, the doctor stitched me up.

A loud ruckus sounded from the waiting room. Then I heard Grant’s voice thundering down the hallway. “Cece, are you back here?”

A nurse stepped through the curtain. “Doctor, I’m sorry, but this gentleman won’t take no for an answer.”

The doctor looked up, clearly aggravated at the interruption. “Call security.”

She turned around and peered over her shoulder. “Oh, it’s okay. A detective in the waiting room is handling him.”

Oh, no! Just what I needed, Alder and Grant in the same place. Again! Both of their voices echoed down the hall in angry tones. It didn’t sound like they were bonding.

I squirmed on the table. “Are you about done? I need to get out there and head off a disaster.”

The doctor slapped a bandage on my arm. “You need a tetanus booster?”

“Nope,” I said. “Had one six months ago. I’m good.”

“Make sure you see your regular—”

“I know the drill.” I fled the room, leaving the doctor and nurse with mouths gaping.

Nancy followed me down the hall. “I called Mr. Hunter. I hope I did the right thing.”

I stopped and turned around. “Why would you call him?”

“I don’t know. I didn’t know where you were, and I . . .” She bit her lip, chewing off her tangerine-colored lipstick. “I figured he needed to know.”

Momentarily forgetting about the apology I owed Nancy, I raised my arms in the air. “This is great! Fantastic even. Can’t you hear them yelling? This is going to be ugly. Come on.” I sprinted down the hall toward the commotion. “We need to run interference.”

I skidded to a halt at the waiting room. Alder and Grant were toe-to-toe yelling, bellowing like two bull moose.

“Stop it, both of you.” I pried them apart and leveraged myself between them. “In case you haven’t noticed, we’re in a hospital. If you can’t calm down, take it outside.”

They both stopped, but they remained locked in a stare down. I knew if I didn’t get their attention quickly, one or the other might take a swing.

I grabbed Grant’s arm and pulled him off to the side. “What are you doing here?”

Out of the corner of my eye, I saw Alder observing, but to his credit he did not intervene.

Grant ran his hand through his hair. “Nancy called with some cockamamy story about you being kidnapped. What were you doing at the dump?”

I put my hand on Grant’s arm and explained about trying to find the boxes I’d sent to the dump, omitting the part about the diamonds and money.

Grant sighed. "What am I going to do with you? You seem to draw more trouble than a pack of rabid skunks. Come on, let me take you home."

Alder must have heard the conversation, because he interrupted. "I'm taking her home. She came with me, and she'll leave with me."

Grant put a protective arm around me. "No, she's not."

Alder reached for my hand. I wiggled out from under Grant's arm and took a giant step back. Alarms were going off in my head. "Would the two of you leave me alone? What is wrong with you?"

Alder crossed his arms and snorted. "Tell him to leave."

"Like hell," Grant said. "I'm not leaving."

"The two of you can duke this out if you want, but I'm not leaving with either one of you." I walked out the door and left them staring after me. Frankly, if they wanted to clobber each other, who cared? I didn't have to stand around and watch.

I started up the sidewalk. It was a long way home, but I wasn't riding with either one of them. Where did they get off acting like a couple of hormonal, puffed-up teen boys?

Halfway up the block a drop of rain splattered on my arm, followed by another and another. I continued walking. Thunder rumbled in the distance. Great! I thought about turning around but decided pouring rain could be the best part of my day. Nothing else had gone right. Clouds rolled in, and the sky darkened, but I kept moving, putting distance between me and the hospital and the two bickering men. The intermittent sprinkles turned into persistent drops. My hair wilted around my face, large raindrops pelting me relentlessly. When a bolt of lightning zapped a transformer on the corner, I decided to turn around before I got toasted. Besides, I'd left Nancy to fend for herself.

Grant's truck and Alder's car were both still in the

parking lot. I sloshed into the ER, and they were still arguing. No blows had been thrown; at least I didn't see any blood.

I walked right up to them dripping and all. "Okay, here's the way it's going to be. I don't belong to anyone. I'm my own person. If I want to go to breakfast with Alder, I will."

Alder puffed his chest out in a he-man way.

"And," I continued, "If I want to have coffee with Grant, I will."

Grant sneered at Alder.

"We've had this talk before, both of you," I said.

"Yeah, when you stuck me in the *friendship* zone," Grant said, hanging his head.

Alder smirked.

A crowd had started to gather in the ER to watch the spectacle. Someone had muted the television in the corner, and our voices echoed through the room. I grabbed both men by the arms and pulled them toward the door.

"It's raining. Carla's van is at the storage locker, and I need a ride. You two had better figure out a democratic way to make it happen. No arguing, no punching, make a decision," I said.

Alder looked at Grant. "You can take her."

"No way. I don't want to overstep my *friendship*. You brought her here," Grant said.

I tapped my foot and waited.

Finally, Alder pulled a quarter from his pocket. "I'll flip you for her."

Grant didn't respond.

I continued to tap my foot. "Well?"

"Works for me, but let's use my quarter." Grant reached into his pocket.

"Oh, for Pete's sake, will someone give me a ride?"

"Go ahead," Alder said to Grant. "We'll use yours. I call heads."

When Grant started to protest, I cleared my throat. "I'm not getting any younger."

Grant flipped the quarter and didn't catch it.

It fell to the floor, landed on edge, and began to roll. All eyes in the room followed the quarter down the hall, waiting expectantly for Grant or Alder to claim it. Instead a young boy, with a cast on one arm, scooped it up and scampered off shouting about candy bars and vending machines.

A collective sigh echoed throughout the room.

"Well, I'll be. Never had that happen before," Grant said.

Alder presented his quarter, but Grant shook his head. "You go ahead. I need to check in on a job site."

"I need to get back and question a suspect," Alder said.

Both men headed for the parking lot.

"Wait a minute," I yelled. "I need a ride. Come back here."

Alder turned around. "Kidding! Get your friend." He pointed to Nancy, who had her body draped across the admitting desk chatting with an intern.

~ ~ ~

Michelle met me in my driveway. The rain had stopped, and she and Delia were unloading luggage when I arrived in the back seat of Alder's car. Alder threw his door open and helped Nancy and me out. Michelle did a double take at the scene.

"Mom, what happened? Are you okay?" She dropped her suitcase and ran down the driveway.

I grabbed her and hugged her to me. "I'm fine."

Michelle pulled away and narrowed her gaze at Alder. "What's he doing here?"

"Not now, Michelle. Your mom's been dealing with a lot. Help me get her and Nancy in the house," Alder said.

Michelle huffed up. "You might be a cop, but you're not my boss." She turned on Nancy, who still wore the sleazy outfit she'd put on this morning. "Who are you? Will somebody tell me what's going on? Why do you smell like garbage, Mom? I leave for vacation, and you go crazy. Honestly, Daddy will blow a gasket."

Ellen Foster, Delia's mom, stood in the driveway, hands on her hips and staring at us. Hazel's smear campaign already had me banned from the country club, so it didn't matter if Ellen witnessed all this chaos. Though, I expected a call from Hazel as soon as Ellen could share the news about me coming home in the back of a cop car with a floozie.

Instead, she met us in the driveway. Smiling weakly, she said, "Michelle, why don't you and Delia carry your suitcases upstairs? Your mom seems like she's had a tough day. Give her a chance to catch her breath."

Michelle glanced at me. I nodded, and she turned and stomped to the house. "Thanks, Ellen. I'll call you tomorrow and explain all this."

"No need, Cece. Life happens. The girls had a good time. We'll expect to take Michelle when we go back in the fall, if it's okay with you."

"It is," I said. "Thanks. I owe you."

"No need. Not everything has to make the rumor mill at the club. Take care of yourself." She walked back to the car and waited for Delia.

Alder walked Nancy and me to the door. "Do you want me to come in for a while?"

My knees were still shaking, and for once, I could say it wasn't Alder's presence. "Yes, please."

I sank into the sofa in the great room and Nancy plopped down beside me.

"How about a glass of wine, ladies?" Alder called from the kitchen.

Nancy kicked off her heels and moaned. "Sounds good to me." When she leaned back against the cushion, I noticed blood seeping through her dressing.

I reached over and checked the bandage. “You’re going to have a nasty bruise. How does it feel?”

“It hurts like crazy, but not as bad a being dead. I guess it’ll be all right.”

Alder handed us each a glass of wine and bent down to take a look. “You have extra bandages?” he asked me.

“There’s a first aid kit in the kitchen pantry,” I said. “Omigod, I’ve got to get dinner started. I invited Brad to meet Jessie.” I jumped off the sofa and started for the kitchen. For the first time since Phillip had left, I had splurged and bought steaks. They were marinating in the fridge. I had planned to grill outside. Now all I wanted to do was crawl in bed and go to sleep.

Alder took me by my shoulders. “Slow down. You need to take it easy. Call them and make it another night. They’ll understand.”

“I can’t. I promised.” I stood on tiptoes and whispered in his ear. “If my divorce was final, I’d invite you to stay for dinner, but I can’t.” I kissed him on the cheek. “Thanks for coming to my rescue.”

He blushed. “You need to thank Mrs. Wafford and Nancy. Without the two of them, I’d have never known where to find you. By the way, we are going to talk about this. Tomorrow. I can’t keep chasing you around the county. You’ve got to quit your amateur investigation.”

I saluted. “Yes, sir. I understand. I’m off duty as of now.”

“Good.” He brushed my cheek with his fingers. “Now I have to go talk to Rhonda Bray and find out how she’s involved in all of this.”

After Alder left, I begged Nancy for forgiveness. She said she could forget everything if she could take a bath in my Jacuzzi. How do you say no to someone who almost died because of you? I carried up a bottle of wine, lit the candles for her, and reminded her to keep her head above water.

While Nancy lounged in my tub, I showered in the hall bathroom and changed into a pair of jeans. I had barely made it downstairs when Carla arrived.

Michelle went to her room to unpack, and I told Carla about the diamonds and money. I also broke the news about Noah being arrested.

"Are you freaking kidding me? What a lowlife, scum-sucking traitor." Carla blew out another few choice names for her brother while pacing the room. "I knew he didn't come here to help Mom!" Carla said. "How could he? This is going to kill her."

"Calm down." I hugged her. "Getting your blood pressure up won't help."

"I know, but it makes me feel good to vent. If I could strangle him, I'd feel even better." Carla sighed. "How do I break this to Mom?"

"Oh, Carla, I don't know. Take it one step at a time, I suppose. How's she doing?"

"She's stable. Her COPD flared. They gave her a breathing treatment. I sat with her most of the day. Then stopped by her house. Noah had been there and ransacked the place."

"How could you tell?" Considering the mess, it would be difficult to determine.

"Oh, trust me, you could tell. He tore through there, looking for the diamonds or money. Who knows? How much of this was he in on? And why didn't he come back after he thought Lloyd had left?"

"He figured Lloyd had double-crossed him and taken off with the diamonds. He had no reason to believe your mom had them stored in a curio cabinet along with all the other junk. Rhonda mentioned that Noah shipped the diamonds to Lloyd. Lloyd had a shipping arrangement set up in the storage locker. The file cabinet had documents, and I found more diamonds there. Apparently, Noah shipped them in the hollowed-out elephant statues."

"I never saw them at Mom's house. Is that what you brought here? The boxes Detective Alder took?"

"Yes. They were in the bottom section of a curio cabinet hidden in the back. Maybe Lloyd had hidden them and had plans to make off with some of them but died before he could. The night I brought them here, I had no idea about the diamonds. I had them on the counter and accidently broke one." I chose not to throw Nancy under the bus. It was my fault Nancy got anywhere near the statues in the first place. "Alder saw the diamonds before I could get them all picked up, and he took them into custody. It was sheer luck he didn't take the cookbooks. I had already put that box under my desk in the alcove, or else he would have taken it too."

"How am I going to explain this to Mom?" Carla shook her head.

"I don't know. I'm sorry we didn't find the rest of the money. Maybe Alder can help. He could talk to the county, and maybe we can go back out to the dump. But we'll do it right this time."

Jessie arrived, and Carla and I put our talk on hold. Michelle came down to greet her sister, but she kept her mouth shut about Alder bringing me home. I knew as soon as the two were alone, Michelle would bend her sister's ear—if Jessie would let her.

Neither of the girls had actually met Nancy, nor did they know she had moved into the apartment. Along with Jessie meeting Brad, Nancy was one more surprise I'd be springing on them.

We were sitting on the patio waiting for Brad. Well, I waited for Brad and worked on a plan to smooth it all over with Jessie. The back door opened, and Nancy strutted out the door with nothing on but a towel.

"Oops. Didn't know anyone had arrived. I didn't bring any clothes down before I got in the tub." She crossed the patio on tiptoe and ran up the stairs.

"Mom, is that the woman from the hospital?" Jessie asked. "And why is she going to the apartment?"

"It's a long story, but her name is Nancy." I took a long sip of wine.

"Nancy?" Jessie asked. "Nancy from Bonafide? The one with the gum addiction?"

I told them about Fletcher closing the business, selling his duplex, and Nancy needing a place to live.

"I felt responsible. If I hadn't maced Fletcher, she'd still be employed. When Carla asked me to help at her mom's, I was already in over my head at Hunter Springs," I told Jessie. "You couldn't help. I needed someone, and she needed the money. It worked out for both of us."

Jessie and Michelle both rolled their eyes. Carla started laughing. "You Cavanaughs crack me up. The eye roll thing is priceless."

While we were laughing, Nancy came downstairs, fully clothed. "I'm so embarrassed. I didn't know all of you were out here."

I got up and hugged her. "Don't worry about it. Get a glass of wine, and I'll introduce you to my daughters."

Michelle and Jessie looked at each other while I made the introductions. I knew when we were alone, I'd get an earful. But what they didn't know wouldn't hurt them. I owed Nancy big-time. As long as she wanted to stay here, she had a home.

Nancy pulled a chair across the patio and joined us at the table. She had a few rough edges, but maybe we'd be able to put a dab of polish on her.

Chapter 22

"I think my efforts to fix Cece up with Alder are paying off. I've seen him at her house a couple of times. And it's not work-related, because they take off on his motorcycle and stay gone the entire day. Here's hoping she finally slams the door on Phillip."
Angie Valenti

The steaks were almost done, and Brad still hadn't arrived. I sent Michelle into the house to set the table after I'd given her a brief overview of what had transpired tonight. At least enough to explain the ride home in the back of a cop car and the bandage on my arm. I'd give her a more detailed explanation at some point in the future when I'd had a chance to digest it myself.

She poked her head out the door. "Are Angie and Dave coming over, and that Nancy woman, is she staying for dinner?"

"Only Angie and Nancy," I said. "Dave has a meeting tonight."

"Why do you have seven plates on the counter? Oh, I forgot you invited a date for Jessie." She laughed and slammed the door.

"What?" Jessie asked. "You invited someone to fix me up with? How many times do I have to ask you to stay out of my personal life?"

"Calm down, it's a young man I met at Hunter Springs," I said. "He happens to be pleasant, and he's also single—a nice combination."

Nancy glanced from Jessie to me. "Brad? He was mean to me the other day at the dump."

"The dump?" Jessie asked. "What's she talking about?"

"Nothing. I'll explain later," I said.

"I think I'll go help Michelle," Carla said and disappeared into the kitchen.

"Did I say something I shouldn't have?" Nancy placed a hand across her mouth. "I'm always opening my mouth when I shouldn't. It's a bad habit."

"Nancy, it's fine. Don't worry. Why don't you go help Michelle and Carla?" I said.

Nancy shrugged and got to her feet. "He is kind of cute," she said to Jessie. "But I'd question the pleasant part."

After Nancy left, Jessie pulled her chair closer. "Okay. I know I'm not going to get you to stop with the matchmaking. What's the deal with this Brad?"

I knew she'd come around. "He's a nice, clean-cut guy. I hoped you two might hit it off. No big deal. End of story."

"Nancy doesn't seem to like him much," she said.

"There's a reason. As you probably noticed, she kind of has a way of grating on your nerves," I said.

Jessie nodded.

"She got on Brad's nerves one too many times, and he snapped at her. I would have done the same thing. Jess, I wanted you to meet him. Nothing nefarious, I swear. At least give him a chance. If you two don't hit it off, you don't have to go out with him. Besides, he might not even like you."

"Wait a minute," she said. "Why wouldn't he like me?"

"How do you feel about poker?" I asked.

"Huh?"

"Never mind. He might not even show up," I said.

"Great. Stood up on a non-date I didn't even agree to. How humiliating."

Before I could comment, Michelle interrupted. "Jessie's date is here."

Jessie jumped from her chair, lunging at Michelle. “I’ll get you, you little snot.”

Michelle flung open the door, and Brad stepped onto the patio sporting a fresh haircut, new jeans, and a green-striped button-down shirt which highlighted his green eyes. The same shade of green as Jessie’s. My grandbabies would be beautiful.

“What were you saying?” Michelle asked.

Jessie ran a hand down her blouse, smoothing out nonexistent wrinkles. “Nothing.”

“Brad, I’m glad you made it. You’ve already met Michelle. This is my other daughter, Jessie.”

Brad shuffled his feet, his face a bright shade of red. “Hi. It’s nice to meet you,” he finally said. “Thanks for having me over.”

Jess, out of character for her, didn’t say a word. She always had something to say. Her eyes did plenty of talking though. I think I saw a few sparks sizzle. Finally, I nudged her arm.

“Uh, hi. You want a beer or something?” she asked.

“A beer would be good,” Brad said to her.

“I’ll have a refill on my wine,” I said, holding out my glass.

Jess went into the house. Brad let his gaze follow her all the way. When the door closed behind her, he leaned in. “You didn’t tell me she was hot.”

“Excuse me,” I said, grinning. “You’re ogling my daughter.”

“Sorry,” he said. “But, wow. I’ve had blind dates before, but none of them looked like Jessie.”

“Don’t worry about it. Just behave yourself. She’s a good girl.” I hoped.

Angie made her entrance through the hedge separating our backyards at the same time Carla came out to check on the steaks and announce that dinner was ready.

"Perfect timing," Angie said. "My stomach is rumbling."

"You always know when the food is ready. You must have food radar." I hugged her. "Come on, let's eat. The steaks look great, and Beatrice made us a pasta salad before she left yesterday."

We went inside and joined the rest of the group. Michelle instructed everyone where to sit, and I noticed she'd purposely left a vacant chair by Brad. Jessie made a beeline to sit next to him, and he didn't complain.

Michelle shot me an *are you satisfied?* scowl. I smiled and cut into my steak. Perfect!

After dinner, Michelle offered to wash dishes, a chore she rarely volunteered for. I usually had to twist her arm to get her cooperation. Nancy excused herself and went to the apartment.

"Who wants to sit on the patio?" Jessie asked.

"Great idea," Carla said.

Jessie's face fell, but she didn't say anything. My heart thudded thinking about my little girl being smitten.

"How about you Brad? Want another beer?" I asked, hoping Carla would get the hint.

"Sure, but I need to talk to you first," he said. "I'll be back in a minute," he said to Jessie.

Jessie shot me a questioning look but followed Carla and Angie to the patio.

"What's up?" I asked.

"There's something in the driveway for you," he said. He grabbed my hand and practically pulled me from my chair.

"What's so exciting?" I asked.

"You'll see. Come on."

When Brad opened the door, I couldn't believe my eyes. His truck had a load in back covered with a tarp.

"Is this what I think it is?"

"Yup," he said.

I gasped and threw my arms around his neck. “Omigod. I can’t believe you did this. How did you find them? When did you find them?”

“Hey, slow down. One question at a time.” He pried my arms from his neck, walked to the truck, and peeled back the canvas. “Larry and I went back to the dump early this morning, before work. It took a while, but I think we found all of them. I would have called, but we were running late for work. I didn’t want to get on the wrong side of Mr. Hunter. He’s a nice guy and all, but we didn’t want to push our luck. Anyway, since I was coming to dinner, I decided to surprise you.”

The smell emanating from the truck brought back my ordeal with Peter Bray. “Did you say you found them this morning?”

“Yep, before daylight.” He smiled, and his dimple deepened.

The boxes weren’t even there when I had taken Bray out there. My stomach did a backflip. If I hadn’t gotten away, no telling what he would have done.

“Do me a favor, will you? Pull into the garage. We’ve got to get these unloaded.” The sky looked threatening again, and I didn’t want these smelly boxes getting wet. “I’ll get Carla.”

“These will stink up your house. Are you sure?” he asked.

“Definitely.”

Carla opened the door. “Angie said to tell you she’d catch you tomorrow. Whoa! Is this what I think it is?”

“Yes ma’am,” Brad said. “Sorry, they got a little wet from the rain earlier, but we covered them with the tarp before they got soaked. I think we got every box.”

Without wasting time, Brad pulled in the garage, lowered the tailgate, and handed down the boxes. “Hey, what happened to your arm?”

I explained about my detour to the dump with Bray in search of the boxes.

"Oh man, we could have gotten you killed." Brad halted distribution.

"Don't stop," Carla prodded. "Keep those babies coming."

Brad continued to stare at my arm.

"I'm okay. Let's get back to work." I grabbed the box he held and passed it to Carla, who ripped it open.

"Oh, these are gross." She held out a handful of books and wrinkled her nose.

Brad went around to the driver's side of his truck and pulled three pair of work gloves from behind the seat. "Here, put these on." He pulled on a pair and resumed his task.

Carla pushed the first box aside. "There's nothing in here but nasty books." She pulled another to her.

I rummaged through one and came up with the same result—wrinkly, old books.

We continued working, Brad slitting the tape on the boxes with his pocketknife, Carla and I fanning the pages of the books and pushing them aside for Brad to return to the dump.

"This is hopeless," Carla said when we were down to the last five cartons.

"Don't give up. Let's get these done," I said. "And we haven't even made a dent at your mom's yet. Who knows what else we'll find."

The next box I opened contained books, nice clean cookbooks. Ones without water damage. I pulled the first one out and flipped it open to a hundred-dollar bill. "Jackpot!" I pulled twenty crisp bills from the book and fanned them out.

Carla grabbed a second book—another cookbook—and pulled out twenty pristine hundred-dollar bills. "Score!"

Jessie joined us. "Hey, what's going on? Why is everyone out here?" When she saw the money, her mouth dropped.

"Get a book and help," Carla said. "Or better yet, start stacking these bills, so we can see how much there is."

"Mother, what kind of mess are you in?" She eyed Brad, who was flinging cash out of the books as fast as he could open them. "And him? You want me to go out with him, when he's mixed up in all of this?"

Brad put down the book he held. "It's not what it seems like." He looked to me. "At least I don't think it is. Is it?"

"Jess, it's all innocent. Delores cashed in all her investments. Apparently, she hid the money in her cookbooks when Lloyd started his affair with Rhonda. I happened across it quite by accident. Then I inadvertently had Brad haul everything to the dump, not knowing there was money hidden in them. Start stacking and counting."

Jessie collected all the piles of cash Carla, Brad, and I had in front of us.

When we finished, Carla pulled off her gloves and scanned the garage. "Can you believe this?

Jessie had the stacks neatly arranged on the hood of Brad's truck. "Holy cow."

"This makes me think of all the stories my mother told me about her grandmother hiding money in canning jars and burying them in the back yard," Carla said. "Only your backyard doesn't catch on fire or get blown away in a tornado. What do you suppose got into her? One little spark. Thinking about it makes me cringe."

Carla was not going to like what I had to say. I went and stood next to her. "We have to tell Alder about this," I said.

She swung around. "Are you serious? No way. I'm not having my mother's life savings locked away in an evidence locker somewhere. This has nothing to do with Lloyd getting himself killed. You can forget it."

"We're giving it to Alder. You know the old saying, 'follow the money.' So, go follow the money. Talk to your mom's investment guy. Talk to the bank. Get your proof.

Then take it to Alder and make a claim. If it's legitimate, and they find it has nothing to do with Lloyd's death, then they have no choice but to return it. Better yet, take Alder to talk to your mom. Go early. She tends to get confused later in the day." I had no intention of backing down. With this much money at stake, Alder would kill me for sure if I let Carla get away without reporting it.

"We can put it in my safe with the rest," I said. "But, make no mistake, I'm calling Alder. Concealing evidence is a crime, and if this money has anything to do with Lloyd, I won't be a party to it."

In the end, Carla conceded, and I put the money in the safe in my closet. We all helped load the boxes back into Brad's truck. Carla huffed off to bed. I could tell she was mad, but I knew she'd do the right thing. The last I saw of Brad and Jessie, they were sitting on the patio. I headed upstairs to call Alder and to take a shower. Not necessarily in that order.

Chapter 23

"The case of the frozen body—closed. The case of the infatuated detective—under investigation."
Case Alder

Michelle hadn't even been home twenty-four hours, and already Hazel was monopolizing her time. They'd left before I woke up for a shopping excursion into the city. While I was pouring a bowl of cereal for my breakfast, Alder called.

"How's the arm this morning?" he asked.

"Sore. But I'll manage." I set the milk down, not wanting to pour it until I'd gotten off the phone. I hated soggy cereal.

"You and Carla going to be around for a while? I'd like to stop by and get this wrapped up."

"Michelle's gone, and I'll send Nancy on out to Hunter Springs, so it'll only be me and Carla. How's Peter Bray?" I hadn't slept well worrying about him. After what he'd done to me and Nancy, I knew it sounded crazy to be concerned, but I didn't wish him any ill will, especially nothing permanent. Other than going to prison.

"He's fine, some scrapes and contusions and a sprained ankle. Hospital released him last night, and he spent the night in the holdover at the station, along with his wife and your friend Noah. Feldman confessed to burglarizing your house, though the way it sits, that's the least of his worries." Alder hesitated. He drew in a breath before he continued, "Any worries your ex was involved can be put to rest. As much as it pains me, he's off the hook."

"What a convoluted mess," I said.

"You got that right. I'll be by in an hour or so," Alder said and disconnected.

Carla came in and filled a bowl with cereal while I was pouring the milk. "Can I have some of that?" she asked.

"Help yourself." I slid the carton to her. "Alder's on his way over with additional questions, so we're grounded until he gets here."

"Figures. I need to get to Mom's, so I hope he makes it snappy. Not sure what else I can tell him."

"For starters, you need to tell him about the money."

"I know." Carla slumped over and leaned her elbows on the counter, looking defeated.

"It's probably not connected. I have a confession to make," I said.

Carla straightened. "This better be good."

I filled her in on the whole Lloyd/Frank Archer scam, along with the fact he'd been married to Rhonda, who was actually Katherine.

Carla's eyes rounded. "Wow!"

I scooted over my laptop and pulled up the article about Frank Archer's escape from prison. "Take a look at this. He was convicted of scamming widows. His wife was implicated but never charged."

Carla scanned the screen and let out a long sigh. "I knew I never liked that toad. Poor Mom. Lloyd and Noah were mixed up in the diamonds? I hate to ask, but do you think Noah was trying to scam my mother?" She pushed her bowl aside. "I've lost my appetite."

"Alder would probably know, but based on what Rhonda—I mean, Katherine—said last night, I don't think so. I think Noah and Lloyd were in on the diamonds, and Noah is the one who broke into my house. Alder said your brother confessed." The grandfather clock in the great room bonged nine times.

"What a jerk! I hope you realize now what an incredible waste all your attention on Noah has been," Carla said.

Feeling chastised, I nodded. "Sorry. Old times are hard to forget, but lesson learned. Believe me."

Carla poured herself a cup of coffee, then leaned down and hugged me. "Contrary to how impossible I've been acting, I do appreciate all your help."

"Thanks. If Nancy stays on the straight and narrow, I'll clear some time to help you at your mom's." I scraped our bowls into the disposal and stacked them in the dishwasher.

"I'd appreciate it," Carla said. "Oh, it seems I have a confession to make too. Would you believe I've been paying for that storage locker all this time? It dawned on me last night after I went to bed. I've been paying Mom's bills all this time, and it was actually her locker. The one she'd rented to store her furniture after she moved in with Lloyd. I checked online this morning, and it was the same place. Why I didn't think of it, I'll never know."

I shook my head and sighed. "Well, Alder's got possession of it now. At least until he wraps up his investigation."

"I'm going to go take a shower before he gets here." Carla shuffled off with her coffee cup.

~ ~ ~

With Alder's arrival imminent, I had about worn a hole in the living room carpet with my pacing. I reasoned if he was angry enough, it might be what I needed to distance myself from him until I could get the divorce behind me. Sitting in Dicky's with Alder's arm around me last night had felt so right in so many ways. But it was wrong, plain wrong—and not just because of the stupid prenup. He made me feel safe and secure in a way I had never felt. Ever. It would be too easy to give myself over without ever standing on my own two feet.

The sound of a slamming car door caught my attention. I owed Alder an explanation, and I'd lain awake all night trying to figure out how to justify my actions. But truly, other than my concern for Delores, there really was no excuse.

The door handle rattled, then a loud pounding sounded on the front door. "Cece, let me in!" Phillip shouted. "You can't keep me out of my own house."

Phillip had to show up now, of all times. I went to the front door and pulled it open. "What do you want?" I asked.

Phillip stormed in. "Give me a key. You aren't locking me out until a judge has the final say."

I faced him and steadied my feet. "You don't live here, remember? You left."

"That's crap, and you know it."

"You might not like it, but you can't do anything about it, Phillip. If there's something you want, let me know. I don't give a fig about your personal stuff. You want your tools, take them. You want your fancy coffeepot, have at it." I blew out a breath and continued, "My home was burglarized, and until I know who did it, I'm securing it. If that means keeping you out, then that's what I'm going to do. For all I know, Willow could have broken in." He didn't need to know about Noah. Not yet, anyway.

"Lay off Willow. She hasn't done anything."

"Nothing but steal my husband," I said.

"Oh, get over it, will you?"

"And another thing. Call your daughters occasionally. They miss you, especially Michelle. You've barely talked to them since you left," I said. "Your mother spends more time with them than you do."

Phillip's face softened. "You're right."

I crossed my arms in satisfaction.

"I'm not sure Jess will even speak to me," he said.

"Have you even tried to reach out to her?" I asked.

"No."

"Then do it. And keep trying until you're successful," I scolded.

For a minute, peace settled over us, then Alder showed up.

Alder got out of his car but stopped.

"Good, the cop is here." Phillip leaned in next to my ear. "You keep this up, and you'll be panhandling on the street. I'll have the house and custody of Michelle. You and the cop can live happily ever after."

"Just leave, and don't make a scene," I said. "He's here to question Carla about Lloyd Redmond's murder."

Phillip took off down the sidewalk at a rapid clip.

I motioned for Alder to come on up. When Alder passed Phillip on the sidewalk, Phillip said loud enough for the entire town of Wickford to hear. "Have at her, pal. Good luck. You'll need it."

Alder stayed where he was until Phillip had driven off, then he came up to the house.

"You okay?" He held one hand behind his back.

My heart did a little pitter-pat at the sound of his voice. It had a deep quality. I could picture him singing bass in the church choir.

I stepped aside. When he walked by, he pecked me on the cheek. I wanted to jump into his arms, drag him upstairs, and have my way with him. Except Carla was here, and I had the whole prenup thing to worry about. "By the way, I got the rose and the bud vase," I said. "Thanks for dropping it by."

"It was nothing, nothing at all." From behind his back, he extracted a single pink rose. "But this one . . . . This one is something."

I fanned myself, willing a hot flash to recede, hoping my face wasn't as red as it felt. "It's beautiful."

"You going to make me stand here in the foyer, or are you going to invite me in and put this flower in some water?"

He followed me to the kitchen, where the pink rose joined the red one in the bud vase. I noticed him glance toward the roses Grant had sent.

"No, they aren't from Phillip."

"Didn't ask," he said. "This is me giving you your space."

"And bringing me a rose and kissing me on the cheek does that?"

"Got to step up my game if I'm going to compete with a dozen roses." He laughed.

"Not funny." I already had a pitcher of iced tea made and poured two glasses. "How about we sit on the patio? It's too nice a day to be cooped up inside."

"How about I talk to Carla first and get the business out of the way? Then we can talk." His jaw stiffened, and his voice lost its playful tone.

"Sure. You two can have some privacy in the living room, if that's what you want." I slid the tea back into the refrigerator. "I'll get her."

When Carla passed me on the way into the living room, I told her, "If you don't tell him about the money, I will. And it will sound a whole lot better coming from you."

"I know, especially considering he arrested Noah. My main concern is for him to believe I had nothing to do with Noah and Lloyd's scam."

I went out on the patio and waited for my turn.

~ ~ ~

Two torturous hours later, Alder opened the door and stepped out. "Is the iced tea still a possibility?"

I nodded and pulled myself off the chaise.

"About the roses," he said. "You don't need to explain."

"They're nothing, I promise."

He followed me into the kitchen, where I poured two fresh teas.

"Did you and Carla get everything ironed out?" I asked.

"We did. She's got some legwork to do for the money. But as far as I can tell, it had nothing to do with the diamonds or Redmond's death," Alder said. "Carla said you have it in your safe."

"I do. Does she have to turn it in?" I asked.

"Yes, until I get all the paperwork ironed out. But it shouldn't take long. And with that kind of money, she can hire someone to clean out Delores' house. I put in a good word for you. If you're busy there, you won't have time to be meddling in my cases." He raised an eyebrow.

"Sorry, one thing led to another, and then bam!" I handed him his glass and motioned toward the door. "Let's go back outside."

When we were seated in the twin chaises, I looked over at him. "They're from Grant. He saw the rose and bud vase the day you left them on the porch."

"Cece, you don't—" Alder put his hand up.

"I do." I swiped at the condensation which had gathered on my glass. "I need to tell you a whole lot of things. And I need you to understand."

Alder placed his tea on the table, swung his feet around to the ground, and faced me. "I told you once before, I'll give you all the time and space you need, but if you have feelings for Grant, tell me. I'm not going to have a repeat of what happened with Joyce. There's a reason I haven't let myself open up to anyone. At least not until you came along. I have feelings for you, and I'm starting to—"

"Stop," I said. "Let me get this out."

Alder placed his hands on his knees and leaned in. "Okay, go ahead."

I wanted to swing around and face him. I wanted to swing around and tell him the same thing he was getting ready to say to me, but I couldn't look at him, or else I would lose all the courage I had been working up.

Swallowing the huge lump in my throat, I said, "I cherish Grant as a friend, but only as a friend. He's kind and generous, but he will never be more than a friend. I told you before, my life is complicated. It's only going to get more complicated in the next few months."

Alder pushed himself to his feet. "I think I see where this is going, so I'll make it easy on you."

"Oh, sit down." I reached up and tugged his hand. "I'm not giving you the kiss-off."

He scooted my legs over and sank down on my chaise.

"Um no, you better go back over there," I said.

He got up and went around to the other chaise, where he sat down facing me again.

"The truth of the matter is." I paused. "I can't be around you."

"What? Now I'm confused." Alder's brows scrunched. "What aren't you telling me?"

"This may come out wrong, but let me get it all out before you say anything. Okay?" I asked.

Alder took a long drink of his tea. "This is your show, so go ahead. I'm listening."

"When Phillip and I got married, I signed a prenuptial agreement."

Carla opened the door and said, "I'm heading over to Mom's. Detective Alder, you have my cell number. If you have any more questions, call me. I'll get the paperwork to you as soon as I talk to Mom's financial planner."

"Sounds good," he said.

"Bye," I called as Carla shut the door.

"Now, where was I?" My nerves felt frazzled and fried. Between the news about Noah, my ordeal with Peter Bray, and my emotions all jumbled about Alder, my stomach had tied itself in knots.

"I believe you were about to tell me how you weren't

giving me the boot, but I could be wrong. You're all over the place." He patted the spot next to him. "Come here."

I moved over to his chaise and let him put his arm around me.

"This is about you needing space, right?"

"Uh-huh," I squeaked out. "There's more."

He sighed and rubbed my hand. "Okay," he said, his voice guarded.

"I can't have sex with you." The words were out of my mouth before I knew it. And I couldn't take them back.

"Oh." His left eye twitched. "Ever?"

"No, I mean yes," I said.

"That could be a deal breaker." He chuckled. "Which is it? Yes or no?"

"No, not forever. Someday, maybe, if you want to, but not now," I said.

"Well." He paused. "I don't seem to recall putting a move on you today, so I think we're good. What's this all about?"

"You make me feel all . . . I don't know. A way I haven't felt in a long time, and I don't trust myself. You know. Because who knows where it will wind up?" Wow, I was blowing this in a major way. "I'm rambling, but the truth is I can't sleep with you. Phillip's holding a prenup over my head . . . Wait, this isn't coming out right." I stopped and took a breath. "I don't want you to think this is about money, because it's not.

"I gave up my career after Michelle was born, so I could stay at home and be a wife and mother. If he can enforce the prenup, I will lose everything, my house, half of our investments, possibly even custody of Michelle. Phillip thinks we're having an affair, and he's going to hold it over my head," I said.

"Joke's on him," Alder said. "He's living with another woman, and we haven't done anything for you to be worried or ashamed of. Not that I haven't wanted to. And as I recall you were kind of fond of the idea a few nights back. Look, I'm not bothered about his threats, and you shouldn't be either. And the money is not important. The important thing is to get this divorce final, so you can move on with your life."

"It's about me being independent. Finding out who I am without Phillip. Or anyone. It's me knowing I can take care of myself. It's about me getting my business off the ground and making a success of it. I may not have gone off to work every day, but I earned half of everything we have, and I'm going to fight Phillip to the mat to make sure he takes me seriously." I forced myself to slow down.

"Phillip had me believing he had made some bad investments and we were broke. I worked my tail off, scared I would lose my house, and here he was stashing money away to hide it from me. As far as you and I go, I want to do this for you. I don't want a relationship with someone who sees me as weak or not able to take care of myself."

Alder laughed. "You aren't weak, and I'm sure not looking to take care of you. You also have a stubborn streak and a serious sense of justice, or else you wouldn't be getting involved in cases where you put yourself in jeopardy. Right now, you're on an emotional roller coaster. I know, I've been there. When Joyce left me, it was gut-wrenching, so I get it." Alder rubbed my back.

"Joyce and I had only been together a few years. You and Phillip have had a lifetime together. You need time to mend, get your trust back, and not rush into a relationship without thinking it through. We can work on it together. Whatever you need me to do or don't do, you can count on me. I'm all in."

The tears collecting in my eyes trickled down my cheeks.

Alder stopped rubbing my back and pulled me tighter. "We have all the time in the world. I'm not going anywhere."

Cece's Grandpa Earl's Best Sweet Tea

Ingredients

2 cups of water

4 cups of water

1 to 1 1/2 cups sugar (Cece only uses 1 cup.)

4 family sized bags (Cece has a favorite brand, but use your favorite.)

1/8 tsp baking soda

Gallon of cold water minus 6 cups

Thinly sliced lemons or limes or both

Fresh mint leaves

Directions

1. Bring 2 cups of water to a boil. Add sugar and baking soda. Stir to dissolve.
2. Bring 4 cups of water to a boil and pour over teabags.
3. Cover and steep 5 – 6 minutes.
4. Remove teabags and discard.
5. Add sugar/baking soda water to steeped tea and stir.
6. Pour steeped tea into gallon jug of water (minus 6 cups) and chill.
7. Add ice to tall glasses and add tea.
8. Garnish with lemon/lime wedges and crushed mint leaves.

If you prefer tea with no sugar (heaven forbid), omit step 1 and 5 and add the baking soda after Step 4.

Delores Redmond's Friends of the Library Buttermilk Pie

Ingredients

1 3/4 cups sugar
1/2 cup softened butter
3 eggs
1 cup buttermilk
3 tablespoons flour
1 teaspoon vanilla extract (Delores sometimes uses almond extract.)
pinch of salt
1/8 teaspoon ground nutmeg for sprinkling on top
1 9-inch deep-dish pie crust, unbaked

Instructions

1. Preheat oven to 350 degrees.
2. In a large bowl, cream butter and sugar.
3. Add eggs, buttermilk, flour, vanilla, and salt. Mix until smooth.
4. Pour in unbaked pie crust.
5. Dust top with ground nutmeg.
6. Bake at 350 degrees for 1 hour (depending on oven.)
7. Let cool and set before slicing.
8. Serve with a dollop of whipped cream.

Also from **Tricia L. Sanders** and **Soul Mate Publishing**

MURDER IS A DIRTY BUSINESS

Between hot flashes and divorce papers, a middle-aged woman reconsiders her outlook on life when she butts heads with a hot detective during a murder investigation.

When Cece Cavanaugh's husband empties their joint bank account, steals her designer luggage, and runs off with a younger woman, Cece must decide whether to ask her manipulative mother-in-law for a handout or get a job. Choosing the easier path, Cece lands a job cleaning a crime scene where a high school coach was murdered. When his wife is implicated—a young woman Cece practically raised—Cece finds herself mopping floors, balancing an empty checkbook, and ferreting out a killer.

Amid all this messy business, Cece bumps heads with a handsome detective. She tries to ignore her growing attraction to the detective, but he gives new meaning to the term "hot flash."

After she stumbles onto a clue that could vindicate her friend, her elation turns to panic when she haphazardly confronts the killer. Through the danger and romance, Cece discovers self-reliance and inner strength.

And that crime—at least, someone else's—does pay the bills.

Tricia L. Sanders writes cozy mysteries and women's fiction. She adds a dash of romance and a sprinkling of snark to raise the stakes. Her heroines are humorous women embarking on journeys of self-discovery all the while doing so with class, sass, and a touch of kickass.

Tricia is an avid St. Louis Cardinals fan, so don't get between her and the television when a game is on. Currently she is working on a mystery series set in the fictional town of Wickford, Missouri. Another project in the works is a women's fiction road trip adventure.

A former instructional designer and corporate trainer, she traded in curriculum writing for novel writing, because she hates bullet points and loves to make stuff up. And fiction is more fun than training guides and lesson plans.

Visit her:
Website: www.triciasanders.com
Facebook: www.facebook.com/authortricialsanders/
Twitter: www.twitter.com/tricialsanders

To keep up-to-date on her current books, new releases, exclusive giveaways, and other news and events, sign up for her newsletter, Sleuth Scoop https://mailchi.mp/23a87d715dc3/tricia-l-sanders-sleuthscoop

CPSIA information can be obtained
at www.ICGtesting.com
Printed in the USA
LVHW011556170119
604290LV00017B/583